PRAISE FOR *OPERATION SUNSET*

"The main character, Alex Hofmann, is interesting, believable, and a refreshing new female 'action hero'."

"I strongly recommend *Operation Sunset* and each of the preceding Alex Hoffman novels."

"I didn't think Leslie Wolfe's heroine Alex Hoffman books could get any better. Consider me corrected."

"Complex, Clear, Insightful, Relevant!"

"Scary and keeps you on the edge. Love the Agency!"

"Very suspenseful, action packed...would make a good movie."

PRAISE FOR LESLIE WOLFE

"A winner once again for Leslie, this is an intriguing plot tracking nuclear weapons."

"Great book. Author made my top ten list."

"Another wonderful, page turner story, it's a must read!"

OPERATION
SUNSET

BOOKS BY LESLIE WOLFE

TESS WINNETT SERIES

Dawn Girl
The Watson Girl
Glimpse of Death
Taker of Lives
Not Really Dead
Girl with A Rose
Mile High Death
The Girl They Took

DETECTIVE KAY SHARP SERIES

The Girl From Silent Lake
Beneath Blackwater River
The Angel Creek Girls

BAXTER & HOLT SERIES

Las Vegas Girl
Casino Girl
Las Vegas Crime

STANDALONE TITLES

Stories Untold
Love, Lies and Murder

ALEX HOFFMANN SERIES

Executive
Devil's Move
The Backup Asset
The Ghost Pattern
Operation Sunset

For the complete list of Leslie Wolfe's novels, visit: Wolfenovels.com/order

OPERATION SUNSET

LESLIE WOLFE

II **ITALICS**
ITALICS PUBLISHING

II **ITALICS**

Italics Publishing Inc.
Cover and interior design by Sam Roman
Editor: Joni Wilson
ISBN: 978-1-945302-05-3

DEDICATION

For my biggest fan, my husband.

Alex shifted in her seat as the Phenom turned gracefully, on final approach to Santa Ana's John Wayne Airport. She stretched her neck, her eyes glued to the plane's small window, to see the sunny coast she called home. The heart-piercing deep blue of the Pacific glittered when sunrays hit its restless surface and reflected back in a million shards of diamonds. The golden sands of shore mirrored safety, warmth, and familiar places. This was home. She'd missed it. She feared she'd never see it again. Her heart swelled and her eyes teared up.

She cleared her throat, embarrassed by her own weakness. *Look at me, the sentimental soldier. Argh . . .*

She turned toward Lou, but shifted too abruptly in her seat. A pang of sharp pain in her sternum caught her breath and reminded her she was still convalescing. The pain was nothing like it had been a few weeks before; it was just a reminder to take it easy still. Three cracked ribs and a hairline fracture on her sternum, the doctor had said. A couple of torn ligaments in her left shoulder, and a really bad cut on her forehead. That, unfortunately, had left a scar. Her first battle scar, hopefully her last. Scars aren't sexy in women . . . only in some men. Damn. Alex hated long bangs, but probably she'd have to consider them now. A curtain of hairstyle camouflage to hide the wounds of battle. Huh. Like that was going to work.

"Hey, Lou," she said, then cleared her throat again, still choked up a little.

His eyes were glued to the window. From his side of the plane, he could see the city, and farther out, the hazy Los Angeles skyline, almost lost in the smog.

"What's up?" he replied, then cleared his throat a little, quietly.

"Are you getting emotional, seeing that we're finally coming home?"

He turned and looked at her, a little surprised.

"Come on, you can admit it," she pushed him, smiling widely, making him frown and purse his lips. "It's just the two of us here."

"Yeah . . . a little," he eventually confessed, shifting uncomfortably in his seat.

"It's okay to be happy to be home, you know," she pressed on. "What are you planning to do in the next few days?"

"As little as possible," Lou quipped, then chuckled lightly.

"Yeah, we got time. I'm planning to work on my tan more seriously. The Japanese doctors told me to spend as much time as possible lying on my back, resting. On the beach sounds like the perfect place for me."

"Then, in about a week's time, we'll resume your training routine, right? They said in five, six weeks you should be back to normal. That's coming up."

"Lou, I hate you right now. Words cannot express." She made a strangling gesture with her right hand, grunting a little.

"Yeah, yeah, right. Heard that one before."

"The doctors said at least two more weeks of R and R," she said. "I won't let you ruin that. Plus, we got some time, until Sam and Blake return."

"We shouldn't have left Japan without them, you know. No man left behind, that's the right way to do it."

"They are fine, well taken care of, and out of harm's way. They're not exactly left behind on the battlefield."

"Yeah, but still."

"Lou, they have protection 'round the clock. The Bravo Team is with them. They are surrounded by top-notch medical professionals, caring for them in one of the most exclusive, most expensive health clinics this world has to offer. They rest, they relax, they do physio; that's all they do. They're probably going to make a full recovery before we do. And they're coming home in a week or so."

"Yeah, I guess . . ."

A chime interrupted them.

"That's it, folks. Buckle up for final descent." The pilot's voice was loaded with the same kind of excitement they were feeling.

"I'm actually impressed with this guy," Alex said.

"Who?"

"Dylan, the pilot," she clarified, lowering her voice a little. The door to the cockpit was wide open.

"Why?"

"I didn't think he'd make it out there without losing his shit. He's not military, you know. He's just a civilian, who landed a cushy job flying a big-shot banker, *the* Blake Bernard, around the world."

"Yeah, he's okay, I guess."

The landing gear made a squealing sound as they touched down, followed by the roar of the engines thrown in reverse. The Phenom slowed, then taxied to the VIP terminal at John Wayne Airport.

Alex unbuckled her seatbelt and jumped to her feet, holding on to the seat for balance. She winced when her ribs reminded her again to take it easy, but that reminder quickly faded under the excitement of being home.

"There they are!"

On the tarmac, lined up to meet them, stood Tom and Claire, and, a little to the side, Steve. Steve looked a little grim; there was tension around his mouth, and a frown line crossed his entire forehead. Alex's smile froze on her lips.

"There's going to be hell to pay, I guess," she said, softly.

"What did you expect? I'm not sure I forgave you either, you know." Lou's words were harsh, but the warmth in his voice softened them a little.

She was the first one to get off the plane, landing in Tom's bear hug.

"Welcome home," he said. "We need to talk."

Ugh.

Then Claire was next to hug her.

"Good to have you back, my dear," she whispered warmly.

She moved to greet Steve next, and she managed to do that awkwardly, averting her eyes, and feeling like she wanted the earth to open up and swallow her right where she stood. Not a word was spoken between the two of them. Just a hasty, hesitant handshake, and she pulled away.

She took a deep breath, bracing herself, and opened the conversation as if nothing ever happened. She turned to Tom and smiled.

"So, what's for dinner?"

"Ah, all kinds of good stuff," he replied. "Portabellas on the grill, skirt steak, and a side of . . . What the hell were you thinking?"

She took a small step back.

"What do you mean?" she managed.

"The flares stunt you pulled." Tom's eyes were dead serious, glaring at her mercilessly.

"I thought I'd bring him out, that's all. I'm tired of chasing a ghost. All this time, and all I have is one letter. One initial, the damn letter V. A letter I've grown to hate."

"He's a terrorist, for Chrissake, Alex, a terrorist! You don't bring out terrorists like that."

"Oh, no? Then how? How exactly am I supposed to bring him out?"

"Why is it your job, to begin with? I'm your boss, Alex, and I'm telling you this is not your job."

"Ah, so now you pull rank on me, Tom, is that it?"

"Well . . ." Tom hesitated, taking it down a notch. His wife reached out and gently squeezed his hand. "You leave me little choice, Alex. This is not what we do. We're not equipped to chase down terrorists. We're a corporate investigations agency, and a small one. That's all we are, all we do."

"I—I know," Alex said with a sigh. "But these cases, I didn't choose them, you know. They chose me, you chose me to work them. Because this bastard's still out there, I can't call these cases closed, and it's killing me. I thought I'd draw him out, that's all. Play on his ego, tease him a little."

Steve approached the two of them.

"Did you stop and think you're endangering all of us by doing that?" Steve asked. His frown grew deeper.

She felt her heart break a little, seeing Steve turned against her. What could she expect? Her disappointment quickly became anger, and she spun on her heels to face him.

"Wait a minute there, Steve. Weren't you the one who lectured me on how I'm becoming obsessed with someone who doesn't even exist? Well? Make up your mind, then. Does he exist? Or doesn't he?"

"*Someone* does exist. Someone who might have been watching that satellite feed when you lit the flares and looked straight up, so he can see you grin at him as you destroyed his operation. In my line of work, that's called adding insult to the injury. You just motivated your enemy, that's all. Whoever that is, V or not." His voice was firm, but sad at the same time.

She still resonated to the undertones in Steve's voice, more than she cared to admit. Damn it to hell . . . the heart doesn't belong in the office . . . or on the battlefield. Lesson learned.

"Yes, I did. That's exactly what I wanted to do. A motivated enemy will come out and attack."

"Sure he will," Steve continued. "He can kill you in your sleep, or rig your car to explode. How are you calling that a good outcome? What if you can't see him coming, to do anything about it?"

She pursed her lips, a wave of deep irritation scrunching her features. She shook her head gently, almost imperceptibly, as she kept her eyes glued to the tarmac.

"I'm still struggling to hear you talk about this, when you were the most adamant nonbeliever in this man's existence. You were the one who reassured me that there's no Russian terrorist leader behind everything. You said it was all in my imagination. You made me doubt my sanity. So, why the change in spirit? Because if you did in fact reconsider, and now you do believe that V is really out there, then you owe me an apology." She ended her ranting in a defiant tone and lifted her gaze to meet his. She drilled her eyes mercilessly into his, until he looked away.

"Truth is, I don't know," Steve conceded. "I don't know if you were right, or if I was right. I don't know if there's a Russian terrorist out there or not. One thing's for sure though. What you did was reckless, because you endangered your life and everyone else's for no good reason. For no clear outcome whatsoever. You've now set a trail, a trail that someone can follow with ease, all the way here, to all of us."

Her jaw dropped. She was stunned and angry with herself for not seeing it, in her egotistical excitement with the possibility of catching V. Steve was right; she hadn't thought of them for a second. High on the moment's adrenaline and only caring about exposing and hunting down her elusive Russian terrorist, she had jeopardized the lives of the people she cared about the most. They weren't just coworkers. They were her family, her friends. *Oh, my god . . .* Her hand went to her mouth, shaking, and cold as ice.

"You're no longer the stealth hunter, Alex," Steve added in a low, conclusive pitch. "You've become the hunted, and so have we. This is the mistake you've made."

She stood there, speechless for a while. Pallor descended on her face, turning her features spectral. As realization hit, she felt a million pinpricks on her skin, as wave after wave of adrenaline hit her insides.

"I'll—I'll just disappear," she whispered. "I'll go away, fall off the face of the earth. That way, you'll be safe."

"You'll do no such thing," Tom intervened forcefully. "We're in this together, no matter what."

She felt her eyes well up, and a tiny smile of heartfelt gratitude appeared on her lips. Then she turned to Steve.

"How about you? You feel the same way?"

"Absolutely," he replied, not a trace of hesitation.

"Lou?"

He'd been leaning against the car for a while, his leg injury causing him some grief. However, he bounced up on both his feet and approached her.

"Hundred percent. Never leave a man behind, remember?" He smiled, then added, "I also happen to trust your judgment, you know. So far, I've seen some really awesome results. Maybe, who knows? You'll draw this bastard out, so we can rid the world of him. Whatever his name is."

She nodded toward Lou, then turned to Claire.

"How about you, Claire?"

"I will repeat what I said earlier. It's good to have you home, my dear. That's all that matters to me. The rest, you will fix together. I have no doubt."

Tom opened the door to his car, inviting everyone to join him with a jovial, wide gesture and a slight bow. She felt a wave of emotion swell her chest. They were her family, and they had forgiven her. She swallowed hard, trying to refrain from crying. She tried to hide it with a quick joke, as she boarded Tom's car, sliding with difficulty on the back seat.

"So, I take it I'm not fired, huh?"

Tom made eye contact with her in the rearview, for a split second, but enough for her to register the smile in his glance.

"Don't tempt me."

The heavy velvet draperies were half-closed, a little unusual for that time of the morning. It could only mean two things. Either President Abramovich had a fierce migraine, or he was mad as hell. Neither scenario showing any promise of a good meeting, Dimitrov repressed a sigh, and continued pacing the carpet slowly, waiting for the man to show his face.

He focused on his steps for a while, taking one step at a time, studying the intricate design of the rich Oriental rug, aligning his fine leather shoe to the delicate curves drawn in wool. No matter how heavily he stomped his foot, the rug swallowed all the noise. The lavish design, a million gold arabesques dancing on a dark, deep red with hues of burgundy, matched the wallpaper, the famous Kremlin gold-encrusted ceilings, and the massive, sculpted hardwood doors, also covered in gold foil.

So much detail for the mind's eye to perceive, register, and analyze. So much gold, infatuation, and pretense. After having spent the past fifteen years of his life serving as Russia's controversial, yet balanced defense minister, Dimitrov craved some simple, white walls, maybe with a wall rug or two, just for the sake of tradition.

"Ah, you're here," Abramovich said, surprising Dimitrov.

He snapped out of his reverie and turned to greet his boss.

"Good morning, Gospodin Prezident."

"Drop the formalities, Mishka, it's just us here, in my private quarters."

He took the invitation and relaxed his demeanor a little. After all, they'd been friends since their earlier days as junior officers in the KGB. That seemed like centuries ago.

"Morning, Petya."

"That's better," Abramovich acknowledged. "Do you know why I wanted to see you?"

"I—no, I don't think I do," Dimitrov replied cautiously. Abramovich was world-famous for his short fuse, irrational thinking, and ultrasensitive ego. Not someone you'd want to assume things about.

"I have the press conference in under an hour."

"Ah . . ." Dimitrov said, before he could stop himself. So that's why the semi-darkness in the presidential quarters. Deeply hurt, Abramovich was hiding from the world. The damn press conference was going to cost a lot of people, dearly.

"Yes, yes, Mishka. Yes, you understand. I have to apologize to the entire world on live television. Can you believe that?"

Dimitrov didn't answer. He let his eyes speak, encouraging the volatile Abramovich, while offering him a cigar. Maybe smoking would soothe him a little.

"I have to explain to the whole world that I had no idea what was happening in my own country, goddamn it. I will be the laugh of this entire globe. They'll think me impotent, clueless, a puppet! A trinket, bounced around by someone else, more powerful than I am!"

Abramovich paused his lament to light a cigar. Dimitrov held the match with steady hands, steadier than he'd expected.

Then Abramovich resumed his deploration, his pitch higher by a notch or two.

"How am I going to explain that such a massive undergoing had happened without my knowledge? Tell me, Mishka, how?"

Abramovich stopped, this time waiting for an answer.

Dimitrov let a second or two pass before speaking. When he spoke, his voice was calm, reassuring yet not dismissive, supporting, and firm.

"Petya, this has happened many times before in history. Today it's harsh, I agree . . . it's humiliating for you and demeaning for our country. But you can say that the terrorist attack was a complete surprise to the Russian people, as it was to the rest of the world. You can say no one knew that, hidden in the forested depths of the Far East, evil had found a place to nest and weave its plans. And you will say that you will not rest until you uncover the roots of this evil. You will say all that, while looking straight into the main camera, believing it with all your heart."

Abramovich stood immobile, following keenly every word that came out of Dimitrov's mouth. Then he turned and took a couple of quick steps to his desk, to jot notes on gold letterhead stationery. He held his cigar between the index and middle finger of his left hand; tiny specks of ash found their way onto the shiny, inlaid hardwood desk top.

"What else?" he asked, still leaning on his desk, ready to take more notes.

"Nothing else, Petya, nothing else. If you wish, you can blame it on the Chechens; we always do that. Whatever you decide, keep it very short. All you need is to make a statement. Once you've made it, you don't need to say anything else. Take a couple of questions though; it makes you appear open, honest, and human."

"Ahh . . . the press and their damn questions."

"Regardless of what they ask, all you have to say is how committed you are to finding and punishing the source of this evil. That's all."

"I am, you know," Abramovich stated, with a hateful glint in his eye.

"You're what?" Dimitrov's eyebrows shot up, aiming to get closer to his receding hairline, and adding a few more transversal ridges on his forehead.

"Committed to punishing this evil. I'll give it to Myatlev; I'll give it to him so badly that he'll never forget whom he failed."

"I see what you mean," Dimitrov said quietly. "You must be mad."

"I am more than mad. I am more humiliated and angrier than I've ever been in my entire life. Do you know why Myatlev's still alive, at this very moment?"

Following along like a good sport, Dimitrov replied, careful to quickly repress an eye roll. "No, Petya, why?"

"Because he's got some balls, this guy. Balls the size of Barents Sea icebergs, that's how big they are. Too bad he failed, and he got caught. By the Americans, no less. For that, yeah, I want to kill him myself, with these two hands," he continued, illustrating by holding both his hands firmly outward. "Nevertheless, can you imagine what the world would have been like if he'd succeeded? Can you imagine? Having the power to dictate what everyone of any importance would do, would think?"

Dimitrov remained silent, a crooked smile twisting his lips somewhat. Then he decided to push the issue a little, just to take a temperature read.

"So, it's not because the two of you go way back, even further back than the two of us?"

"Nah . . . no. He screwed up really badly, but he meant well. He's loyal, dedicated, and trustworthy."

"Then he's forgiven?"

"No, not at all. He still didn't deliver, and neither did you. The two of you work together every day, share the same floor, and have promised me one thing. Yet I get nothing, after so much time. Only promises and failures."

"Petya, we are both trying to avoid the nuclear option. We don't want to bring radioactive air on top of Russia, for our children to breathe. That's why he's been thinking up all these ballsy plans, to give you what you want without destroying the entire planet."

"While in the meantime the Americans grow more arrogant, more defiant, and their superiority is pissing me off!" Abramovich bellowed, the sound of his voice reverberating in the huge room. "Is it too much to ask? For a power like Russia is today?"

Dimitrov swallowed hard. "No, sir."

"Don't sir me, Mishka; don't be an idiot. You've done well rebuilding the Army, the arsenal, everything. The Armata tank is a thing of beauty. But I want the Americans on their knees, defeated, begging for my mercy! *My* mercy! How do you plan to deliver on that, you and your dear friend, Myatlev?"

Abramovich's anger was ramping up again . . . Dimitrov suddenly realized he was too old for this job, too old for the Kremlin, and too old for Abramovich's tantrums. He considered it for a split second, but then decided it was the absolute wrong moment to hand in his resignation right then and there. Abramovich still took pride in throwing the insubordinate few to Siberia, where remnants of the Gulag still existed, under new, reformed names, but the same leadership, employing the same methods.

Dimitrov's eyes darted at Abramovich, then looked away. He was afraid the sociopath standing combatively in front of him would see right through him and hear his thoughts. *God help us all, and forgive us the cowardice we are showing by letting this man live.*

"He surprised me a little a few weeks ago when he ordered some backpack nukes," Dimitrov eventually said, hating himself. "We delivered the order. I don't think he's planning to hold on to them for too long."

"He did? Really?" Abramovich's voice bubbled with excitement.

"Yes . . . I was surprised to see he finally adopted the nuclear path. You've been trying to convince him for a long time, and he held strong. He was afraid we would ruin this world for all of us, for generations to come, not just teach the Americans a lesson. But he came around; he changed his mind, recently. He must have thought of something. He must have a plan."

"It was about time," Abramovich replied serenely.

"You should speak with him, see if you agree with his new plan. No more surprises for you this time, right?"

Vitaliy Myatlev's office was abuzz with activity. Myatlev himself directed traffic like an effective street cop, while his aide and personal bodyguard, Ivan, took notes impassively on his plastic clipboard.

"All right, boss, what else?"

"Um, let's make sure the safe at the house is emptied out. I think it is, but check to make sure," Myatlev ordered, a little impatient.

"I cleaned it out myself just a few months back, but I'll drop by tonight and take another look."

"Good. Have the jet fueled and the pilot on standby, day and night."

"Done."

"Who's taking care of the stuff at the house?"

"I am, after dark, just like you said."

"Good. Leave the bulky stuff behind. Leave the furniture; just take my clothes, documents, that kind of stuff. How about Kiev? Is the villa prepared?"

"Yes, it is. Everything is ready for your arrival."

"Good." Myatlev sighed and allowed himself to calm the frenzy of his just-in-case departure preparations. They were good on time. He was prepared to leave at a moment's notice, should the case present itself. It was better to be safe than sorry.

He also needed to be very discreet in his preparations. Abramovich wouldn't take too nicely to him getting ready to run, albeit only to Kiev, to his favorite residence. However, Kiev was now in a foreign country, Ukraine. Abramovich would consider his departure to a foreign country as desertion, and everyone knew what Abramovich did to deserters, lifelong friends or not.

His thorough preparations were more of a precaution than anything was. He wasn't planning to run, just for the sake of becoming Abramovich's next hunting target. No matter how rich and powerful Myatlev was, once Abramovich had decided he wanted him dead, he couldn't survive for long. Division Seven had the best cleanup crew a secret service had ever had. Myatlev knew just how good they were, because he'd trained some of them himself and seen most of them in action.

Nevertheless, he intended to carry out the president's vengeful plans, without hesitation, even if that meant the detonation of numerous nuclear devices within the continental United States. Now, more than ever, Myatlev shared Abramovich's lust for vengeance, after having been bitterly humiliated by that Hoffmann bitch. Fuck her. Fuck that bitch from hell.

He felt alive again and thrived in the feeling, rejoiced in it. For almost two years, he had believed he was losing his mind. Crippled for months by rampant anxiety and bouts of paranoia, at times he believed he had an imaginary enemy, who saw through all his strategies and ruined all his plans. Other times, he'd feared it was the hand of God himself. Senseless fears had crept up on him, augmented by the very alcohol he had used to try to silence them. Thus, he'd forgotten who he was: a powerful energy and weapons magnate, who never failed and never took no for an answer. He had no enemies, because the moment an enemy would surface, that nemesis would soon find an early demise. Now, he finally remembered, with every bone in his body and every breath he took, he was back in the power seat.

Once the source of his irrational anxieties had gained a name and a face to go along with it, he transformed overnight, returning to his old self. His drinking habit almost entirely gone, the dark circles under his eyes and his swollen abdomen were soon to follow. His stomach recovered on its own, as his paranoid worries disappeared. He felt twenty years younger; his refreshed blood pumped strong in his veins, ready to fuel his rekindled ambitions of infinite wealth and power and a tireless lust for vengeance.

That bitch, she almost killed him. She was going to pay, and then some.

"Um . . . anything else, boss?"

The rest of the staffers had left, after diligently packing resource lists, deployed agents' networks, asset banks, maps, organizational charts, and every single useful document Myatlev could think of. The last of them had vanished quietly, closing the door behind him.

"No, you can go, Ivan. We're set. Thanks."

Ivan approached Myatlev, extending his clipboard for him to view.

"What about her? Should I take care of her?"

A picture of Alex Hoffmann was attached to Ivan's clipboard, held in place by a large metallic clamp. A little grainy and blurred, that was the image captured via satellite when the bitch had delivered her latest blow. Smiling defiantly, sure of herself, Hoffmann had laughed in his face. Her time to die was now.

"Yes, Ivan, take care of her, and of everyone she's ever loved, ever met, ever set eyes on. You hear me?"

"Yes, boss. I'll get it done myself."

Myatlev stared into the grainy eyes of the woman in the photo. Not watching those defiant eyes blur as life left her body, not hearing her whimper and weep, not having her lying at his feet, begging for her life, that just didn't seem right. Why should Ivan have that privilege?

"Never mind, I'll take care of this one myself."

"You sure, boss?"

"Yeah. I want to hear her scream."

The backyard table had been extended and set with the utmost care. Covered with starched, white linen, arranged with matching napkins, and complete with the Isaacs' best serving set, Bohemian crystal glasses, and silverware, the table arrangement would have been worthy of an embassy reception or an inaugural gala. However, much to Claire Isaac's visible chagrin, the refined elegance of the meal stopped there. Her significant other, Tom, still wore jeans, a checkered shirt, and his most cherished grilling apron, the one that read, "The man, the myth, the legend."

As for the guests, their attire varied a lot, from Adeline's elegant dress to Steve's faded jeans. Their plates held burgers and fries, an unceremonious yet incredibly tasty meal that no one would have traded for something fancier. Alex contained her smile when her amused glance met Claire's, but not for long. Without a word, they both cracked wide grins. This was their crew; nothing could be done to change who they really were.

Tom stood and cleared his throat, drawing everyone's attention. Their lively chatter ceased as they all turned to hear what the man had to say.

"Dear friends, we are reunited again around this table, and nothing makes me happier. Welcome home, Adeline, Sam, Blake! Welcome home, kids!"

Cheers erupted around the table and everyone raised their glasses.

Then Blake Bernard stood, a little hesitant on his feet. He leaned against the table with his left hand for support and balance. His right hand met Adeline's and squeezed it. He still looked awfully pale. That tends to happen when you get shot and lose a lot of blood. You need more than three weeks to be fully recovered. Pallor aside, he and his wife, Adeline, looked quite well, considering what they'd just been through.

Blake seemed to hesitate in finding the right words; that never used to happen. The banking magnate could speak for hours in front of presidents and kings and not skip a beat.

"Um . . . it's really hard for me to express what I feel right now. I'm at a loss for words. You gave me my life back, and you risked yours in the process. You sacrificed beyond anything I had imagined. Somehow, thank you doesn't quite cut it . . . but let's start there anyway. Thank you all, thank you all for everything you've done for my family and me. I am forever in your debt."

Adeline stood and embraced her husband, tears running down her cheeks. She turned to look at the people around the table and placed her right palm above her heart in a silent, heartwarming gesture of gratitude to each one.

Alex fought back her tears and swallowed with difficulty. She took a sip of wine to wash down the knot in her throat. All these people . . . Did she bring doom to all of them? Was her recklessness going to cost them their lives? Was she going to take away the very thing she had fought to regain for the Bernards— their lives, their happiness, their family?

She suddenly became aware that people were looking at her, and the conversation had simmered down a little.

"Um . . . what?"

A couple of them laughed.

"I was asking you if there's anything wrong with your burger. You seem to prefer eating keratin instead," Tom said jovially, but with a look of concern on his face.

"Eating what?" Alex replied, confused.

"Keratin. Fingernails. You're biting your fingernails."

"Oh . . . I apologize," Alex said quickly, hiding her offending hand behind her back, like a child.

"What's on your mind?" Tom pressed.

She frowned a little. How can he even ask, and with everyone here? She sighed, letting out with her long breath more sadness than frustration.

"You know what I'm thinking about, nonstop since we got home and you opened my eyes."

"We discussed that," Tom said. "I thought we'd completely cleared the air."

"The air, maybe," she said thoughtfully. "My conscience? Not so much. I don't think I can forgive myself that easily."

"You should," Steve intervened. "You acknowledge your error, learn from it, and then you move on."

"To what?" Alex replied, the bitterness in her voice apparent, instantly regretting her question. The last thing she needed was a psychotherapy session with Steve, with everyone there to listen in.

"To damage control," Steve replied impassively. "To doing what you do best. To solving this case."

"Oh, so now it's a case?" she pushed back, sounding edgy.

"Maybe not yet," Tom replied. "We do need to discuss countermeasures."

"Yes, we do," Alex agreed. "But before we do that, I'd like to ask everyone here for your forgiveness, for endangering your lives with my stupid actions. I really believed at that time it was the best thing to do, to let V know we're out there, watching his every move. No one here truly believed he existed, so I felt . . . I felt

I wasn't doing any harm. I was terribly wrong, and I apologize."

"Accepted," Sam said in a cheerful voice. "I, for one, wouldn't even be here today if it weren't for you. That's who you are; you never give up. You didn't give up on me back there, and you won't give up on catching this bastard either."

"Same here," Blake added.

"See? Problem solved," Tom added. "As for the rest, we'll sort through it. Not before you eat your burger though." Tom took a big bite out of his burger, chewing happily. She followed suit, taking a tentative bite out of hers and pairing it with a fry or two.

"Lou, you're in charge with our safety and self-defense training," Tom said. "What are your thoughts?"

Lou cleared his throat and wiped his mouth with his napkin before speaking. As a former Navy SEAL, he was the most capable of orchestrating the team's tactical response.

"It depends on how far you want to go with this. I'd recommend going deep under. Change our identities, appearances, locations, activities, everything about ourselves that could make us recognizable. Pair that with 'round the clock protection from pro-grade tactical teams. We'd have to maintain that until we catch this terrorist, V. I have learned to accept his existence. If Alex says he's real, I believe her. She's saying he won't stop. I agree. People like that never stop. Born killers, who take any defeat as a personal insult, never stop. He'll come for us with all he's got, to make us pay."

Silence engulfed the small gathering, as they processed the implications. Sam nodded gently in approval.

"Reality is, we're exposed," Lou continued. "We can expect our cars to blow up, a wet team to show up on our doorstep any day, and so on."

"Oh, my God . . ." Claire whispered.

"I still think I should be the one who disappears," Alex said. "It's me he'll be coming for. I defied him; I made it personal."

"No, that's out of the question," Tom replied firmly. "We're not splitting the team."

"I agree," Lou said.

"Me too," Sam added. "Together we're stronger, even if some of us are still recovering."

"Then what would you like to do?" Lou asked.

"I think Alex should tell us what she thinks V will do," Sam says. "So far, she was accurate in guessing this man's next moves. Let's continue on this path."

Sam's opinion weighed a lot to everyone on the team. His background as a CIA operative, his three decades of working in the most danger-ridden places on Earth, and his sharp intellect made him a treasured asset for their team. He and Tom went way back, since their military service days. Sam was grateful to Tom and his crew for pulling him out of the boredom of retirement and giving him another whiff of action now and then.

"That's actually smart," Blake said.

Tom nodded gently, inviting Alex to speak.

"Oh, wow, talk about no pressure," she said, a crooked, tense smile fluttering on her lips for a second. "Well, I made it personal. A car bomb, a wet team, setting the house on fire, or whatever other means of remotely eliminating us won't work for this guy. He has to be personally involved." She paused for a second, thinking. "If I were to guess," she continued, "I'd venture to say he wants to see me defeated before I die. Maybe not just me . . . maybe all of us, but still. He'd want revenge, but in a meaningful way, one that makes reparation for his defeat."

"If he really exists, I think your description is close to what I'd expect to see from someone with his psychological profile," Steve said.

"If he really exists, Steve?" Alex pushed back. "You still don't believe me, huh?"

She clenched her jaws, angry with herself at the sorrow that had crept into her voice as she questioned Steve. No matter how much time had passed, his betrayal still hurt as if it was yesterday. That doubt, that lack of trust in her, his misplaced loyalties had crushed their relationship, and still hurt like hell.

"I believe there's someone out there, Alex, I really do. I definitely don't believe that it's the same man, over and over again. You see a mastermind, a global conspirator of incredible reach, a terrorist leader like none other before him. My background as a psychologist tells me that these people, terrorists in general, are small-minded and not as powerful; even terrorist leaders follow the same rules. Those who have means and power don't want to risk it all for some political statement or another. Those with means and power have achieved their status by being self-centered and focused, by being motivated by money, not by being dedicated to some political cause, no matter how just. That's why I can't comprehend the individual you're describing, Alex. He doesn't exist."

She suddenly felt tired, immensely tired. His argument made sense, had logic, yet she knew it was wrong. She knew V, and she understood him better than anyone had ever understood him, even if she had never met him. By pulling that flare stunt, by drawing his attention to her, she wanted to signal to him that she understood him. Surely, that would draw him out.

If she'd only known his name, she'd go about it in a much different way. She'd hunt him down like the vicious killer he was and have him meet his maker. At her hands. Yes, this was personal all right. Way personal.

She refocused her attention on Steve. She wanted to have an intelligent debate with the man she still loved, but somehow she couldn't find the words. She'd lost all hope of ever persuading him to see her point. His obstinacy drained her of her strength.

"Yeah, Steve, whatever," she uttered sadly, refusing to engage.

A long second of uncomfortable silence engulfed the table. Blake interrupted it, standing up and clearing his throat.

"I think I can say it's this crew's tradition to pop a bubbly and celebrate the successful completion of a case," he said.

"Yes, that's right," Tom said. "We have something on ice, I'll bring it out."

"If you'll allow me," Blake said, "this time I'll do the honors."

Steve stood to help Blake, who was still a little unsure on his legs. They went inside the house together and came back out pushing a serving cart with glasses and a big bottle on ice.

They all gathered on the patio, lit gently by cream-colored lanterns.

"It was hard to find a bottle that would rise to the occasion," Blake said, lifting the large bottle with a cringe of pain.

"Let me help you with that," Steve offered.

"Nah . . . let me try," Blake replied. "So, let's celebrate tonight with a Dom Pérignon Rosé Vintage 1996."

Tom whistled in appreciation.

"I don't think I've ever seen a bottle," he said.

Blake uncorked the gold-rose bottle with expert hands. The loud pop was met with a round of cheers. Then he insisted on filling everyone's glass.

They raised their glasses in anticipation, waiting for Blake to voice his toast.

"Thank you again, from the bottom of my heart. Santé!"

Their glasses, raised high, met with cheerful clinks.

Then Blake turned to Alex, handing her an envelope.

"This is for you, a small measure of my gratitude."

She accepted it with hesitation; she hadn't expected anything.

"Thanks, Blake, but you know you shouldn't have."

She opened the envelope and looked at the amount written on the check, her eyes rounding in surprise.

"Holy crap," she reacted, "Blake, this is way too much!"

She offered him the check back, but he shook his head with a smile.

"You earned it, Alex. Enjoy."

"That changes things a little, Tom," Claire said humorously. "Now you'll have to see if Alex still wants to work for you."

"Nothing I'd rather do, and nowhere else I'd rather be," Alex replied. "Therefore, Tom, I'm sorry, but you'll have to fire me to get rid of me. As for this," she said, pointing at the check, "let's all share it."

"No need," Tom replied. "We've all received what was our due."

"Hmm . . . all right then," she said, "now that we're rich, let's focus on not being dead."

Vitaliy Myatlev hated his Ministry of Defense office more and more, despite its Western décor and lush furniture. He wasn't an employee. He hadn't been one since the old days of the KGB, and he hated having a master again. However, Abramovich, the constantly irate, unpredictable Russian president, wanted him to work from the office, so he had no choice and complied.

Like many mornings before, Myatlev had to revisit the reasons why he complied. He was rich and powerful; he owned multibillion-dollar businesses around the globe, so why wasn't he telling Abramovich, "Thanks, but no thanks; go fuck yourself"?

The answer, as with everything else he'd done in his life, was money. Abramovich was worth a lot of money to Myatlev. Defense contracts, tax exemptions, easy and free permits for everything he wanted to do on Russian territory, even land. Land that wasn't for sale suddenly became available for cheap if Myatlev wanted it. Money was the key to it all. Money was the reason why Myatlev had enrolled his support behind Abramovich.

He sometimes liked to think there was more to it; deep inside, Myatlev loved Russia and wanted the best future for his country. Yet, in all fairness, he wasn't that sure that Abramovich as president meant a good future for Russia. However, Abramovich meant a great future for the Myatlev business empire. How reliable were Abramovich's favors though? That was another issue altogether.

Myatlev repressed a sigh and wiped his brow with a small towel. He'd ordered an elliptical trainer installed in his office, and every morning his routine started with at least one hour of variable-effort cardio conditioning. Checking the time, Myatlev hopped off the machine with a satisfied grin. It was time to get down to the business of the day.

"Ivan," he called, loud enough to make it through the thick walls of his office.

"Yes, boss," Ivan replied immediately, bursting through the door.

"Who's the best in Cyber Division? Find out and bring him here," he ordered, wiping sweat off the back of his head with the same small towel. "Better yet, find out who Smolin was using in Cyber. That man was shrewd; he knew his assets well."

"I'll find out, boss."

Ivan disappeared. He was effective, that young man. Myatlev had been patient with Ivan, while patience had never been his strongest suit, and he didn't regret his hiring decision. He'd recruited Ivan from the top ranks of Spetsnaz, the Russian Special Forces, to be his personal bodyguard. After becoming impressed with Ivan's skills, but most of all his loyalty, he started relying more and more on him as a personal assistant of sorts. Ivan got stuff done, even if, at first, he required a little coaching on how to get things done the right way. After all, his background was commandos, not business.

Twenty minutes later, just about when Myatlev was starting to lose his patience, a quick tap and Ivan stepped in, holding firmly the arm of a young girl. Her hair was unkempt and her clothing dirty; she looked like one of the many strays, omnipresent on Moscow's streets.

"What's this?" he asked, irritation seeping in his voice.

"Boss, this is who Major Smolin was using. Her name is Valentina Davydova."

"Huh . . . all right." He made eye contact with Davydova. He liked what he saw in the dark eyes brewing with anger and throwing daggers of hate. He saw spirit, the material that winners are made of.

"Sit down," he said, gesturing to a deep red velvet armchair, that would probably need a thorough steam cleaning after she'd used it.

She obliged quietly, throwing him a fuming glare.

He sized her up quickly and smiled. She was young, and, under the layers of grime and neglect, she was attractive. She was obviously smart, if Smolin had used her instead of Cyber Division's top-notch programmers. The day could yet be interesting after all.

"You live in the streets?" Myatlev asked.

"No . . . in the slammer."

"In prison? What have you done?"

Davydova made a gesture of irritation with her head, as if saying, "Are you kidding me?" Then she removed a rebel strand of dirty hair from her face with thin, long fingers.

"I got busted, that's all."

"For what?" Myatlev insisted. "Prostitution?"

Her jaws clenched and the glare she shot him could have burned through concrete.

"No. Some cybercrime, can't remember."

"Yeah . . . must have been *some* cybercrime, to get you Smolin's attention," Myatlev said, amused. "So where are they keeping you? Downstairs? In the basement?"

"No. I am staying at a house, under guard 24/7. Still a prison, but not here."

"How come?"

"So I can work. I have equipment, computers there. But that won't last for much longer, with Smolin gone."

"Ah, I see. Well, if you live in a house, why not take better care of yourself?"

"Pfft . . . 'cause the fuckers want to watch."

"The guards?" Myatlev clarified.

"Who else? The assholes claim they have to watch every move I make. They watch me piss and crap; well, I can't help that. Some sick fucks jerk off right there, in front of me, while I'm on the can. Sure as hell I ain't gonna let them watch me take a shower. If I did, what do you think would happen next? Since I've been in your so-called detention, I've had way past my share of unwanted male attention, if you get my point."

"So-called detention, huh?" Myatlev laughed. "What would you call it?"

"Forced labor, because that's what it is. I never had a trial; I never got sentenced. I just got taken."

"How old are you?"

"Nineteen."

"Will you work for me?" Myatlev asked, more and more fascinated by her.

"Like I have a choice," she replied bitterly. "What do you need done?"

Myatlev didn't immediately respond. He felt his anger rising inside, fueled by the stupidity of the Russian grunt who'd risked a valuable cyber asset over a jerk off. Where did Russia find such cretins? Why were they even born? He remained thoughtful for a while, then turned toward Ivan.

"Ivan, get a cleaning crew inside that house. Have them clean it well, top to bottom. New sheets, new carpet. Have all guard shifts arrested and interrogated. Whoever didn't keep it in his pants will be doing hard time. Then get someone to pick up clothing, cosmetics, you know, everything she might need. Finally, have a good security system installed on the premises. Going forward, guards will not be inside that house. They will guard the exterior, and she will be the only one with the access code to enter."

Ivan took notes. "Got it, boss."

Turning to face Davydova, Myatlev saw a faint glint of surprise in her eyes and a bit of gratitude.

"Now, will you work for me?"

"Yes, I will," she replied, more enthusiastically than before. "What do you need?"

Myatlev stood and pulled a photo from an envelope on his desk, then handed it to Davydova.

"This woman's name is Alex Hoffmann. She's an American. That's all I know. I need to know everything there is to know about this woman. I need to find out who she really is, who's pulling her strings, and who signs her paychecks. You'll be her ghost, following every move she makes and reporting to me, and only me, once every day—weekends included."

"You want image recognition run against the Internet, to get past history and a profile of activities?"

"Everything."

"You want me to trace literally where she's going, or just city and state?" Myatlev looked a little confused.

"I could trace her via street cameras, ATMs, traffic, and so on, so you see even from what store she buys her groceries and what she bought."

"Yes, everything."

"How about financials?"

"Again, everything you can find. Report to me on a daily basis."

"What did this walking corpse do to you?"

Myatlev chuckled, impressed with how fast Davydova had read his intentions.

"Remember Smolin? He was a victim of Cold War stealth," he said.

"Cold War stealth? What's that?"

"It's a cold war that no one sees or recognizes is happening. I know better than anyone, because I started it. This woman," he said, tapping his fingers against the photo, "is my Cold War stealth enemy. One of them, anyway. You'll find the rest of them for me. You'll find everyone she speaks with, she meets with, and everyone she crosses paths with."

"Got it," Davydova confirmed calmly. "What resources do I have?"

"Unlimited, just ask."

Davydova thought for a while. Myatlev felt a wave of excitement watching how her mind worked, how she negotiated. He'd like to have her by his side, in more ways than just that.

"I'll need more powerful equipment. I'll need a stack of six-core i7 Intel processors; tens of gigs of RAM, the best Radeon video cards out there, and at least a dozen monitors."

"Write down the specs, give them to Ivan."

"He won't find this at the local store, you know. I'll need fiber optics Internet access installed, and huge bandwidth."

Myatlev shrugged indifferently. "What else?"

"I need access to satellite imagery feeds, real time. I need a satellite under my control."

"Fine. What else?"

"I don't want to be a prisoner anymore. Set me free."

Myatlev didn't see that one coming. That would be the day . . . She'd disappear in a nanosecond.

"Now, why would I do that? Why set you free?"

"I can give you the best that I can, the way things are set up right now. You seem decent, you have arranged to clean up the house of all that filth, and you give me good equipment. But I'm still a prisoner. I miss the sun, the wind. In time, I'll get depressed, lose my edge. Set me free, and every single neuron I have will work for you in ways you can't even think of."

Myatlev took a couple of steps, approaching her. He saw a lot of himself in this young woman. He saw an equal, and that was new to him. Would he ever dare set this woman free? Probably never.

"Let's see how you do for a while, then we'll discuss," he said, as encouragingly as he could.

"Ah . . . you lie," she said, lowering her head.

He reached out and lifted her chin up.

"What would you say if I told you I wanted to fuck you?"

A glint of rage shot from her eyes.

"I'd say there's plenty of pussy out there for you to choose from, but only one brain like mine. Be careful what you want in the long run."

He let her go instantly, as if her skin had burned his fingers. He gave her a long, admiring gaze, while his mind churned with the possibilities of the future with such a formidable resource on his side. Such spirit.

Tom's small den was filled with sunshine, coming through the fine, white sheers with light blue hues from the perfect California morning sky. Indoors, the fumes of fresh-brewed coffee filled the air, a constant presence for almost every one of the work sessions.

There weren't any notes or images pinned to the walls; the room had been cleaned after their last adventure, its walls and whiteboard pristine, waiting for the team's next case. Yet there was tension in the air; unspoken tension, the type that creates deep stress lines on everyone's faces.

"Why won't you consider it, Alex?" Lou asked, a little irritation seeping into his voice. "Anyone in your position would jump at the opportunity. It's right, the logical thing to do."

"I just don't want to have some goon with me 24/7," she replied sternly, crossing her arms. She had a stubborn look in her eyes, and she wasn't budging.

"That's how you see me, Alex, a goon?"

"Ah, Lou, don't go there, for Chrissake. This isn't about you."

"But it would be someone just like me," Lou continued to insist. "It would be someone I know well and I trust with my life, someone I've served with."

Their argument was escalating, and she felt anger and irritation churn inside. He did have a point; getting 24/7 protection was the sensible thing to do under the circumstances. But who, or what, would that make her? Feeble? Unable to take care of herself? Worse, even, what if she got used to trusting someone else with her safety and then slowly lost her edge? How would she be able to do her job then?

More than anything, she dreaded the moment Tom would set his foot down and make it mandatory. As his employee, she could only negotiate that to a certain limit. For the time being, though, Tom watched the exchange quietly. He probably wanted to give her the opportunity to say yes on her own, without pressure from him. She took a quick look at him. His jaws were clenched and his thick, salt-and-pepper eyebrows ruffled by a deep furrow. Not a good sign at all.

"He does have a point," Steve intervened. "Lou would never assign you a bodyguard he doesn't trust with his own life. Please consider it, for all of us. Just for a short while, until you nail that bastard and we all can feel safe again."

She glared at him for a split second; Steve and his overbearing concern for her safety drove her nuts. She just wished he would treat her as an adult, a responsible one, and trust her judgment.

"It wouldn't even be for you," Steve continued to press on. "It would be for our peace of mind. For Tom's, for Claire's, for mine."

Alex remained silent, desperately trying to contain her bout of anger. She didn't say a word, just shook her head a little.

Claire reached out and squeezed her hand gently.

"He's right, you know," she said. "It's more for us than for you. You're very capable of taking care of yourself, my dear. It's to make us feel better. To help us sleep at night."

She couldn't bear to snap at Claire; she'd never met a kinder, more supportive human being.

"Claire, I wish you—"

The doorbell chime froze all of them; no one breathed for a second.

Then Claire stood and headed for the door.

"I'll get it," she said, sounding calm and sure of herself.

Lou drew his weapon and followed her closely. "No," he whispered, "let me."

"Don't worry, Lou," Claire whispered, "they wouldn't ring the doorbell if they were here to kill us, now, would they?"

Lou ignored her, and moved quietly to the left of the door, where narrow windowpanes covered in white sheer gave him a sliver of view to the street. Alex joined him, peeking over his shoulder, her Walther in her hand, ready to fire.

They saw a black, unmarked SUV pulled in front of the driveway. There was one man in front of the door, dressed sharply in a dark suit, carrying a small, black briefcase.

Could that be a bomb? Alex wondered, feeling sweat break at the roots of her hair.

The doorbell rang again. This time, Claire called out, "Just a second!"

She opened the door widely.

"Yes?"

"Claire and Tom Isaac?" the man asked.

"Yes, this is us," she said, her voice showing just a tad of emotion as it trailed off.

"I have a delivery for you."

The man opened the briefcase, holding it on his forearm, and extracted a large, white envelope, with cursive, gold lettering.

Claire accepted it, not taking her eyes from the man's face. "Thank you."

"I was instructed to leave with you the deliveries for Alex Hoffmann, Louis Bailey, and Steve Mercer."

Alex saw Claire's blood drain from her face. Their cover was blown. Tom

Isaac's corporate investigations firm, The Agency, had a cover front, a real estate agency with very few clients, if any. Their cover, built carefully to protect everyone, involved maintaining that there wasn't any real association between The Agency executives, other than a client visiting with their Realtor, and occasional gatherings, typical for real estate agents who keep close ties with the community. Nevertheless, in all fairness, they'd grown more and more relaxed about those safety precautions. They'd gotten sloppy. Maybe it was too late now to fix anything.

"I—I don't know why you'd assume that," Claire said. "They—they don't live here."

"Those are their cars on your driveway, ma'am," the man replied forthright, making Claire wince and Alex strengthen her grip on her Walther. "Will you accept delivery?"

Speechless, Claire took the three envelopes from the man's hand. Her own hand shook a little, and she barely managed to whisper, "Thank you."

The man bowed his head slightly. "Have a good rest of the day, ma'am."

Then he turned on his heels and walked straight to his car. Seconds later, he was gone.

Claire closed the door gently, and walked back into the den, as Alex and Lou holstered their weapons. She sat, still holding the envelopes.

"I'm a bit shook up," she said with a tentative smile. "I never thought the day would come when I'd be scared to open the front door when the doorbell rings."

Tom touched her shoulder, reassuringly. "It's all right, my dear. Let's see what this is about." He grabbed the envelope addressed to him and Claire, and whistled while opening it.

"Are we getting sued?" Alex asked.

The envelope was a heavy silk paper, cream-colored, with metallic, gold lining. He extracted and unfolded the letter, written in black, cursive letters on the same high-end silk paper. The letter held a single paragraph, centered under the White House logo, embossed in gold foil.

"Nothing like that," Tom replied in an excited voice. "You're not going to believe this."

He handed the letter to Alex, whose hand had been reaching out intently. She read it in a split second, then whispered faintly, "Jeez . . ."

"What's it saying?" Lou asked impatiently.

"It says," Alex replied in a voice strangled with emotion, "'The President of the United States requests the pleasure of the company of Mr. and Mrs. Isaac, at a reception to be held at the White House, Friday evening at seven, June the ninth. Southeast entrance.' Holy shit, you guys." She put the letter on the table, then grabbed the envelope addressed to her and opened it. "Yup, same thing."

"Wow, that's something," Lou said, staring at his own letter, unopened.

"What the hell am I going to do?" Alex said, unable to refrain from voicing her wave of anxiety. "Can I just . . . not go?"

"That's nonsense, my dear, you've earned it," Tom replied in his paternal voice. "Why would you not want to go? This is important, for all of us."

"I don't know what to wear. I'm probably going to behave badly, curse, or who knows what stupid thing I'm going to say or do. Spill my drink, maybe, or address the wrong people."

"You'll be fine, Alex," Claire said encouragingly. "You'll be with friends; all of us will be there."

Steve chuckled lightly, then covered his mouth with his hand, but the smile was still there, in his eyes.

"What?" Alex asked.

"You. It's just you, you're so funny."

"Really? How do you figure?" She was getting irritated again; she hated being put on the spot.

"You have no fear or concern going into battle in a foreign country, or running one of the world's largest exfil operations, but you freak out over a party at the White House."

Alex's jaw dropped. Her initial anger melted, taken over by the warmth she felt as she looked in his eyes. She saw in them all the admiration and the respect she'd been longing for.

"Ahem . . . if you put it like that," she conceded, "yes, it *is* kinda funny. Yet I'm still freaking out, you know."

Her phone rang, startling everyone and bringing one more time a frozen silence around the table.

"Unknown," Alex muttered and frowned while checking her phone's display. She picked it up in hands-free. "Hello."

"Alex Hoffmann?" The caller's voice sounded very familiar.

"Yes, that's me."

"This is Henrietta Marino, with the CIA."

"Yes, hi. Good to hear from you," Alex said excitedly. "How are you?"

"Yeah, well, we need you to get on a plane and come see me at Langley for a series of conferences, Miss Hoffmann. How soon can you arrange that?"

"Um . . . what's this about?" A wave of worry swept over her, as she processed Marino's cold, almost threatening inflections.

"You understand we can't discuss any of this over the phone. How soon?"

"I—I can be on the first flight out tomorrow," Alex offered.

"Good. Let's meet on Thursday morning at 10:30AM."

Marino hung up, not waiting for any confirmation.

"Oh, boy," Alex said quietly. "I got a bad feeling about this."

Vitaliy Myatlev headed toward Abramovich's cabinet with a spring in his step. No matter how unpleasant, the meeting was not going to take too long. For a change, he could make commitments that he could keep and support his statements with action and data, with facts.

He knocked twice, then entered the room. Abramovich sat behind his desk, sifting through a pile of paperwork. He didn't even lift his eyes when Myatlev entered. He simply ignored him, leaving him to stand waiting. What an asshole.

Finally, Abramovich threw a glance in his direction.

"Ah, Myatlev."

"Gospodin Prezident," Myatlev replied with caution, noticing the tone of formal distance set by Abramovich.

He continued to stand, as President Abramovich returned to his heap of paper. He let his eyes wander, admiring the traditional yet luxurious Russian setup. The vaulted ceilings, with their signature lattice patterns highlighted in fine gold lines, shimmered discreetly. The inlaid hardwood had intricate geometrical designs, covered in part by a thick area rug with oriental motifs. On the wall behind Abramovich, high on the wall and nested on a hardwood panel, stood the double-headed eagle, Russia's coat of arms, in solid gold. A crystal chandelier with hundreds of light bulbs cast a soft light above their heads.

"Sit down, Myatlev, what are you waiting for?" Abramovich said, almost giving him a start.

He complied, smiled politely, and remained silent.

"Myatlev, what the hell am I going to do with you?"

"Sir?" Myatlev said, feeling uneasy, almost afraid.

"Nothing I ask you to do ever gets done. Nothing! Whose side are you on, anyway?"

Myatlev dreaded these diatribes; they were always a sign of Abramovich's bad mood setting in. Such a mood swing could bring unpredictable results of immense consequences. His mood swings were something Myatlev had learned to fear many years before, when they used to study together at Dzerzhinsky Higher School, and then work together for the KGB, building their careers with each other's help. He'd seen people crushed by his temper attacks, destroyed over nothing. Abramovich's response to stress was that of a three year old. That, combined with the unlimited power he controlled, made him terrible, dangerous, and unpredictable. Myatlev braced himself and let Abramovich continue.

"I had to apologize to the entire damn world, you know that?" Abramovich bellowed. "To the entire world! I had to humiliate myself because of you! Instead of having the Americans begging for their lives, on their knees, defeated, I had to beg *their* forgiveness. You promised me my war, Myatlev! You promised me I'll have the Americans crushed, finished! How many times before have we had this conversation? How many times, huh? What have you got to say?"

Myatlev held his breath. It was serious this time. He'd been smart to clean up his office, pack everything, and get ready to run. What more could he say to this maniac? He'd made every promise in the book, and, against his careful planning, had broken most of them. That fucking Hoffmann bitch. Every time he thought of her, he ground his teeth spasmodically, without even realizing it until he heard the noise that made inside his head.

"Gospodin Prezident, forgive me, please," he said, as humble a voice as he could muster. "I am truly sorry I have caused you such embarrassment. Whatever you choose to do with me, I will respect your wish. All I am asking for is a little more time. I am getting ready to deliver the war you wanted: fast, devastating, and nuclear."

"You're not lying to me, Myatlev?"

"No, sir. I have the nukes ready. Within two weeks, they will be set up for detonation, deep inside the United States. The effects will be devastating and long-lasting. I am foreseeing fifty years of nuclear winter for America. I hope you'll find this scenario satisfying."

Abramovich stood, stretching his back, probably a little stiff from tension, from sitting too long for hours.

"You saved my life, Vitya, I do remember. I will never forget that; I would have been dead now if it weren't for your courage," Abramovich said, his rage visibly subdued. "But I also can't wait forever. They had me apologize to the entire world . . . they and you! It can't happen again; do you understand?"

"Yes, sir," Myatlev replied, knowing better than to give up his formal, respectful tone.

"This is your last warning. You said you'll be ready in two weeks. For the sake of our friendship, I give you three months. But that's all."

"It will be more than enough, Gospodin Prezident. Thank you for your generosity. You won't regret it, I swear."

Abramovich came toward Myatlev and stopped right behind him, putting his arm on Myatlev's shoulder. He stood there for a few long seconds, while Myatlev turned and looked him in the eye, not knowing what to expect.

"What happened, huh?" Abramovich finally spoke. "We were friends; we shared the same goals, the same ideals. Why did you fail me?"

"I still do," he replied. "I still share all your ideals, now more than ever. Now I realize what pure genius drove you to seek this war. We could rule the world. We could *own* it, together. Again!"

Abramovich remained cold and deathly silent, not responding to Myatlev's enthusiasm.

"But I have—I had an enemy, a very powerful and cunning enemy. One who made sure that all my plans failed."

"Who?" the president asked. "Are they your enemy or an enemy of Russia?"

"I don't know yet, not for sure. But I do know, for sure now, that they exist. Before, I used to doubt that, doubting my own sanity. Now I know they're real, and they're powerful. More powerful than anyone I've faced before. I have information; a face, a name, who can lead me to their entire organization."

"Americans?"

"Americans, *da.*"

"Fucking Americans . . . I'm telling you, Vitya, we have to rid the world of their entitled arrogance. What do you know about this enemy of yours, of ours?"

"They're the ones who crashed my operation in the Far East. They are very resourceful and very well organized. They seem to have access to secrets that only you and I know. Yes, I know what you're going to say but no, I've swept all offices, my home, my car, and everything was clean. I almost ripped the entire building to shreds. No bugs, none. We couldn't find any recording devices."

"Who knew about your Far East operation? I didn't even know, Vitya," Abramovich said, his voice filled with bitter reproach.

"No one; that's the problem. That's why I thought I was losing my mind. Now it's different. Now I know about them, I'm on to them. This time will be different, I promise."

"Different, how?"

"Now they can't surprise me anymore. Our mission will be a success. America will have the punishment you've always envisioned for it. Crippled, defeated, kneeling for your mercy, and crying for your help from the depths of a nuclear winter that will set its sun forever."

"Cry for my help, you say?"

"Yes. Just imagine. Americans' land, devastated by our attack, covered in radioactive ash. How will they eat? How will they survive, those of them who won't die in the first days? Their only hope will be Russia. We can feed them, for a price. If you decide they're worth feeding at all."

"Uh-huh," Abramovich said, deep in thought. He rubbed his bony chin.

"Just as you wanted them, begging for their lives, at your mercy."

Abramovich patted him twice on the back, but said nothing. He circled his desk slowly, then took a bottle of vodka from the ice bucket and poured the liquid into two cut crystal glasses.

"You promise?" Abramovich asked, smiling for the first time in days. He handed Myatlev his glass and raised his in a silent toast.

"I swear it to you on my life, Petya. On my life."

"*Ura!*" Abramovich said, then gulped the vodka, exhaling loudly as the liquid burned his esophagus.

"Ura," Myatlev replied, then took a small sip.

The first chance he had, he discreetly poured the rest of his vodka at the root of a potted plant. Abramovich didn't notice a thing, as he turned his back and headed to his massive leather chair.

"Now let's talk details, Vitya. I won't be surprised again. Tell me, what exactly are you planning to do?

Myatlev waited for the two men to settle in their seats before talking. While the two high-ranking SVR officers poured their coffee and took out their notebooks, he studied them carefully. He had known them personally for some time, but people change.

Colonel Anton Lagunov, SVR's head of Border Intelligence Operations, had definitely changed. He must have added at least five inches around his waist since they last met. His uniform fit well though, probably made to order. His pudgy fingers and bulldog jowls spoke of his many indulgences. At this rate, soon he'd have difficulties walking through the door. He must have recently become one of the heaviest men in the Foreign Intelligence Service.

Lagunov was a capable intelligence officer though. He'd distinguished himself on several occasions, and Smolin had spoken very highly of him. His team gathered valuable intelligence about border screening processes in all countries of interest. He knew what procedures were used to screen incoming visitors, cargo, private aircraft, or marine vessels. What could or couldn't be transported across which borders, and how—he was the man who knew.

Myatlev's other visitor, also Foreign Intelligence Service or SVR, was Lieutenant Colonel Aleksei Slutsky. He was in charge of nuclear logistics and response. Although the SVR focused on intelligence operations outside Russia, Slutsky's responsibilities sometimes crossed that borderline, much as a radioactive cloud would.

The two men finally seated at the small conference table, Myatlev waved Ivan out of the room. He waited for the soundproof door to come to a full close.

"Good morning,"

"Good morning, sir," they replied in unison.

"The operation we are about to discuss is above top secret and has the full endorsement of President Abramovich. Very few people know anything about it. Please treat this as highly confidential. Don't take any notes or discuss anything with anyone. Code name, Operation Sunset."

"Understood," Slutsky replied.

Lagunov nodded in compliance, closed his notebook, and pushed it to the side.

"The problem at hand is the transport of several small-size nuclear devices across the border into the United States. They have been designed to fit in individual backpacks. They're heavy, but manageable."

Myatlev stopped talking for a little while, allowing both men to process the information. He looked them one by one in the eye, and both men held his gaze unperturbed. Good. He liked what he saw, their unwavering commitment to their country, to their superiors.

"The question is, what's the safest, fastest, most reliable way of doing it?" Myatlev continued. "Ask any questions you need; I'll answer everything I can."

"How big are these nukes?" Slutsky asked.

"Just the nukes? About 50 pounds, or 23 kilos each."

"And yield?"

"Three kilotons."

"Ah, relatively small," Lagunov commented.

"They're almost a fifth of Hiroshima," Slutsky clarified. "Each."

"How many are we talking about?"

"Fourteen."

A moment of silence engulfed the room. Myatlev allowed it to take its course for a little while, then continued.

"How do we deploy them? We need them on the ground, within the American borders."

"Where do you need them? East Coast? West Coast?" Lagunov asked.

"West Coast," Myatlev replied. "Anywhere on the West Coast is fine."

Lagunov pushed away from the small, round conference table and stood with a groan. He paced thoughtfully, clasping and unclasping his chubby hands and rubbing them against each other.

"We can do this several ways," he eventually said. "One way is to pack them all in a small, motorized, underwater container, like an automated sub. We drop that sub from a low-flying plane in international waters, close enough to the American territorial waters, but not too close. We rig this sub to head to shore as soon as it hits the water. Then we retrieve the cargo with a private marine vessel. The vessel can lock and track its beacon, find it right—"

"That's risky, though," Slutsky interrupted. We'd be having all our eggs in one submarine basket, in an area that's heavily patrolled by members of the US Coast Guard. They have issues with Mexicans smuggling drugs. They'd be all over any private marine vessel pulling cargo from the sea.

"I say it can work," Lagunov insisted. "They don't have the resources to look at all the craft sailing near shore. If we do the drop at higher latitude, then we're farther out from the Mexican border. We'd have fewer issues with the Coast

Guard.

"You're forgetting this is a big piece of cargo someone has to hoist out of the sea," Slutsky clarified. "It's heavy. We're talking fourteen times 50 pounds, 75 pounds with the rest of the gear, plus the sub. That's almost 1,000 pounds. You'll need hoisting equipment to pull that out of the water. That draws attention for sure."

"What if we pull them out one by one, using a diver?" Lagunov asked. "Can these nukes be underwater? Can they be submerged?"

"Probably it's not a good idea. They have electronics, a timing device, and a satellite receiver," Myatlev replied. "What else can we try?"

"We could try smuggling them in aboard cargo containers," Lagunov said. "Cargo containers remain the biggest vulnerability in the US border security, although the agents are getting much smarter, and fast."

"That could work, Lagunov; give me more," Slutsky said.

"High-volume maritime ports process millions of cargo containers each year. Most of the ports are now modernized, with security measures built to prevent exactly what we're trying to do. Containers go through an X-ray gate, like luggage does at airports. The agents have sniffing dogs, that'll sniff almost any type of drug or explosive. The latest technology they deployed takes air samples from inside the containers, through the air vents, and analyzes that with a mass spec. Within minutes, they know every single compound that's inside that container."

"That's not good," Myatlev commented. "If we use containers, my agents have to each carry their own backpack. We can't risk the cargo on one single container."

"There's also the issue of nuclear radiation sensors," Slutsky added. "Maritime ports are strategic objectives, so all ports are probably fitted with multiple sensors. The backpacks would have to be perfectly insulated with several layers of lead packaging. And that will add to the weight."

"What if we tried one shipment by container, to see how it goes?" Lagunov asked.

"That's not going to do it for me. If that one is caught, it would raise security levels, keeping all the others from getting in. No, we need all of them to attempt entry simultaneously. Probably some will get caught, but most will make it. I've provisioned for that scenario."

"Uh-huh," Lagunov mumbled, thinking hard. "I think I have a solution. Please allow me a few hours to think through it in detail, check my most recent data, and come back with more information. We might need a diversion. Or something."

"Agreed," Myatlev replied, pushing his chair away from the table and standing, ready to leave. "You got 'til tomorrow morning."

Alex parked her rental and took a minute to breathe, to recompose. Her heart was racing, and her sweaty palms had been a nuisance on her drive over. Quite surprisingly, she'd slept well through the night, although she didn't expect to get little more than a wink.

"Well, this is it; let's get this show on the road," she mumbled to herself.

She'd expected a warmer tone from Marino, considering their recent collaboration. Alas no, the woman was cold as ice, almost mean. Tom, in his infinite wisdom, had taught her there was no way she could guess what was on Marino's mind. "Stop worrying, go out there, and find out," he'd said. "Whatever it is, we'll deal with it." Right. "We" was not here, at Langley, about to enter Marino's home field. Only she was.

She strengthened her posture and arranged her jacket, running a sweaty palm against the side to smooth some invisible wrinkles. She checked her reflection in the car's tinted windows. She looked sharp, wearing a black Anne Klein business suit, combined with a white silk shirt, to underline the image of cold, effective professionalism. Her black Prada shoes and matching briefcase had set her back four figures at Nordstrom. She looked exactly how she wanted for that morning's meeting. She breathed a little easier and couldn't contain the hint of a smile. Her self-confidence was creeping back up.

She walked the considerable distance to the main entrance and entered the lobby, realizing it was her first time to enter the CIA building. That was another first, to add to the growing collection of many recent others. First time discharging a weapon in a foreign country. First time breaking into a foreign military base. First time on an aircraft carrier. Now, first time visiting the CIA. Huh . . . it should be easy-peasy by comparison.

She walked straight to the reception desk and presented her ID to one of the officers, announcing her name and referencing Marino as her appointment. The officer promptly stood and escorted her, at first, through security screening. The security person x-rayed her briefcase and had her walk through metal detectors. Then the officer led her to a small conference room and asked her to take a seat and wait.

She sat on the simple, uncomfortable chair and placed her briefcase on the table. There wasn't much furniture in that room. As she started absorbing and processing the details of the room, Alex realized it looked more and more like an interrogation room. Barren, grayish walls, and an active video camera in the corner, right under the ceiling. Rugged, simplistic furniture, easy to clean but not easy to scratch or destroy, made of laminate panels on stainless steel frames. The traditional mirror was there too, most likely a one-way.

She regretted not noticing what the room was labeled. Was it called "Conference Room X"? Or "Interrogation Room X"? The officer had opened the door for her, covering the tag with his body. She walked to the door and tried to open it, but it was locked.

"Uh-huh," she muttered. "Just what I expected. Damn it, Marino . . ."

She looked straight into the camera, her hands on her hips, and said loudly, "Really?"

Then she sat back on her chair, pulled her iPad from her briefcase and started reading to keep her mind from going crazy with anxiety.

A few minutes later, the door opened and Marino walked in. She looked her normal self; her hair was loosely tied in a ponytail, and she didn't wear any makeup; except maybe a touch of lipstick, but it was hard to tell. She wore her nails trimmed short and clear of nail polish. She was dressed in a brown polyester suit and a light blue, low-cut top. For a moment, Alex worried she'd overdressed, but then remembered she'd been locked up in an interrogation room and thought, *let her take it.*

Marino slammed a file folder on the table, then pulled out a chair. The chair made a loud, shrill, grating noise that made her cringe.

"Miss Hoffmann," Marino said by way of a greeting.

"Agent Marino," Alex replied, smiling warmly.

"I'm an analyst. Definitely not an agent. CIA doesn't have that nomenclature, not for home-based employees, anyway." There was no warmth in Marino's tone.

Alex's smile died, frozen, as she felt a pang of fear.

"What do I call you then?" Alex replied coldly.

"Marino is fine."

"All right." Alex closed her reader and put it in the briefcase. "I'm all ears. What is this about?"

"In short, Miss Hoffmann, we want to know who's your source."

"Who's my *what*?"

"Source. You have a source in Russia. We're talking about the person who's been feeding you the information that you've been acting on."

"I—I don't have a source," Alex stammered, shocked. She'd never seen that coming. She'd expected heat for acting without sanction, without an official role, but she didn't see this question coming.

Marino stood abruptly and slammed both her hands against the table, palms down.

"Oh, come on, Hoffmann! You're a smart woman! You know people don't just dream this stuff up! People don't just wake up one morning and find missing people, based on their sheer luck, all the way behind enemy lines. People have sources, who tell them where to find what they're looking for. Who's yours?"

Alex leaned back against the backrest of her chair and almost smiled. She'd seen worse illogical arguments, not even in interrogation rooms but in corporate conference rooms.

"Honestly, I don't have a source, Miss Marino. I wish I did, I really do."

Marino sighed with frustration.

"Need I remind you you're not a journalist? The law doesn't protect your sources."

Alex pursed her lips, feeling her rage build.

"Miss Marino, with all due respect, there are only so many ways I can tell you I don't have a source," she said, her speech barely stronger than a whisper. She did that in an effort to refrain from yelling the woman's head off in a cocktail of cuss words. She was getting angry, fed up with this nonsense.

Marino shook her head, unimpressed.

"Do you realize what's at stake here? Huh? Do you? Do you realize you could be charged with treason? Do you realize I can throw you in jail without process, without any rights, under the PATRIOT Act? You're conspiring with a foreign national, trading information. He's obviously feeding you great intel. The question is what are you giving him in return?"

"What?" Alex stood and started pacing the room. "You people are insane! I don't have a source!"

"Sit back down," Marino commanded. Alex complied, with a shrug and a grimace of disappointment.

"No offense, but if you were a little more open-minded, you might be able to have the results I did, on your own," Alex said, making Marino turn red as a beet. *Great job, Alex*, she thought, *make your interrogator angry. Great strategy.*

"How dare you?" Marino growled. "I bailed your ass out of there, and I thought we could collaborate, we could work together."

"You call this collaboration? Really?" Alex said, her tone loaded with biting sarcasm. "How about thanking me for dropping everything and flying across the country when you needed me? How about offering me a cup of coffee and asking me how I did what I did, before throwing these ridiculous accusations in my face? How about not locking me up? Huh? How about that for collaboration?"

Marino shook her head, her eyes steely, harsh, piercing.

"Nice . . . I still believe you have a source, and if you're any bit as smart as you like to think you are, you have to tell us who that is."

"All right, keep going down that rabbit hole, Marino," Alex said angrily, throwing her arms in the air. "It's going to be a very long day, because I have no damn source to give you to make this end!"

"Somehow I doubt that," Marino replied calmly.

There was nothing more prone to get Alex to blow up than to have an intense argument with someone who remained calm. It felt like the person had manipulated her, with her buttons pressed in the right order to get her to be emotional, lose her cool, and start reacting instead of thinking. This time was no exception. The seriousness of her situation, where she was, the fact that a video camera recorded every word she said, suddenly made no difference.

"Don't you think I would have loved to have a source?" Alex bellowed, jumping off her chair. "Huh? Well, guess what? I would have loved to have a source, 'cause then I'd know this guy's name!"

"Sit down, Miss Hoffmann," Marino said.

"Ah, shove it, Marino!" Alex replied, yelling from the bottom off her lungs. "I don't have a goddamn source, so I have to spend day and night wondering who this guy is. Where is he going to strike next, do *you* know? I don't! If I had that source, I'd know who he is, and I'd go out there and . . . *retire* the son of a bitch!"

"You'd go out and kill him? You?" Marino asked, almost snickering. "You, an uncredentialed, unsanctioned civilian, you'd go on a clean-up op, all by your merry self, and kill a man?"

Alex turned and put her palms on the table, getting in Marino's face, only inches away, close enough to feel her breath on her skin.

"I'd kill a terrorist, not a man. Wouldn't you? 'Cause that's *your* job!"

No one spoke a word for a few seconds. Then Alex sat and took a long breath. *Okay . . . that probably wasn't very smart,* she thought. She rubbed her forehead a little, then the back of her neck, embarrassed with her lack of self-control, trying to compose herself.

Marino sat too, closed the file she'd brought and recomposed herself as well. She looked flushed, with dark shades of red coloring not only her cheeks, but also her neck and chest. She probably should have her blood pressure checked. Alex thought to recommend that, but then decided against it and remained silent.

"Let's start over," Marino said in a softer, almost polite tone. "Can we please do that?"

"Um . . . sure," Alex replied, a little intrigued.

"Here goes," Marino said with an uncomfortable, timid smile. "Alex, thank you for flying here on such short notice. We appreciate it."

"Sure, anytime," Alex replied, frowning in disbelief. What was that all about? Was it time for good cop? No one changed that fast. Who was that woman, and what had she done with Marino?

"We need to know everything you know about the terrorist you call V, and how you acquired the information. You see, we have a spike in chatter, chatter of the Russian flavor. These days, everyone's keeping their eyes and ears on ISIS, but we've registered heightened activity on the Russian side, and we don't know what to make of it."

"Interesting . . . what are you hearing?"

Marino frowned briefly before responding, probably more used to asking questions in that room rather than answering them.

"Well, we're not sure, not yet. But there are mentions of travel plans, arrangements of all kinds, and some references to a 'family gathering.'"

"This is much better, thank you for doing this," Alex replied, then added, seeing how confused Marino looked, "for treating me like an ally, a partner. Even if you don't believe in it, maybe you will, with time."

Marino nodded with a sigh of resignation.

"Will you help us?"

"With everything I can. I'll tell you everything I know. I hope that it will help. But there are some rules to our cooperation," Alex said and winked. "There are some actions of mine for which I'll take the fifth. I hope you'll understand."

"Okay, let's see how it goes," she said, then opened her notebook.

"I'm sure you know by now I work as a private investigator specialized in corporate investigations. Business owners or boards of directors who see troublesome signs in their business operations, or results that they can't comprehend, typically contract my employer's company, The Agency. That's when they call us and I go in and work for that client company, undercover, posing as one of their leadership level employees. I conduct my investigations from within the troubled company. This is the norm; this is how I work. Any questions so far?"

"No, please go on," Marino said, not lifting her eyes from the notes she was jotting.

"A couple of years back, I was asked to investigate a certain company. The investigation led me to uncover a global conspiracy of unprecedented proportions. From here on, I take the fifth, up until the point where we had identified all the conspirators except their leader. They were retired, and, in the process, interrogated."

"By you?" Marino's eyes were round, and her eyebrows high, creasing her forehead.

"No," Alex chuckled, "by Mossad."

"Jeez!"

"Yeah . . . Well, Mossad interrogated the one conspirator it could get close to, but he died before giving more than one initial, V. That's how we learned about his initial. We also knew we didn't catch him, obviously. We knew we were missing one key terrorist, the leader of their cell. We tried . . . we tried everything we could, including foreign travel associations, money trails, everything we could think of."

"Do you trust this information to be accurate?"

"Yes. Mossad would have no reason to deceive us. It was a good partner."

"I still can't get over the fact that Mossad worked with you. Who the hell are you, people? How did you even get to Mossad?"

"Long story, where I have to take the fifth on behalf of someone else."

"You know there's no such thing, right?"

"Yeah, I do," Alex replied dryly, "but it's as good as it gets."

Marino nodded and let out a frustrated sigh.

"The other thing worth mentioning about that case is that all the terrorists involved, all the conspirators, were loaded. They were of different nationalities, most of them Arab, but all of them rich, successful business people—not fitting the traditional terrorist profile."

"Hmm . . . interesting. Got it. What else?"

"I've encountered V's fingerprint, MO, or style, whatever you want to call it, during another case, for which, of course, I'll take—"

"The fifth, I get it. Move on."

"Again I couldn't find out his identity, but it became apparent that he's the master puppeteer again, the man operating from the shadows. Again, we were only able to capture the second line, but never got to the first. I worked with the FBI on this; I think my credentials are still valid."

"Jeez, Hoffmann, do you have a limit?" Marino reacted, amazed and chuckling lightly, shaking her head.

"None that I've uncovered so far," she quipped. "Anyway, so that's why, when I was asked to find those people, and I saw the greatness of the plan, the strategic prowess of the master puppeteer, his brilliance, I believed there was a strong chance it could be V again. Therefore, I went on with my search, very open-minded, and found them. After all, I had no definitive proof that V was behind it. I still don't, but it fits. From there onward you know what happened; you bailed my ass, for which I remain eternally grateful."

"You also did a number with some flares? Why?"

"To draw him out, in case I'd been right. I wanted him to take it personally and I called him out. Made it personal. Showed him that I knew who he was."

"But you don't know, do you?"

"No, I don't, but he doesn't know that," Alex said, smiling with a devious look in her eyes.

"You know he could probably kill you in your sleep, right? If he really is this global-reach, master orchestrator and key strategist, he could easily get to you. That was one stupid thing you did, so you know."

"Oh, I've been told that, more than a few times already, but I need to find him no matter what. Who knows what calamity he'll think up next?"

"One more thing, Alex. Do you have any idea what this 'family gathering' that we're hearing about could be?"

Alex thought for a moment.

"No . . . sadly I don't. But I'll keep thinking and I'll be in touch."

Alex's head was on a swivel, taking in every detail of the ride to the White House. Yes, it was yet another first, and quite a notable one. She wore a permanent smile of excitement and anticipation and still felt a little uneasy after extensive coaching sessions offered generously by Claire. She'd patiently taught her how to use every cutlery utensil invented, how to sit properly, and how to eat like a lady. Apparently, her education had been quite lacking.

Raised by engineers of German heritage, that finding came as no surprise. Now she had several more things to worry about. Was her back straight enough? Were her elbows close enough to her body? Was she spilling her soup? Maybe they'd have the common sense and not serve any soup, or any food that struggles dearly to escape from the plate. Ugh . . .

Tom's advice also came to mind. He recommended she focus on the evening, on having fun and feeling good. She should take in the experience and enjoy one of the highest forms of recognition offered to American citizens. Tom seemed a little stiff, though, in his impeccable tux and his shiny, pure silk, white shirt. He sat in the huge limo across from her, his legs crossed casually, looking like blue-blooded royalty.

Alex was a new generation young woman, more comfortable in jean shorts and sneakers than wearing the expensive evening gown she had donned that evening. The dress hugged her form gracefully, and the shimmering black fabric was a thing of wonder. Of course, Claire had helped her choose it, after a brief but determined exchange about going strapless. Claire had insisted, calling the strapless black gown the ultimate reception elegance, but Alex didn't want to worry about things sliding out of place. By the look Steve had given her when she was ready to leave, she knew she hadn't compromised by much. She looked fabulous, and she loved how Steve's eyes reflected that acknowledgment.

The black limousine pulled in at the southeast entrance and came to a stop. Tom opened the windows on their side, and she looked outside, curious to take in all the details, to breathe the air, and enjoy every bit of scenery. Secret Service agents approached the limo and greeted them respectfully, then interacted briefly with the limo driver. The limo was part of the White House fleet and had been sent to pick them up at their hotel.

Alex looked out the window, observing the details of their screening procedures. It must be hard to need this kind of security all the time. Even if a Secret Service agent drove the limo, it still underwent screening procedures. It must be hard, knowing there are people who want you dead. *But wait*, she thought humorously, *I already know how hard that is.*

They were cleared to proceed; within seconds, the limo pulled in at the entrance, and the door was held open for them. Alex felt a little overwhelmed, strangled with emotion as she walked inside. She noticed very few details as they were led to a meet-and-greet area, where they were invited to taste the aperitifs, readily offered by a white-gloved waiter. They were the first guests to arrive.

She accepted a small glass of champagne, and when she turned around, she locked eyes with Marino.

"Alex," she greeted her with a nice smile.

"Miss Marino," Alex replied, unable to hide her surprise. Although she'd recognized her at first, after giving her a second look, she didn't recognize her anymore. Dressed with class in a blue silk gown, her hair done up with style, she wasn't the same person she'd spoken with the day before.

"Henri. I think it's about time you called me Henri," she offered.

"Henri," Alex acknowledged with a nod, and shook her hand. She appreciated the invitation, but it didn't sound right. To Alex, she'll always be Marino, tough as nails.

"Let's go meet my boss, Director Seiden."

A few steps toward the entrance, a tall man with intense eyes under a solid frown looked their way, then nodded slightly, inviting them to approach. He didn't look a day older than forty. *How does one become so powerful, so young?*

"Director, this is Alex Hoffmann," Marino said, "Alex, meet Director Seiden, head of the Central Intelligence Agency."

"Ah, the famous Alex Hoffmann," Seiden said, the smile on his lips not matching the coldness in his eyes. He shook her hand firmly, and then turned on his heels to face the door, right as President Krassner was coming in.

Alex swallowed hard and flashed her megawatt smile, resisting the urge to wipe her sweaty palm against the delicate fabric of her gown.

"Welcome, everyone," Krassner said. "It's a pleasure to have you all here this evening." He took a few steps forward, and greeted her warmly. "Miss Hoffmann."

"Mister President," she croaked, strangled by emotion, then cleared her throat. "It's an honor to be here. Thank you for having us."

Krassner shook her hand firmly, then moved to greet Tom and Claire. She breathed, irritated with her own emotions. How could she be such a wuss? How could she feel so insecure? It was just a dinner, for Chrissake. She took a deep breath, straightened her back, and decided she was going to be just fine.

A few moments later, the guests took their seats in the dining room, in front of impeccably set accoutrements. Fine china plates with thin, gold borders were set on white, octagonal place mats. Simple crystal glasses, set directly on the shiny, lacquered finish of a hardwood table brought a slight frown to her forehead. *I better not spill my drink then, not even a drop*, she thought. The impeccable silverware didn't contain any troublesome tools, like snail tongs, crab crackers, or fondue forks. Claire had been spot on when she'd reassured her that the president didn't want pieces of crab flying through the air, or people going into anaphylactic shock over their seafood allergies, too intimidated to refuse any part of the presidential meal. Claire had anticipated the meal would be exquisite, but not exotic, and that was exactly what was printed on the cursively written menu resting on her plate. They were going to enjoy a small salad with fine cheeses, followed by Beef Wellington with three mouthwatering sides, and dessert. All courses were served with different, well-assorted wines.

Alex had expected Krassner to take the seat at the head of the table, but he sat across from her, in the middle of the table, flanked by Tom on his left, and Seiden on his right. Marino sat next to Seiden, and looked significantly less sure of herself than the day before, in that so-called conference room. With that thought at the back of her mind, Alex reflected briefly on Krassner's single status. Had there ever been an unmarried American president? The times were definitely changing.

Claire was seated next to Alex, to her right, and Steve to her left. Lou flanked Claire's other side. Alex had managed to not come that close to Steve since they parted ways as a couple and remained simple coworkers. She was painfully aware of his proximity. Good thing Krassner was seated right across; she had good reason to not look to her left at all.

"I am privileged to find myself in such company," Krassner said, the first to speak after they'd taken their assigned seats. "It's not often that I have my dinner table surrounded by heroes."

Alex felt a rush of blood burn her cheeks. Thank goodness for makeup. No one was going to see her blush. At least that. As for knowing how to react, she had no idea; she just followed along, watching Tom and Claire for hints. They listened calmly, smiling politely, so she did the same.

"Some heroes can never be recognized the traditional way, with medals pinned to their chests, in public acclaim. Some heroes will remain unknown to the public, for reasons you all understand. However, our country's debt of gratitude to all of you is immense. Please accept my heartfelt thanks for your dedication, sacrifice, for fighting for our citizens' freedom, no matter where that fight took you."

Tom nodded once, slowly, keeping his head lowered for a split second more than usual, conveying respect. "On behalf of my entire team, thank you, Mr. President," he said. "It is an unexpected honor to find ourselves seated at your table, an honor we will cherish for the rest of our lives."

She followed suit, and placed her hand on her chest when thanking him.

Several servers brought delicate bowls of spring salads, and the president picked up his fork, getting ready to eat.

"How do you do it, Miss Hoffmann? How do you do what you do?" Krassner asked.

"It's Alex, please," she blurted, instantly aware that it might have not been appropriate. *Damn!* "I—I just keep an open mind, I guess. I don't eliminate any scenarios, and I don't recognize any obstacles. That was a valuable lesson I learned from this guy—um . . . this man here, my colleague, Steve Mercer."

"Obstacles?" Krassner probed, while Alex locked eyes with Tom searching for his silent approval, and found it.

"Um . . . like another country's borders," she said, instantly regretting it as soon as she registered the chuckles going around the table, "or, not having satellites."

"Would you care to elaborate?" Krassner asked.

"Yes, sure. For me, when I'm doing my job, no scenario, no outcome, and no methods are too extreme. Let's say, for example, that I need satellite imagery for a certain location. This is the point where most people would throw their arms in the air and say, 'Sorry, we don't have satellites. We're not the government, we're not military, and we're not CNN. We'll just settle for Google maps, no matter how old those images might be.' Instead, I just go get me a satellite or two."

Krassner chuckled once, then asked, "How? How do you get what you want?"

"I just solve it, that's all. Instead of saying, 'No, I can't,' I just solve the problem, for example, 'What needs to happen for me to get access to satellite imagery?' Such problems typically return multiple solutions. I just take the easiest, fastest method, and execute it."

"I like your style, Alex," Krassner said. "What else goes into your recipe?"

"Um . . . once I figure out what the enemy or the target thinks, what his motivations are, I like to ask, 'What would I do if I were the enemy?' That's all."

"Whew, Alex, then I'm glad you're on our friends list," Krassner said, and everyone laughed with him. "I, for one, if I hear you're worried about something or someone, I will pay attention."

"Thank you, Mr. President," she said, bowing her head a little.

Krassner turned his attention to Claire, asking her about life with a husband with such an interesting line of work. Alex missed Claire's answer, as she noticed Seiden's keen interest in her, making her a little uncomfortable. His eyes drilled into her as if trying to pry her open. Then she watched Seiden lean into Tom's ear while touching his shoulder.

"Is she available? CIA needs assets like her," Seiden whispered.

"You'd have to ask her. As far as I know, she's not a huge fan of large, organized environments with lots of politics going on," Tom replied warmly. "But even if she won't come work for you, you're welcome anytime to ask for her help if you need it. As far as I know, she won't say no to a good challenge."

"Ah, I see," Seiden replied dryly, frowning more than his usual. "Thank you."

"You're welcome," Tom said graciously.

Alex locked eyes with Seiden. They held each other's glances for a few seconds, and Alex fought the urge to look away, feeling still irritated with the treatment she'd received the day before. Seiden's drilling gaze fueled her irritation.

"So, what makes you tick, Alex?" Seiden asked.

"People's rights," she replied, almost harshly. "I guess deep inside I'm an idealist. I believe in people's freedom to live good lives in fair, lawful environments."

Her jaws clenched; was she being interviewed by the CIA again? This time for a job she didn't even want? She didn't like Seiden; not at all. His type used anyone and everyone to get what he wanted, then spat them out, used, destroyed, and emptied shells with no future, like crushed soda cans thrown to the curb. She'd seen it before.

"How so?" Seiden pressed on.

"I have an intense sense of right and wrong, and I feel strongly about it. For instance, locking someone up without due process is wrong. I hope you agree, at least in principle?" Alex asked with a sweet smile that failed to cover the storm brewing inside.

Marino rolled her eyes discreetly, but Alex noticed it. She nodded briefly in her direction, amusement fluttering on her lips. *Yeah, what did you expect, huh? I still remember yesterday.*

"I absolutely do," Seiden's surprised answer came, just as Alex felt Claire's hand discreetly touching her thigh. She took that as a message to cool off and calm down. She gave Claire's hand a quick, reassuring squeeze, then turned to Seiden and buried the hatchet.

"That's exactly what I thought. Great, because that means we could do great things together."

Marino looked at her with round, consternated eyes; her confusion was hilarious.

Alex sighed. The president's dinner table was no place for arguments on principle, especially with powerful men who might come in handy sometime. Claire was wise, as always.

"You're flying back to the Golden Coast tomorrow, Alex?" Krassner asked, surprising her as she was taking a bite of incredibly tasty crème brûlée and savoring it with eyes half closed.

She swallowed quickly and replied, "No, not yet. I've decided to stay in town for a few days, see some old friends, and maybe do some shopping. I'm between assignments right now."

...Chapter 11: Eruption
...Saturday, June 10, 11:47AM Local Time (UTC-8:00 hours)
...46°32'19.2"N 121°30'04.8"W
...Old Snowy Mountain, Near Mount Rainier, Washington

The man climbed with little effort, although he didn't follow a trail, and he carried a heavy backpack. He made his own way up, choosing carefully where to set his next footstep. He'd left the last beaten path climbing the northwestern versant of Old Snowy Mountain and kept on going. Every now and then, he checked his handheld GPS and the time. Then he kept climbing at a steady pace, taking deep breaths of rarefied air with each step.

At first, his climb took him through the lush forest, where ascending had been easier, his footing firm against tree roots. Then he left the forest behind and his ascent slowed somewhat, requiring him to make often use of his climbing axe and his rope loop. Barren rock, here and there, covered by patches of sparkling snow, let him know he was close to reaching his destination, the highest peak of the versant.

A quick walk on the crest and he'd made it to his destination, Johnson Peak, 7,487 feet high. The air was clear and crisp, the view breathtaking, and the sun shone brightly on an intensely blue sky. The man paid no attention to any of that, and, after setting down his backpack, turned his attention northwest, squinting a little against the blazing sun.

In the distance, the magnificent silhouette of Mount Rainier stood high and proud, the upper half of its approximately 14,400-feet-tall cone still covered in snow, a dazzling view for anyone who'd ever laid eyes on it. An active volcano of the modern era, Rainier had been quiet for more than 120 years, showing little or no recent signs of seismic or volcanic activity. Reassured by the mountain's quiet mood, hundreds of thousands of people had chosen to live on older lahars, the now hardened flows of pyroclastic material, mud, and molten rock proud Rainier had spewed centuries before, when it had been awake and angry.

The problem with lahars is that where one has flowed before, another will follow, as they typically flow through naturally formed valleys or along riverbeds. However, lahars only happen in case of an eruption, not otherwise; that was the shared truth that people who had made the area their home had told themselves. Rainier was sleeping soundly; they were safe.

Thirty miles farther northwest, following such lahars-filled valleys, one would find Tacoma, home to more than 200,000 people who loved to wake up in the morning and admire Mount Rainier as it adorned their horizon line.

The thirty miles were not devoid of populace though; charming little towns like Carbonado, Fairfax, or Buckley map the road from Rainier to Tacoma, following the natural valleys and built on hardened lahars. North of Tacoma, a short twenty-five miles of beeline, Seattle is home for more than 650,000 people. The Seattle-Tacoma metro area is home to almost four million people, who are betting their lives on Mount Rainier's deep sleep.

What a colossal mistake.

Mount Rainier's conical peak also stood at more than 20 miles away from Johnson Peak. Just what the man wanted; not too close, but not too far either.

The man checked his time, then sat on a big boulder, getting some rest. He carefully checked his surroundings, his head turning in the direction of any sound, no matter how tiny. Satisfied with his privacy, the man unpacked his backpack and extracted a seismometer and a laptop. He crouched, setting the seismometer down carefully, then attached the laptop and powered everything on.

The device immediately started displaying lines on the screen; tiny oscillations visible, so tiny they didn't mean much. The man stood and stomped his foot down forcefully. The seismometer recorded a spike. Satisfied, the man checked his watch again and looked briefly at Mount Rainier. Then he extracted a chocolate bar from one of the backpack's many pockets and sat on a boulder, eating slowly, savoring it.

The alarm went off on his watch as he was stuffing the chocolate bar wrapper in his pants left pocket. He grabbed his binoculars and hung on to a nearby boulder, for balance.

There was a loud explosion, sending the seismometer's digital needles off the charts. In the distance, Mount Rainier spewed a puff of dust, ash, and vapor. Then a second explosion ensued, this one a deeper pitch, yet stronger than the first. The seismometer's needles oscillated off the charts for a long time, and the man held on to the boulder tightly, wrapping his left arm around it and crouching lower against it.

He watched the mountain through binoculars for a while, then gave up on those and watched the mountain directly. Rainier spewed ash and vapor for a few minutes, then erupted in a series of aftershocks, sending fire-embedded smoke, ash, and gas toward the blue sky in a column miles high. Parts of the column fell back, collapsing to the sides of the mountain in pyroclastic flows to accompany the fiery lava overflowing the edges of the caldera.

He couldn't see much anymore; angry Mount Rainier had shrouded itself in a dark, threatening cloud of ash and smoke, covering the sun and darkening the day. There wasn't much left for him to do. He needed to get going before ash covered the trails, making them slippery and treacherous to climb down.

He checked the seismometer's readings again, shut down his equipment, and packed everything in his backpack. Then he pulled out a satellite phone and retrieved a number from the phone's memory.

"It's done," he said, the moment his party picked up his call.

Then he started his descent off Johnson Peak, leaving Mount Rainier behind, shrouded in ash and smoke, hidden from view. There was nothing left for him to do there; his job was done.

Mount Rainier was wide awake and angry as hell.

Before his morning exercise routine, Myatlev liked to enjoy a cup of fresh-brewed green tea. Part of his recent transformation, tea had replaced his morning coffee, with difficulty at first, despite being one of the world's finest brands. No matter how tasty, green tea was no coffee, and Myatlev needed some time to get used to that. Nevertheless, the effects were visible after only a couple of weeks; his skin grew tighter, his flab started to fade away, his mind became more alert, and his appetite for physical exercise was surprising.

He heard clamor outside the door of his office. He made a quick move to put the teacup back on its saucer and spilled some hot fluid, scalding his hand.

"Fuck . . ." he muttered, wiping the tea with a tissue he pulled from a desk drawer.

Ivan stormed through the door, followed by Davydova.

"Sorry, boss, she said it was urgent."

"Yeah, yeah," he said, waving her in. Ivan remained by the door, alert.

Davydova didn't look like a bag lady anymore. She was clean, dressed neatly to her age in jeans and a T-shirt, all tidy and new. Her hair had recovered its shine and looked much healthier than before.

"What's going on?" Myatlev asked.

Davydova pushed in front of him an enlarged, grainy photo. The image showed the Hoffmann woman peering out the window of a black limousine. The picture had been taken from above, probably via satellite, when it was almost full dusk. The woman's face was clearly distinguishable though, lit by security lights at what appeared to be an entryway into some heavily guarded compound.

"Where is this?" Myatlev asked.

"The White House," Davydova replied, "southeast entrance."

"What?" Myatlev sprung off his chair, pushing it against the wall behind him. "You tell me she works for the American president? *Bozhe moi . . .*"

That explained everything. The unlimited resources the woman had. The fearless nerve she had to cross Russia's border and snatch away what was his.

Her private jets, her money, and her friends in high places. Her resilience, her attitude, her balls of steel.

He rubbed his forehead, forcing away a threatening migraine cloud.

"Could this be true?" he asked.

"No, I didn't say that, did I?" Davydova replied, remaining calm.

"How else do you explain this? This, and what's happening to me, to us, to everything we've been trying to do?"

"I can't, no, sir. Not yet. But we don't have enough information in this picture to substantiate that she is under the American president's orders."

"Then what the hell do you think is going on here?" Myatlev shouted, tapping the picture angrily with his fingers.

"We only see that she's visiting the White House. We don't know why. I also determined she wasn't alone in that limo. There was at least one other man with her."

"Who?"

"A man by the name of Tom Isaac, a Realtor from southern California."

"A Realtor, my ass," Myatlev snapped. "That's the oldest cover in the business, goddamn it!"

He felt a wave of that familiar, ugly feeling of overwhelming anxiety wash over him. No, he wasn't going to let himself fall prey to that anymore. Not now, not ever. He took a deep breath and refocused, regaining control over his logical brain function.

"You said there was at least one other man, why? What else—who else did you see?"

"I only saw Tom Isaac, no one else. But here," she said, pushing another image over the desk toward Myatlev, "in what appears to be Secret Service checking IDs, the security officers take more than two ID cards from the driver's hand. I made out at least four."

"Whose?"

"No way of telling, sir. I couldn't zoom in that much; low resolution."

"Find out. Find out who the fuck else is the bitch taking with her when she visits with the American president."

"I will find out, sir. It will take me some time though."

"There is no time!" Myatlev bellowed.

Davydova flinched, then recomposed and replied, "I understand, sir."

"What are you doing to find them?"

"I've been watching Hoffmann's every move, mostly tracing her movements through available camera systems I can easily hack into: ATMs, traffic lights, that kind of thing. I pull satellite only when I need to see perspective or trace the movements of a fast-moving vehicle in areas where typical cameras are not frequent enough. I also keep an eye on all her spending:

credit cards, bills, cash withdrawals. I can tell you what she likes to eat and where. What brand of toilet paper she uses, and how much of it I can—"

"You think I care how often she wipes her fucking ass?" Myatlev said. "I need to know what she's working on, and how's she planning to screw me again."

"She's not really working on anything right now, sir. Her Internet searches are mostly clothing, shoes, Facebook stuff, Pinterest—where her interests vary, stuff like that. Nothing significant. She goes to a massage therapist twice a week and does physiotherapy twice a week. She appears to have been wounded or some kind of health issue. Again, it doesn't seem that she's working on anything, sir."

"But this?" Myatlev pointed at the grainy, dark photo shot from above at the White House entrance. "How do you explain this?"

"Um . . . you don't know much about women, sir, do you?" Davydova asked. "Look at her face. She's joyriding. She's happy and excited. She's dressed in a revealing evening gown, and wearing long diamond earrings. This woman is going to a party, not to work."

"Huh . . ." Myatlev said, picking up the photo and studying it carefully.

"Oh, I forgot to mention," Davydova said, frowning and cringing in anticipation of Myatlev's reaction. "She visited the CIA yesterday."

"And you didn't deem that important enough to tell me?" Myatlev asked quietly.

"It was going to be in tonight's report. I'm sorry."

"Well, what would be your conclusion?"

"Hmm . . . I'd say she's definitely well connected inside the American government, that's for sure. She doesn't work for them; there's no financial trail whatsoever. She definitely has their ear, though, including the president's. That's still bad."

"Yeah, it's still bad. Maybe even worse."

"How's that, sir, if I may ask?"

"CIA, FBI, we know how those organizations work. We know what to expect. We know who most of their agents are, and we understand their methods. This one, we know nothing about. That's much worse," Myatlev clarified, pensively.

In a few steps, he crossed the large office to where Ivan was standing.

"I want her followed night and day, on the ground. Send a team. Video and computer tracking isn't enough anymore. I want her house and her car bugged, and clone her phone! I want to see and hear everything she says and does, and with whom."

"Yes, sir," Ivan replied.

"Work together, the two of you. You continue everything you do," he said, pointing at Davydova, "and you, Ivan, you'll be in charge of that team. How long before you can have them onsite, tailing her around the clock?"

"Twenty-four hours, sir."

Myatlev pursed his lips in disappointment.

"That's not goddamn good enough, you hear me? Make it happen sooner than that."

Alex moved as fast as she could, walking briskly, almost running toward the entrance to the CIA headquarters. Once through the massive doors, she headed straight to the reception area, her heels delivering a loud, echoing staccato on the shiny mosaic marble floor inlaid with the CIA seal.

Shiny lobby floors were an old enemy of hers, since her early corporate days. She saw them as the supreme form of passive-aggressive discrimination against women in professional settings. Make it almost mandatory for career-driven women to wear high heels, and then shine the floors to the point where they can barely maintain their balance.

She finally reached the reception desk and got the attention of an officer, a young uniformed woman.

"Excuse me, I need to see Henri Marino immediately, please," Alex said, showing her ID.

"Do you have an appointment with her?" the officer asked.

Alex ground her teeth in frustration. If she had an appointment, she would have mentioned that. But the woman followed procedure, not logic. Sometimes the two paths have very little in common.

"No, I don't," Alex replied. "Please call her, and let her know I'm downstairs. My name is Alex Hoffmann, and this is urgent. She'll understand."

"Let me see what I can do."

Incredibly slowly, the officer dialed an internal extension and hung up soon thereafter.

"I am sorry, ma'am, I'm getting voicemail. She might be in a meeting. Please call and make an appointment next time; people are quite busy and hard to track down in this building."

"Yeah, I'll call and make an appointment, right now," Alex said, yanking her cell from her pocket and dialing Marino's cell phone.

"Hey, I'm downstairs, and I need to see you," Alex said, as soon as Marino picked up.

Then she handed her cell to the officer. She took it reluctantly, with an expression of infinite disdain.

"Yes, ma'am. Yes, ma'am, I understand."

The officer handed Alex back her phone, holding it with two fingers, then said, "Please, follow me." She led Alex to the same conference room she'd been in last. Alex couldn't contain a chuckle.

"Something funny, ma'am?"

"Nah . . . just that I know this room quite well, that's all."

"She'll be right with you. Please take a seat."

As soon as the officer left, Alex checked the door to see if it was locked. This time it wasn't; apparently a sign of her improved status with the CIA.

Marino walked through the door looking a little unsettled. She didn't wear her typical jacket; just slacks and a shirt, her sleeves rolled up to her elbows.

"What's up?" she asked, skipping the pleasantries and getting straight to the point.

"I think I know what V is doing these days," Alex said. "The volcano eruption, I'm fairly sure that was him."

Marino threw her arms in the air with frustration.

"Now why on God's green earth would you think that? Why do millions of people watch the news, see the eruption on TV, and think it's an act of God, of nature, or whatever you want to call it, while you instantly think it's Russia? Why?"

She shook her head almost violently, while looking at the cement floor, with her hands firmly on her hips.

"Here we go again," Marino mumbled.

"How many times do I have to be right until you give me the slightest benefit of the doubt?" Alex asked.

Marino stared at her intently, probably weighing options. "Go on," she finally said, grinding her teeth.

"Look, I'm not even sure it's him," Alex said. "I can't be sure at this time, but if he's somehow behind this, wouldn't you want to know?"

"Sure I would. However, why do you say that the eruption is manmade? That's where you lost me. No one said that . . . none of the volcanologists, the seismologists, none of the scientists who are studying the eruption even hinted to that."

"Sure, but I heard yesterday on TV that there weren't any warning signs before this eruption. No earthquakes, no increased activity in gas emissions, no sulfur discharge, no changes in shape, not a single sign of magma buildup or activity."

"So now you know volcanoes?" Marino asked cynically.

"I read up on the subject," Alex replied dryly, "all day yesterday."

"What's your point?"

"My point is that volcanoes don't suddenly kill people anymore. There are always warning signs, when nature is the only culprit. That's why, when a volcano eruption is imminent, people are evacuated with plenty of notice. But that's not what happened on Saturday. Almost 20,000 people died, trying to escape the lahars, trampling one another, or drowning in Puget Sound, desperate to get away after the bridges had jammed. Being that this time, all warning signs were simply not there."

Alex paused for a few seconds, giving Marino time to absorb the information.

"That led me to believe this was not an act of nature. This was foul play. This was a manmade disaster," she continued.

Henri whistled, amazed. "Do you realize what you're saying?"

"If someone killed these people, I'd want to know who. I, personally, think it was V. It fits his profile, Henri; it's big, it's mind-blowing, it's unprecedented."

Marino looked at her intently, as to gauge how serious she was.

"Listen, you asked me to tell you how I work. This is how I work. I spot something that doesn't fit the norm, that's out of order. Then I find a solution, an answer to that puzzle. In this case, V fits the bill. Who else would have done something like that? The eruption was clearly artificial. Someone killed tens of thousands of people on Saturday, and caused tens of billions of dollars' worth of damage. Has anyone claimed the attack? No, because that's not how V works. He doesn't advertise."

"What about the scientists? Why didn't they say it's manmade?"

"Give them time, and you'll see they'll probably figure it out at some point. For now, they can't, because they can't even imagine how someone could blow up a volcano. They can't conceive the possibility. Their minds are closed; they're trying to fit the Mount Rainier event into their traditional standards. It doesn't fit, but they don't see that yet. So they're still trying to explain the lack of warning signs through some natural circumstance, or collusion of naturally occurring events."

"By the way, Alex, since you brought it up, how does one cause a dormant volcano to erupt?" Marino asked serenely, almost patronizing her.

Alex pursed her lips, frustrated.

"Well, that's the problem; I don't know yet."

"See? That's why I'm saying you're wasting my time," Marino said. "No offense, but I think this time you're dead wrong."

"Okay, so let's say maybe I am," Alex conceded. "Don't you want me out of here? If you want to be rid of me, get me in touch with the team of scientists working onsite. I need to get all the facts behind this eruption. That way, I won't be wasting any more of your time. I'll be wasting theirs. Everyone's happy."

Marino considered it for a second or two.

"Yeah, sure, why not? That would definitely work for me," she said. "Let's get you on your way."

"Um . . . one more thing," Alex said with the sweetest smile she could muster.

"What?" Marino asked, her patience visibly running out.

"If this was indeed V, he's watching me via satellite. I need to disappear. I need a new face, new documents, new credit cards, the works."

"You've got to be kidding me," Marino reacted. "Really?"

"Yeah . . . I really need to fall off his radar. Trust me. If he's out there, he's watching me just as I watched him."

"But why?"

"Because I don't think this is over."

"What isn't over?" Marino asked, her pitch picking up a level of two.

"This whole thing . . . Mount Rainier. This doesn't feel like it's over. This eruption wasn't his end game."

"What is, then?"

"I don't know, but I believe Rainier was just the beginning, and he'll be watching my every move, to make sure I don't screw things up for him anymore. Plus, he'll probably want to kill me at some point."

Marino paced the room thoughtfully.

"Do you realize just how paranoid and crazy you sound right now?"

"Paranoid?" Alex asked with a chuckle. "Nah . . . maybe just careful. How about realistic?"

"All right," Marino conceded, turning all of a sudden to business, in her typical fashion. "You have statistics on your side; so far you've been right more than you've been wrong, so I'll help you get what you want. We'll set you up with temporary credentials, a new identity, and fly you out to Portland tomorrow first thing. Seattle-Tacoma International Airport is out of commission due to ash. You'll need to drive from Portland. We'll have a truck waiting for you there—one that can handle the volcano ash. Sounds good?"

"Awesome," Alex said, smiling widely. "I do need one more small favor, please."

Marino rolled her eyes. "I'm listening."

"Can I borrow your car? By now he probably knows what I'm driving."

"Seriously? Hell, no."

"Ah, come on, you'd probably be trading up. I've rented a nice convertible Beemer."

"Of course you did."

"Drive mine around, keep V's people busy chasing the wrong gal. You'd be safe . . . I don't think anyone is going to kill you while I'm gone."

"Pfft . . ." Marino snorted. "You're even crazier than I thought, Hoffmann . . . God help us if you're right again."

...Chapter 14: Samples
...Monday, June 12, 1:21PM Local Time (UTC-8:00 hours)
...46°51'10"N 121°45'37"W
...Mount Rainier, Washington

The man drove to the base of Mount Rainier in his truck, fitted for the occasion with a snorkel. A big, circular air filter had been fitted on the snorkel's opening, to prevent the falling ash from clogging the engine's air filters. So far, the entire improvisation had worked just fine. The truck hadn't sputtered once on the road, although ash fell from the sky thicker than snow, settling everywhere. When he drove his truck on the ash-covered roads, he'd raise the ash in the air in mini-squalls, visible in the rearview mirror like angry, gray monsters chasing his truck. They were barely visible though, as artificial darkness had set, making high noon seem like the last light of dusk on a rainy November day.

He wore one of those white, industrial, dust-protection coveralls that are typically light and thin as paper. This one appeared bulkier, although the material seemed light enough. He moved with a little difficulty wearing it, but his steps were firm and steady, helped by heavy, steel-toed boots.

He wore a dust-protective helmet, taped with pieces of duct tape on top of the coveralls' hood to ensure a perfect seal. He'd tightened the string on that hood, and it surrounded his face securely. It covered his forehead, down to his eyebrows. The helmet, in fact a full-face respirator dust mask, was fitted with a clear shield that he cleaned with his gloved hand every time it accumulated specks of ash and dust.

He looked at Mount Rainier, still spewing ash and pyroclastic materials high into the atmosphere. It had only been two days since it erupted. The eruption had been massive, taking off part of the mountain's peak. The northwestern side of the peak was gone, leaving a gaping, asymmetrical hole at the top of the volcano, that led the lava, lahars, and pyroclastic clouds to form and flow toward the most populous areas of the region.

Not bad for a day's work.

He decided he was close enough to the mountain. No need to push his luck any further. He stopped his truck and hopped out of the cab, raising more ash in the air. He checked his suit carefully; he made sure it was zipped fully and all hermetically sealed. Finally, he touched the emblem atop his left breast pocket, to see if it was still there. The emblem, the commercial logo of a well-known construction company, depicted a bear wearing a green hard hat.

He took a small toolbox from the truck and opened it. He extracted several glass vials, and collected ash samples in each one, tightening their caps carefully. Then he measured the ground's temperature, at first with a surface thermometer, then by inserting a probe several inches into the ground. Satisfied, he jotted the readings onto a small notepad.

Finally, he took a handheld Geiger counter from his toolbox and took some readings. The device crackled. The man moved it around a little, until he registered the most frequent crackles, then read the device's display and jotted down the number on the same notepad.

He was ready to leave. He packed everything back in the toolbox and placed it on the truck's floor, behind the driver's seat. Then he brushed off the ash from his suit, trying to get as much of it off before getting into the truck. He patted and rubbed his gloved hands against his head, shoulders, chest, and legs, clearing as much of the ash as possible. When he thought he was clean enough, he hopped behind the wheel and slammed the door shut.

A round, Velcro patch, depicting a bear wearing a green hard hat, had dropped to the ground, soon to be covered into oblivion by the heavy falling ash. On the man's chest, where the bear logo had been, the original marking of the suit was now visible: a black on yellow trefoil, the bone-chilling symbol of ionizing radiation.

Myatlev slammed the door to his office and went straight for the window. He felt restless, after a sleepless night, paying dues to a ferocious attack of anticipation anxiety. No meditation, no drinking water, not even sleeping pills had done anything to calm him. How could he calm down, when he was literally days away from owning the entire world?

He had forty-three land purchasing agents out there with access to unlimited funds, instructed to purchase all the farmland they could grab. Most of them scouted Russia, Ukraine, even Turkey. But he had others acquiring massive surfaces of land in China, India, Brazil, and Argentina. His cash reserves were depleting rapidly, but this was going to be the masterpiece of his existence.

He'd started this project with forty-eight billion dollars in cash; that was the extent of his cash deposits and reserves, together with any assets he was able to liquidate in a hurry without taking too much of a loss. Half of it he was investing in farmland, and he had set aside 10 percent for new, efficient farming equipment, irrigations, and fertilizations. The fact that his new farmland was in China didn't mean he was going to farm it the old Chinese way. He was going to bring innovation, productivity, and modern farming methods to Myatlev's Farmland Asia.

Russian farmland sold for dirt-cheap. Negotiations typically started at $400 per acre, but typically closed at under $200 per acre. In some regions, even $70 per acre was too expensive. He had to be careful and plan every move though, to ensure that the price of farmland wouldn't go up due to the sudden increase in demand.

To do that, he had hired land-purchasing agents and synchronized their activities to the last detail. They each deployed in the targeted regions; then identified land that was good, rich, yielded good crops, and could be negotiated. Then, on a set date, they all made offers. A week or so later, Myatlev owned more than two hundred million acres of farmland, and his agents had secured farm management teams as part of the sale deals. Most previous owners, willing to stay on as managers, made it very easy for Myatlev to have those farms up and running, without him worrying about the details.

Of course, the smarter agents had figured out he was on to something big and had purchased land in their own names, even if they hadn't figured out why. He expected nothing less; he hired smart people and he wanted them to act as such. He couldn't buy all the land in the world, even if he wanted to. His agents were fine running their little enterprises alongside his, as long as they remembered whom they really worked for in the end. At some point in the future, he could buy them out.

Then he shifted his attention to the futures market, where he secured immense quantities of food futures, also in a synchronized attack to ensure prices didn't go up. He secured massive options for grains and rice, at the day's fair market price. In a few days, clean food was going to become scarce overnight, and half the world's grain fields would turn radioactive for decades to come. That's when those futures would sell for an immense profit, immediately replenishing his depleted cash vaults.

That's why he couldn't sleep at night. Wide awake with anticipation, and obsessively going over the plan's details in his mind, he grew more restless by the minute. His plan had taken weeks of preparations, carefully orchestrated in the utmost secrecy by Myatlev himself. He couldn't risk letting anyone in on his global strategy this time. Not even Ivan; not for now, anyway. Not even President Abramovich had all the details. No one knew what he was up to, so no one could betray him. The game pieces had been carefully set on the board, and he was ready to play.

A knock on the door disrupted his all-consuming thoughts.

"Da," he said.

Valentina Davydova came in, followed closely by Ivan. She looked gloomy and scared.

Shit, he thought. What now?

"Um . . . sir," she said, hesitantly, "I lost Hoffmann."

He sprung to his feet, clenching his fists until his knuckles hurt, turning white.

"What do you mean you fucking lost her?" he bellowed. "Don't tell me that!"

"I—I can't find her anywhere, sir. For a few hours now, I just can't find her anywhere. It's like she fell off the face of the earth."

A pang of familiar fear twisted Myatlev's gut. Could it be possible she knew? How? She couldn't. No. Not this time, not now. No one knew what he was planning.

"Tell me what happened."

"I was tracking her just fine yesterday, her time. She gassed up her car, had coffee and a croissant at a coffee shop, that kind of thing. Nothing out of the ordinary. Then she went to the CIA headquarters and came out of there a couple of hours later. She went straight to Langley Oaks Park. She strolled casually down an alley, where trees are large and thick. There were no cameras on those alleys, and the foliage was too thick for satellite to penetrate. She . . . she never came out of there. I lost her. Her car is still in that parking lot, the last one there. I have facial recognition software running nonstop, cycling through all street camera feeds, traffic, ATMs, airports, railway stations, everything I could think of."

He stared at Davydova with his jaw dropped, unable to speak, suffocated by a wave of intense anger. She cringed under his glare.

"The problem is with the onsite team. They're arriving this afternoon, and I don't know where to send them," Ivan explained. "I will send them to check the park, her hotel, everywhere. But if they can't find her, what would you like us to do? Of course, Davydova will keep on looking, watch her credit cards and all that."

"Huh . . ." Myatlev said, almost pensively, still in shock. "I can't believe it!" He rubbed the back of his neck, trying to figure out what he could do next. How could this have happened? Why? Why now?

"Fuck that woman! Damn that bitch!" he yelled.

They both flinched.

Myatlev was angrier than he'd been in a long time. He didn't need that . . . he needed peace of mind so he could focus on his plan. He had more important things to worry about. That goddamned bitch!

He'd been daydreaming about his hands closing around her neck as she drew her last breath, begging for his mercy. That fantasy was not worth the risk anymore.

"When the ground team finds her," Myatlev said, "have them kill her and bring me proof of death."

Alex pulled a small, four-wheel suitcase across the shiny floors of Reagan international airport, walking casually. She had plenty of time until her flight's scheduled departure. The airport seemed less crowded than usual and eerily silent. The PA interrupted the silence every now and then with announcements, while most travelers huddled quietly in front of TVs displaying news from the Mount Rainier eruption, and the ensuing disaster that had engulfed Seattle. Twenty thousand people presumed dead. Thousands more missing, and more than ten thousand wounded, in need of medical assistance. For days, millions struggling to survive, while trying to get away from the devastation. No water, no food, no clean air, no basic social services, pure hell.

She refocused on her current situation; she had to make it to her destination alive, without V learning anything about her whereabouts. Every time she passed by a storefront, she checked her reflection in the window and didn't recognize herself. Her hair was long, black, sleek, and shiny, with long bangs covering her forehead. A wig, of course, but a good quality wig, made from human hair that looked the part. She wore large sunglasses, not too dark, so she could wear them inside buildings that were likely to have video cameras everywhere, such as airports. The frames were colorful, rhinestone-encrusted plastic, flashy as can be. Normally, she wouldn't be caught dead wearing something that kitschy. But it worked well on her new look, and it served a purpose.

She wore a black, silky ensemble of pants and a top. The pant legs were generous, and fluttered and clung around her shape as she walked. The top, not too revealing, was worn with another sparkling accessory, a black belt with enough rhinestones to start her own BeDazzler franchise. Her shoes, black kitty heels, matched the ensemble by having a few rhinestones of their own, right on the heel line.

Complete with dark lipstick and some eyeliner, the entire look gave her a somewhat trashy look, memorable yet easy to change out of and disappear in a second. Everyone seeing her only remembered the sexy brunette in all those rhinestones and nothing else. By drawing attention not to herself, but her accessories, she ceased to exist, hidden in the background like a faceless department store mannequin.

She passed another storefront on her way to the gate and gave her reflection a small, tense smile. *I could learn to like this*, she thought. *I look like an overly adorned, brunette Barbie doll.*

Alex arrived at the gate and checked the monitor. The destination city on the gate monitor read, "Portland, OR." That name brought back memories. The city where she'd moved when she left her native town, Mt. Angel, behind and with it, her estranged parents. The city where she'd held her first real job, albeit crappy and underpaid, and got her college degree in computer science. The city she left behind only a couple of years later, making her big move to southern California. No regrets for having left Portland; none whatsoever. It had been little more than a steppingstone. Her home was now San Diego.

She was leaving DC later than she'd anticipated, but there had been no more negotiating with Marino after she'd agreed to help her test her theories and cover her tracks. The woman had rules for everything. In all fairness, she couldn't expect the makeover, complete with new ID, new credit cards, everything, to be complete in an hour. The CIA wasn't exactly bored with nothing better to do, waiting for Alex Hoffmann to need a new ID. Nor did they have clothing her size, just waiting on the racks for her. Everything took time, and she needed to learn to respect that.

But did they actually have that time? What was really going on in V's mind right now? What did blowing up Mount Rainier do for him, other than the obvious destruction of lives and property? Was it really him? Or was she finally losing her mind, seeing him where he was not?

Yet no one could explain why Rainier's eruption had no warning signs. She was hoping to get to the science team stationed near the mountain and work with them on validating her theories. Of course, there'd be a wall of arguments against her theory at first, and she'd have to fight their narrowmindedness until they'd be willing at least to consider the possibility. Only at that point, she could hope to find out how a man can make a volcano erupt.

Ever since the mountain had erupted, she'd had this feeling of imminent doom. The fact that her own life was in danger didn't give her much trouble, no matter how surreal that felt. She wanted to draw V out of hiding so badly she didn't care about the danger it posed to her. She deeply cared about the rest of her team though, and she hoped they'd be careful, take whatever precautions Lou deemed necessary, and stay alive and well until this was over.

This . . . whatever this was; still hard to tell.

What would a man like V do, if scorned badly, the way she did before leaving Russia? Were there consequences for him, once his operation had been exposed to the enraged public opinion? After all, V was Russian . . . Would the Russian president have punished him in some manner for his actions? Was he dead or serving time somewhere for his actions? Or for his failures? Maybe that's why she was still alive, because he was locked up and couldn't get to her.

Nah . . . she dismissed the thought with a shrug. No way could someone as powerful, as arrogantly bold as V be subject to normal laws. Somehow, his actions depicted him as a man who had no fear of being held accountable for his criminal actions. How was that possible? How was he above the law? Or, better said, why was he behaving as if he were above the law?

Then, this volcano. How can someone be so ruthlessly bold to think something like that? No way of telling. She remembered Tom's reaction when she'd called and shared her theories, and told him she was headed west. He kept silent for long seconds, then he warned her about looking too closely into the abyss. He hadn't expressed any doubts about her theory regarding V. None of the team had really doubted her since she'd returned from Russia. Not openly, anyway.

But Tom had been right, as always. When she twisted her mind to try to decipher what could lie in the folds of a brain capable of blowing up a mountain and killing 20,000 people like it was nothing, a little bit of who V was rubbed off against her. To understand how his brain worked, she had to embrace who he was. To stop him meant to understand him to the point where her own mind could conceive the same plans, think the same way, see the world through the same eyes. She had to think like the brilliantly strategic psychopath who V was.

Steve had given her pointers in understanding how the psychopathic mind works. He had the background, as a trained, licensed psychologist, to decipher and analyze such behaviors in detail, extracting valuable pointers from every bit of information she could gather and validate. He'd told her the person she described V to be had no conscience, and killing was as easy for him as going to the grocery store was for her. Just a means to an end. He was mean, bold, and unhesitant to do and say whatever served his needs. Most likely, he held a big appetite for blood, for defeating others to assert his superiority. He was callous and manipulative, and that, combined with a superior intellect, made him compelling, dominant, bone-chilling, and invincible. Or almost invincible, she hoped.

She had encouraged Steve to not hold back and give her as much insight into the darkest recesses of the psychopathic mind as he could. She reassured him she could take it; she was a big girl. But late at night she went home and curled up in her tub, hugging her knees, and let the shower's hot water cleanse away the ugliness of the abyss. It was necessary for her to harden her heart and remove the emotional layer, so she could think like him, understand him, and foresee his actions. That was the only way she could hope to trap and kill V one day. Soon.

"Miss? Aren't you on the flight to Portland this morning?"

She snapped back to reality, enough to see she was the only passenger left in the gate area.

"Oh, shit," she reacted, then grabbed her wheelie and ran down the jetway. "Thanks!"

She boarded the flight and went to her assigned aisle seat, absentmindedly registering people's reactions to her appearance. Most men were appreciative, most women envious, several passengers glared at her for not boarding the flight on time and holding everyone back. Oh, well . . . she deserved those glares.

The middle seat next to her was empty, and the man taking the window seat instantly focused his attention on her, smiling widely, welcoming her aboard, the whole works. She repressed a sigh. Men are so superficial. *It's just rhinestones and fakery, bud. Take a break.*

She put on her headphones, trying to isolate herself from the man's attention to convey the message of no availability. But no; the man was insistent if nothing else. Probably also not used to being unsuccessful in his advances, considering he was good-looking, charming, and seemed well off.

As soon as they climbed to 10,000 feet, she decided to take her laptop out and go through the massive amount of reading she had to do to understand the most important details on how volcanoes work. The moment she stood and reached up to grab her wheelie, the man offered his help and didn't take no for an answer. She let him help her put her wheelie back in the luggage compartment, but then opened her laptop and immersed herself in a document describing magma movements, magma chambers, buildups, and the formation of pyroclastic rock.

"So, where's home?" he asked. "By the way, my name is Paul," he said.

He was not giving it up.

"Hi, Paul, nice to meet you," she said. "Hey, listen. I have to study this entire flight. I know it sounds boring, but the only thing I can discuss with you today is volcanoes. Are you a volcanologist, by any chance?"

"No, I'm sorry," he laughed, "but I can sell you medical imaging equipment if you'd like."

"Nah, that won't work, I'm afraid."

"So you're with the volcano people, huh?"

"No, just a student who has the opportunity to do some field research, that's all," she replied, and fixed her eyes on the subject matter.

"When we land, do you want to grab a drink, or lunch maybe?"

She turned a little toward him, thinking what she could say to let him down easy.

"Listen, um . . . I don't think I can do that, but thanks for the invite. I'm spoken for."

"Oh, I see," he said, a little red-faced. Rejection always hurt, no matter how gently one applied it.

A few minutes later, he'd fully recovered.

"Hey, what do you think, will that volcano erupt again? Or others?"

Henri Marino waited in line at the nearest Starbucks from her office. As always, during that time of day, people chose the coffee shop for their early morning day-starter and rushed in to get their fix. So did Henri.

"Can I help you?" the barista finally asked her.

"Yes, please give me a grande macchiato and an apple fritter."

"Name?"

"Marino," she said, then watched the barista write her name on the cup as Maria. She swallowed her chastising comment.

She went to the end of the counter, where other people's drinks were brewed ahead of hers. She waited, a little impatient, tapping her left foot quietly against the floor.

A chime alerted her that she had a text message. It was from one of her analysts, and it read, "Check your email NOW!"

Irritated, she opened her work email and saw a new email marked "Urgent" and red-flagged. It came from Director Seiden. She opened and read it, unaware her jaw dropped and her pupils dilated.

"I'll be damned," she muttered as she read the message, "I'll be fucking damned!"

She turned away and headed hurriedly toward the exit.

"Miss? Your coffee?" the barista called.

"Doesn't matter," Marino replied without looking back, before the coffee shop door closed behind her.

A few seconds later, her car was leaving a double trail of burnt rubber in the parking lot.

The large conference room was rearranged to accommodate a theater-like setting. The conference table had been pushed to the back, and the chairs lined up in rows, facing the front of the room. A small podium was placed at the front, and Myatlev paced behind it patiently. His earlier turmoil and anger were gone, at least on the surface. He focused with every fiber of his being on the mission at hand, not letting any other concern or worry distract him. His entire future depended on how well he could motivate and inspire these young men to sacrifice for their country.

Fifteen young Division Seven agents took those chairs, dressed as everyday Americans. Jeans, T-shirts, golf shirts, running shoes, baseball caps, all just a little worn to make it more authentic. They'd been through the most rigorous of drills, including a stay in one of Russia's famous mockups of American towns, built entirely for asset training. A perfect replica of any town in the American Midwest, the location, off limits for any civilian, the majority of the government, and most military forces, enabled assets to become familiar with the daily routine in America.

They learned everything, from garbage day rules, to operating the HVAC thermostat, and the proper use of the self-cleaning function in a stove. They learned about lawn mowing and the all-consuming obsession that Americans have with their grass. An updated remnant from the Cold War, the mock town still had benefits, even if everyday life in Moscow resembled more and more the Western life, with its vast array of small appliances, tools, TV channels, and incessant lists of chores. As such, these men, after their arrival in the United States, would instantly recognize everything and fit in seamlessly, ready to fulfill their mission unperturbed.

Their eyes were glued on Myatlev, who remained standing, walking slowly from left to right and back again, sizing them up. Ivan stood by the door, watchful and alert as always. Myatlev scrutinized every one of their faces, looking to see the determination to serve with honor, courage, and boldness. He had handpicked them one by one, from Division Seven's best agents and was happy with his selection.

Rumor had it that young agents were fighting over the opportunity to serve with the great Myatlev—that's what they called him—on the new secret mission. No one knew what the new mission involved. Not yet. But they were about to find out.

Myatlev stopped his pacing and took center stage, facing the men. The silence was absolute; they held their breaths in anticipation of the revelation they'd been waiting for.

"Are you ready," Myatlev asked, "to serve your country in one of the greatest acts of bravery Russia has ever known?"

They sprung to their feet at attention, and shouted in one voice.

"Yes, sir! Ura!"

"Are you ready to die, if necessary, to complete your mission?"

"Yes, sir! Ura!"

Myatlev stared at them with fierce determination, and they held his gaze. Not one of them flinched. Good.

"You make me proud, all of you," he said. "I wish I were younger, so I could join you in your brave endeavor. I am confident you will succeed and return home as heroes of Mother Russia."

"Ura! Ura! Ura!" they cheered, stomping their feet with each cheer.

"Take your seats," Myatlev ordered.

Myatlev switched on a projector and displayed on the wall a map of the northern Pacific Ocean.

"Before noon tomorrow you will be inside the United States. All of you. You will leave tonight."

Their eyes lit up with excitement and a touch of fanaticism, the perfect mix Myatlev wanted to see.

"You will execute a mission of the utmost importance. You will carry with you small-size nuclear weapons, which you will deliver to an assigned set of coordinates and prepare them for detonation."

The silence was thick, palpable.

"This is not a suicide mission, people. Agents like you are too valuable to waste. The weapons will be detonated remotely, when you're at a safe distance, out of harm's way."

The silence remained thick.

"Make no mistake . . . This mission is historic. It will shift the balance of power in the world in ways you can't even imagine. It will restore Russia's position as the strongest, most-powerful, most-feared nation in the world. And you, all of you, will be the artisans of Russia's rebirth. We are brothers, united, serving our mother. Ura!"

"Ura!" they shouted, back on their feet at attention.

"Our enemy," Myatlev continued, "the United States, deserves every bit of what's coming to it. For the past thirty years, Russia has endured great famine and destitution because of the United States and the rules the leaders imposed on us, a sovereign country. They have the arrogance to dictate to us what we can and cannot do with our former Soviet republics. They had the supreme audacity to humiliate our own President Abramovich over that meager issue regarding Crimea. If President Abramovich wants Crimea, what do we say?"

"Ura!" they replied wholeheartedly.

"If President Abramovich wants to rebuild Russia, what do we say?"

"Ura!" they repeated, with even more zest.

"If President Abramovich wants to nuke those arrogant, impotent bastards, what do we say?"

"Ura!" they chanted forcefully, under the scrutinizing eye of Vitaliy Myatlev.

He pursed his lips with disappointment. One man, at the left side of the front row, showed signs of hesitation, averting his eyes.

"Any questions?" he asked, looking in the general direction of the man. "It's all right to ask, people. This is not a routine mission."

The man he was targeting raised his hand, a little unsure.

"Sir, won't we be killing ourselves with all that radiation? Radiation won't stay in America. Radiation moves with the wind and can destroy us, here, in Russia."

"What a disappointment you are!" Myatlev bellowed. "You don't trust your leaders to have thought of that. You think we're all lame idiots."

"No, sir, I'm sorry—"

"You are a detriment to the spirit of this unit. Look at them! Not even one of your brothers here has the thinnest shred of doubt. Only you."

"But sir, I—"

"You're a liability to this mission. You're excused."

Unexpectedly, Myatlev pulled his weapon and shot the man in the head. He fell right where he stood.

Then he holstered his gun calmly and asked, "What do we say?"

"Ura!" the remaining agents replied, in deafening unison.

"Ura!" he responded. "Let's discuss the details of your mission. Take your seats."

He gauged their expressions again, and found no more reasons for concern or disappointment. He considered asking them to remove the body from the room, but then decided against it. It would serve as a reminder to the rest of them.

He almost chuckled remembering how well he'd seen that coming. He only needed fourteen agents to deploy in America, yet he'd selected fifteen, knowing one would cave and serve only as an example for the rest. That's why he was the great Myatlev; he knew people better than they knew themselves.

He turned toward the map projected on the wall.

"From now on, you'll know each other only by numbers. You," he said, pointing at the young man who sat on the first seat of the first row. "Start counting."

"One," the man said, then looked to his right.

"Two," the next man said.

Myatlev watched them count, and nodded his approval with each number spoken.

"You will enter the United States through multiple channels and points of entry. You will enter at roughly the same time. Should one of you be captured, chances are the Americans will raise the alert levels and make entry much more difficult for the others. We can't risk that. We don't want to give the enemy time to think, figure things out, and get organized. We will strike fast. Crossing that border is the number one priority and is an attack of its own. Understood?"

"Yes, sir!"

"Good. You will be flown in via military jets to our aircraft carrier there, in the northern Pacific," Myatlev said, directing his laser pointer at a small pin on the map. "Refuelers are standing by along your route, Ilyushin Il-78s. Our carrier, *Admiral Yankulov*, is in position, seventy nautical miles outside of the American ADIZ, or air defense identification zone, in international waters. Make no mistake. We might be in international waters, but the Americans are watching that carrier. It's too close to make them comfortable. That's why we have deployed other military vessels close enough to the US ADIZ to cause concern, but in different locations. Those are only for diversion. They won't know which location to watch first."

He checked their facial expressions again. They were listening intently, not a shred of worry on anyone's face.

"Any questions?" Myatlev offered, not expecting anyone to speak.

"Sir, if I may," a young man said, hopping up on his feet. "This is a carrier, and ADIZ is for aircraft, right? Or is it for sea vessels too?" He was the man who'd called out number ten earlier.

"Number Ten, ADIZ is for aircraft, that's true, but it also marks the area the US monitors very closely. Even if the ADIZ regulations don't really apply to an aircraft carrier, anything within the ADIZ makes the Americans nervous."

"Thank you, sir."

"From there," Myatlev continued, "as soon as it gets dark and they lose satellite, helicopters will pick up you and your baggage and drop you onto cargo ships getting ready to enter the territorial waters of the United States."

Surprise was the common denominator of their facial expressions.

"We don't have enough Russian cargo ships scheduled to enter the United

States tonight or tomorrow morning. But we do have allies who have agreed to assist us. They don't know what or whom they'll be helping land in the United States. We didn't share; you shouldn't either. Several cargo ships, sailing under various pavilions, will allow you to sneak inside one of their containers and be unloaded in ports with the other containers. These commercial vessels are registered in China, India, Thailand, Malaysia, Colombia, and Chile. These ships are headed toward various ports on the western seaboard of the United States, and are scheduled to arrive anywhere after 3:00AM tomorrow, all through midmorning. Understood?"

"Yes, sir!"

"Whether you arrive in San Francisco, San Diego, Long Beach, or wherever, as soon as you're off the cargo vessel, move fast. Go to your assigned coordinates, and complete your mission. You will each receive a packet containing cash, a valid American ID, credit cards, a satellite phone, a detailed map of your targeted region, and everything else you need to know. Study everything on the way to the *Admiral Yankulov*, and then destroy the map and the instructions. Keep the rest."

He finished explaining and switched off the projector, then turned his attention back to them.

"This country is counting on you. I am personally counting on you to fulfill this mission and make it a glorious success. So listen carefully. Every one of you who successfully delivers the package at your destination and makes sure it blows up when it should will receive five million dollars from me. If you don't make it back, if you are killed or captured, but you still fulfilled your mission, your family will receive five million dollars from me. That's how important this mission is for me, for us, for Russia. What do you say?"

"Ura! Ura! Ura!" they cheered, the fanaticism in their eyes all-consuming.

"All right people, you leave within the hour. Good luck, and dismissed!"

Myatlev and Ivan waited for the young men to clear the room. Then Ivan closed the door, and approached Myatlev hesitantly, his eyes riveted to the corpse left behind on the floor.

"Yes, Ivan?"

"Sir, may I speak freely?"

"Always," Myatlev encouraged him.

He'd anticipated some questions from Ivan. Myatlev hadn't even shared with his trusted right hand what he intended to do. He still couldn't share all the details of the plan, not yet, not even now. Not with anyone.

"Boss, I've always been on your side, no matter what. I still am, and you can count on me."

"Good to know, Ivan, good to know."

"But how sure are you, boss? Pardon me for asking, but radiation . . . I know you never wanted to mess with nukes before. Fourteen . . . that's a lot of nukes. But it was Abramovich who always wanted nuclear war. You always said no, and tried something else."

"Yes, yes, that's true, Ivan. Abramovich had the vision a long time before I did. Then, one day, I finally saw it! The power we could have over the entire world. We will rule, Ivan, you, me, Russia!"

"I—I don't understand, boss. How?"

"With America locked in decades of nuclear winter, we will be the only ones holding clean food, Ivan. My people bought hundreds of millions of acres of farmland, did you know that?"

Ivan's face was petrified. Myatlev slapped him on the shoulder for encouragement.

"You and I, old buddy, you and I will be richer than anyone has ever been, or dreamt of being, ever before. We will own the entire world, my friend."

"But—but it was Abramovich who wanted the nuclear solution, right? He insisted, right?"

"Yes, he did, at first, but now I see it too. The man was right all along."

"Boss, how about Canada? It's not our enemy, but the people will get some of the fallout," Ivan said in a hesitant voice.

"Canada will be collateral damage. Too damn bad. And considering how much agricultural land it holds, that's actually going to help us in the long run."

Myatlev took out his checkbook and leaned on the table, writing fast. Then he tore the check out and handed it to Ivan.

"Do you still trust me?" Myatlev asked.

"Yes, sir," Ivan replied, "absolutely."

"Then trust me on this too. It will work out just fine. Now let's get the hell out of here; let's go to Kiev. We're better off there, and I'm sick of this damn office. Let's go back to making money!"

He handed Ivan the check with a smile. Ivan took it, not believing his eyes.

"Boss! That's a million dollars! I—I don't know what to say, boss . . . *Spasiba*! Thank you!"

"I know," Myatlev chuckled. "Once we're all done, you'll get ten times more, and that's a promise."

Alex earned herself a frown from a tall, blonde flight attendant with tired eyes, who wore a nametag reading, "Hey Miss." That *was* funny and creative—things rarely seen on commercial airliners these days.

She gave up trying to irritate the crap out of Hey Miss, proceeded to shut down her laptop, and got off her seat to stow it away, as per the final approach instructions voiced earlier through the PA. Before she could reach the luggage bin, Paul, her window-seat neighbor, was already there to help.

"Please allow me," he said, smiling widely.

She stepped back, making room for him to get her wheelie down. She put her laptop in the outer pocket, then zipped everything back and let Paul be of service once again.

"Now that you can't study anymore, maybe you can tell me your name?" Paul asked.

"No, Paul, what would be the point in that? We're about to part ways forever in about ten minutes or less."

"You are too rational, you know. Has anyone ever told you that?"

"Just the way I am, Paul. No need for anyone to notify me."

"So, what's the scoop with them volcanoes? Are we all going to die?" he asked, still smiling, but somehow only half-joking.

Intrigued, she decided to probe a little in that chain of thought.

"Why would you think that?"

"Just . . . you know, 20,000 people gone in an instant. I'm hearing thousands more are wounded, who knows how many more could die if another eruption would happen. Or maybe earthquakes, right? I heard somewhere that after volcano eruptions, the—the stuff that's underneath there turns unstable. The plates move or something. Big earthquakes could happen. Did you read that in your study materials?"

"Yeah, something like that," she replied, deep in thought.

Something in what Paul had said was tugging at her gut, but she couldn't tell precisely what. The man obviously didn't know much about the subject matter at hand, but it was something in how he'd phrased it. *20,000 people gone in an instant . . . who knows how many more could die?* he had put it. Could that have been it? Could Mount Rainier have been a—

Her phone chimed, letting her know she had a text message. Hey Miss shot her a killing glare as she moved by with a trash bag, collecting empty bottles and used napkins.

Alex pulled her phone out of her bejeweled purse and showed it to the flight attendant.

"It's a sat phone, Miss," she said, feeling the need to explain.

"Doesn't look like a sat phone to me," Hey Miss replied. "Looks just like an iPhone."

Alex extended the distinctive, thick antenna and showed her.

"How about now?"

"Yeah . . . maybe. What's that?"

"It's a SatSleeve. It turns your own device into a sat phone when you need it. Really slick!"

Hey Miss smiled and moved on with trash collection.

Alex opened her messages and frowned. The new message was from Marino. It read, "Things have changed. Call as soon as you get this."

Before she could switch to the dialer, another chime warned her. She opened the newest message. It was from Sam, just as cryptic and as worrisome as Marino's. Sam wrote, "Hey kiddo, just in case you're headed west, there's something you need to know before stepping out of that airport. CALL!"

Great . . . What the hell was going on? She looked out the window, triggering a smile from Paul, who, obviously, thought she looked at him. The plane bounced a little, descending on its final approach. She extended the full antenna and retrieved Marino's number.

"Sat phone or not, you can't be on a call right now. Turn that off, please."

She grunted, but complied. Last thing she needed was trouble with the TSA. It wasn't going to take much longer anyway. Hey Miss had taken her spot on the jump seat.

The moment the aircraft wheels squealed while touching the runway, her phone was in her hand, ringing Marino with full encryption.

She picked up instantly.

"Hoffmann," she said, "I got some news for you. NEST found traces of manmade radioactive materials in the volcanic ash cloud."

NEST, or Nuclear Emergency Support Team, was a group of scientists and engineers trained to identify, track, and respond to any type of nuclear emergency. Hearing the name hit Alex in the gut like a fist, freezing the blood in her veins. She'd never seen that coming. Nuclear changed the name of the game, changed everything: scale, implications, death tolls, and response strategies.

"Oh, my God . . ." she whispered, painfully aware Paul was staring at her with his mouth gaped open.

"*Traces* is the operating word here. They're small concentrations; they almost missed it."

"But that means—well, I don't know yet what that really means," Alex blurted.

"Yeah . . . so what do you want to do?"

"Are they deployed yet? Onsite? Those guys?" Alex said. She avoided using their acronym while on a taxiing plane full of people.

"Hoffmann, isn't this call encrypted?" Marino asked, almost growling.

"Yes it is, but I'm still on the plane."

"Jeez, Hoffmann! They're deploying now. I have that location."

"Great, because that's where I should go first. The volcanologists can wait."

Marino fell quiet for a second.

"I'll make the calls. But suit up, and do as you're told. Don't be stupid, all right?"

Then she hung up before Alex could say anything else. Seconds later, the NEST deployment location was in her text inbox, with GPS coordinates, and a contact name: Edward Zoller, engineer.

Alex walked through Portland International as fast she could, heading for ground transportation, where her rental truck was waiting. Pushing her wheelie with one hand, she hung her purse on its handle to free up her other hand and called Sam.

"Hey, kiddo," he said, his voice heavy with worry.

"Hey, Sam, how's it going?"

"I—I heard a nasty rumor," he said, hesitantly.

She stopped abruptly and let go of her wheelie's handle to cover her mouth with her hand. The man walking behind her almost ran into her. He moved past, throwing her a fiery glare and cussing under his breath.

"Radiation in the ash cloud?" she whispered, then resumed her hurried walk. "Yeah, Marino just told me."

"There's something else," Sam added. "The signature of the radioactive compound is Russian. It came from the nuclear power plant in Rostov."

"How the hell do you know that?" The man was nothing short of amazing. He might have been a retired CIA operative and convalescing on top of it all, but he had connections everywhere in the world of intelligence.

"Well, let's just say the NEST nuclear forensics expert is an old friend of mine."

"I kinda figured out that part, Sam," she said with a faint smile. "I meant, even the precise power plant? Really?"

"Really, kiddo. It can get that precise. They're still working on figuring out precisely from which reactor within the Rostov plant it came. He's feeling uneasy about his findings. He said the signature is very close to the Rostov power plant signatures they have in their database, but it's not precisely the same."

"Is he at least sure it was Russian, though?"

"Absolutely. He's also sure it came from Rostov. He just can't figure out why it doesn't match precisely either one of Rostov's reactors' signatures."

"Wow," she whispered, as the implications of his words sunk in. "That means it was Russian foul play, Sam. I was right."

"Yeah, kiddo, you always are. That's the scary part."

"Trust me, Sam, I wish I was wrong on this one, I really do. I never expected nuclear. Never saw that one coming. Why aren't they afraid though? The Russians? They must know we'd figure that out and retaliate."

"That's a good question, kiddo. I can't come up with an answer. The moment I know, you'll know."

She was approaching the ground transportation terminal, and saw a red truck pulled right in front of the entrance. A man leaned against its hood, wearing a sign with her name on it. Next to him, a family huddled on the sidewalk; they were all sobbing.

"Hey, Sam, I got to go. Keep your fingers crossed. This time, you know, I— I'm a little scared," she confessed. "I could be way in over my head. What am I even doing here?"

"You're the bravest human being I ever met, kiddo. I'm not worried. That Russian bastard should be worried, though," he chuckled quietly. "Be careful, and remember to call home every now and then."

She hesitated a little, then texted Marino with the radiation source information. Seconds later, a chime, and she read, "How the hell do you know that before we do?"

Alex scoffed and decided to ignore that question.

The randomness of fate that made him choose a certain chair that morning had also chosen a code name for him. He was Five. For the duration of the mission, until he received the five million dollars from the great Myatlev, he was going to remain Five and nothing more.

He was happy with his number. It harmonized well with the bounty Myatlev had promised, making him believe there was destiny's hand mixed in somewhere, ready to make it happen for him.

He'd been high on dreams about how that money would change his life forever, not stopping for a second to ask himself if what he was tasked to do made any sense, or if it was the right thing. For five million dollars, he would nuke his own mother.

He saw the carrier in the distance, on the ocean's choppy surface, just as his pilot's voice crackled through the radio.

"Get ready, we're landing. The sea is rough, and we have high winds. It's going to suck."

He braced himself. He was past ready for the flight to be over. It had been long, forcing him to stay put in a very small space. *Rehearsal for hell*, he thought, feeling the plane decelerate and descend, getting ready for the carrier landing. They said carrier landings are the worst. He was about to find out.

The sailors had to help him get off the aircraft; his legs were numb, his neck stiff and painful. Fighter pilots have a height restriction, so they can fit comfortably inside the jets. Five was tall; his three extra inches hadn't disqualified him for the mission, thank goodness, but it did make for an uncomfortable flight, with his helmet almost forced against the canopy and his neck crooked.

He wanted to kiss the deck when he stepped on it, finally freed from the confinements of the jet. Within seconds, he was unloading his stomach content on the same deck instead, fighting to maintain his balance against the carrier's strong roll, while tens of deck maintenance crew and techs laughed at him and called him all kinds of names.

He wiped his mouth with his sleeve, and gave the support crew the middle finger, which only caused another roar of laughter and expletives. Hearing their comments and watching bet money exchanging hands, he understood he was the third agent to spill his lunch on that deck. Third out of twelve who had arrived already.

An alarm sounded, and he was ushered off the deck in a hurry. Another jet was coming in for landing. He took the opportunity to get out of the flight suit, and spend some precious time alone in the can. When he came out, the rest of his unit was being assembled on deck. He rushed and managed to get in line before the commander started speaking.

"Welcome aboard the *Admiral Yankulov*," the commander said, raising his voice to cover the howling wind. "We are proud to be part of your mission."

In the background, crew were lowering the jets on lifts and bringing up helicopters from the hangar below deck, getting ready for the next stage of the mission.

"As soon as night falls," the commander continued, "we will fly you to your designated cargo vessels. We will do so in the order of the vessel's proximity to the territorial waters of the United States. Use the remaining time to inspect and organize your backpacks. The cargo jet has already landed."

Five looked to his left, where deck crew unloaded the cargo jet carrying all their backpacks.

"Your country thanks you for your bravery and your sacrifice," the commander said. "God be with you! Ura!"

"Ura!" they cheered forcefully in one voice, overpowering the wind for a second.

Five went straight to the cargo jet, and found his backpack, labeled neatly with his number. They'd done a good job with those backpacks. They were actually brand-name packs, colorful, built on an aluminum frame, real heavy-duty mountain-climbing equipment. Five smiled. His first concern had been walking through America with a Russian-drab backpack, guaranteed to get everyone's attention in seconds.

He tried his pack on for weight. It was heavy, but manageable. The aluminum frame fit nicely, distributing the weight of the pack to the strongest areas of his back without limiting his movement. He put it down again and started the inventory of its contents.

Attached to the backpack's exterior, much like any mountaineer had, were loops of climbing rope, gloves, and a bunch of carabiners, some 6,000-pound weight class, more than enough to hold him and his baggage.

Inside the backpack, the main cargo was about the size of a crockpot, wrapped securely in lead-coated foil. On the inside of the backpack's flap there was a wearable dosimeter attached, what was called a radiation badge. Its sensor showed a passive, light gray color, the color of no radiation leaks. It could turn yellow for minute amounts of radiation, or red for hazardous levels. Gray was great; gray was the best.

A thick, heavy, corrugated plate was aligned to the back of the pack, slid in a custom-size pocket; it sat against his back as he carried it. On top of the main cargo, as Five liked to think of the nuke itself, was another package, wrapped tightly in layers of metallic foils. He didn't open that one; he'd been instructed to not touch the shielding wrappers of any of those items.

A small canister with a rubber seal was on the list of must-have items. The air inside was carefully formulated to return a specific combination of chemical compounds. In case he pulled a short straw and his container was fitted with an air valve for testing, he was supposed to attach the canister to the valve before the container was unloaded from the cargo ship. Then, Customs and Border Protection would sample the air in that canister, instead of the air in the container itself, which might have trace amounts of explosive or radioactive materials floating by.

A large sheet of lead-coated, thick, plastic foil was neatly folded in its packaging. As soon as the cargo container lined up for unloading, Five would wrap himself in that protective foil blanket, to reduce his exposure to the X-rays normally used to screen containers, and to ensure the screeners didn't distinguish human features in the image. They would only see a dark gray shape, much like the rest of cargo that traveled in sacks.

Five had to remember to wrap his weapons in the lead-coated plastic. A Beretta 92 handgun, three ammo clips, and a combat knife completed his outfitting. As Five had been told, if he ran out of bullets he could easily find more, from the nearest Walmart to any hunting store. It was the weapon of choice for American cops, very popular. However, he had to be careful; any one of these items seen on a container X-ray would immediately trigger a search order.

A container egress toolkit was next, adding a few pounds to the backpack's weight. Complete with a miniature blowtorch, the egress kit had everything he needed to get himself out of a locked container, and a padlock with steel wiring to secure the container doors shut again.

A pup tent was packed so tightly it took less space than a loaf of bread. It was light too, probably fiberglass rods with very light fabric.

A couple of food and water rations completed the backpack's load, in case unloading the cargo ship took more time than expected. The trip itself didn't take more than a couple of hours, once he was aboard. That's typically how long it takes a cargo vessel to navigate about fifty nautical miles.

Satisfied, Five reassembled his backpack the way he found it and leaned against it for a bit of shuteye.

Alex drove her truck north on Interstate 5, from Portland heading to Olympia, where NEST had set up its mobile response unit in a restricted area of the Olympia airport. Sadly, though, the airport was closed for operations due to unsafe levels of volcanic ash, so she had to drive the distance, wasting precious time.

As she drove north, she noticed how the day seemed to fade into an early, gloomy dusk as she entered the ash cloud. The road surface became slippery and she had to reduce her speed. It reminded her of driving through winter whiteouts, where she could only guess where the road was. Only this whiteout had a larger granulation, and it wasn't going to melt away under the sun's warm rays. Driving on it was like driving on millions of tiny little ball bearings.

The number of crashed or abandoned cars increased with every mile she drove north. No one had the resources to deal with that anymore. Urgent needs, like emergency response, food and water, evacuation, and survival were the top priorities. No one cared about the chunks of metal on the side of the road.

Everything was a deep, murky shade of gray. Ash had covered the landscape, bringing to memory the forgotten days of black-and-white television. One hour into her drive, and no other color could be seen anywhere, except for the hood of her red truck, where airflow had swept away the falling ash particles. There was an eerie feeling of death, of doom in the particle-filled air. Ash and dust absorbed all noises, and her truck whooshing by was the only sound she heard. No one else was driving the northbound Interstate; a few cars drove south though, probably the last ones to evacuate.

She had kept the truck's ventilation on recirculation, in a lame attempt to shield herself from whatever radiation there was in the surrounding atmosphere. She knew that wasn't going to do much, but it was the only thing she *could* do. *They said* trace *amounts of radiation*, she encouraged herself. She should be fine driving through it.

The landscape didn't change much once she exited the Interstate, but there was something else, infinitely more disturbing. She saw people, with their faces covered by surgical masks, trying to make sense of what was going on, walking on the ash-covered sidewalk. A woman swept ash off her porch, in a useless attempt to regain some degree of control over her existence. Her broom lifted a cloud of dust that settled back right where it came from. One man, dressed in a light nylon hoodie, was carrying a bucket, but stopped and watched her truck turn the corner with empty, hollow eyes. They were quite far from Mount Rainier, safe from the lahars, but ash had changed their lives forever. They were stuck, their cars rendered useless, unable to get food or water. FEMA was probably focused on the immediate disaster area, miles north of there.

She reached the Olympia Regional Airport later than she'd planned, and headed for the restricted area, marked clearly with 8-foot fencing and "No Trespassing" signs. She approached the gate slowly, noticing how heavily guarded the area was. Soldiers guarded the entire perimeter of the airport, armed with automatic weapons. A uniformed guard approached her window immediately.

She lowered the window and he gave her a quick look. Then he smiled with a smug air of know-it-all.

"Miss, I believe you're in the wrong area. Where do you want to go?"

"There," Alex replied, pointing at a hangar, barely visible in the ash-covered landscape. Then she pulled out her FBI credential, and placed it under the man's eyes.

"Oh," he said, raising his eyebrows. "Sure, please go ahead." He pressed a button, and the access gate rolled open with a long, painful squeak.

She drove a beeline for the hangar NEST had taken over. There was no way she could distinguish where the road was, under all that ash. Right in front of the hangar, there were two unmarked UH-60 Black Hawk helicopters, fitted with heavy equipment. They had modified air intakes to accommodate additional filters, most likely to keep ash and dust from stalling the engines.

She pulled her truck as close as she could to the hangar's entrance and then hopped out, painfully aware of how she looked. She was dressed more appropriately for a dance party than a visit with a NEST mobile unit, and she raised an unforgiving cloud of gray dust as she walked.

She opened the hangar door and walked right in, closing it fast behind her. The hangar, powerfully lit, held several folding tables covered with equipment. A small number of people hustled among them, comparing readouts, consulting digital maps, or discussing. She counted seven men and one woman, most likely scientists, not military, judging by their looks.

One of them lifted his eyes from a bulky device that spat a long, continuous printout, and saw her standing there, by the hangar door.

"This is a restricted area. You need to leave," he said, approaching her. He looked uncompromising and critical in the look he gave her attire.

"No, I don't," she replied. "You're NEST, right?"

"Ma'am, you need to leave. Now," the man said and took out a radio.

"Don't judge a book by its cover," she quipped. "I'm looking for Edward Zoller. I'm here on business, believe it or not." She pulled out her FBI ID again, but the man's frown and critical glare remained.

"That's him, over there," he said, pointing to a tall man in his thirties. "Eddie, you have a visitor," he called, a shred of dark humor tinting his voice.

Edward Zoller approached her suspiciously, with an eyebrow raised, making his frown lines appear crooked and out of balance. She extended the same FBI credential again, and he studied it intently.

"We were expecting you," he said, "but . . ." he gestured vaguely at her, probably referring to her unusual attire.

"Do you have any video surveillance cameras active in this hangar?"

"N—no, I'm fairly sure we don't," he replied. "Why?"

She took her sunglasses off with a sigh of relief and replied, "That's why."

"Huh?" he asked, confused.

"Never mind. Long story. Let's get down to business."

Edward scratched his balding head, unsure what to do next.

"We're scientists here, you know. We're trained to challenge everything, ask questions."

She invited him to continue with a hand gesture.

"We received a call announcing your arrival," he said. "The call came from the CIA. Yet you have an FBI badge? How come?"

"Ah . . . long story. Maybe some other time."

"You say that a lot, you know."

"Yeah, well, everything these days is a long story. We have no time for that. I have specific questions about the radiation found in the ash cloud."

"Shoot," he said.

She looked at him, noticing his tall forehead; bright, intelligent eyes; and his intrigued expression. NEST probably worked with a number of alphabet agencies, the FBI, CIA, and DHS for sure, maybe others. The members were used to that, but probably they'd never had to deal with someone like her. He obviously didn't know what to make of it. She decided to pace herself and structure her questions in a manner more likely to elicit support rather than anxiety.

"Eddie, um . . . may I call you Eddie?"

He nodded, while a tentative smile fluttered on his lips.

"I'm Alex, by the way."

His handshake was firm, but brief, maybe just a hint of awkward.

"What's your specialty?"

"I'm a nuclear engineer; I run mathematical models for contaminant spread and effects, among others."

"You run fallout simulations?"

"Precisely."

"Excellent," she said, "you're just the man I needed to speak with. First, please talk to me about the radiation levels you found in the ash cloud. Your report said trace amounts, right? What does that mean?"

"Yes, trace isotopes are what we found. We have numeric thresholds for what constitutes trace amounts. We found one cesium isotope to be more prevalent, but still at trace levels. Would you like to see the numbers?"

"Maybe later. So are these levels of radiation safe?"

He rubbed his nape before answering and creased his brow.

"With an underground explosion, essentially all of the fission products condense on ash and other solids and remain buried in the ground. Since this coincided with a volcanic eruption some fission products would be in ash and lava that were released but the levels are within variations in natural background radiation; they will dissipate and decay in a few days. The primary issue is that some of the ash will be inhaled or ingested by people both locally and wherever the winds take it and if it is ash with condensed fission products, some people could experience health risks. Radioactive materials that enter the human body pose a higher danger than low levels of external radiation a person might receive."

She was confused. Did that mean the manmade radiation spilled with the ash cloud was just as bad as the normal air? That wasn't so bad, then.

"I don't see you wearing protective gear, though."

"We wear these," he said, showing her a clip-on badge. "They're dosimeters. If they shift colors, we get to wear the astronaut suits. Otherwise, we choose not to. They make our lives miserable."

"So it's safe," she insisted.

"Let me explain," he offered. "When thinking of the effect of radioactive materials on a human's health, you have to think of the combination between the strength of the radiant energy, combined with the duration of the exposure. That's why we say, in this business, that there aren't any safe levels. Does that help?"

"Um . . . a little," she replied. "I think I get it."

"Let me try again. Think of ionizing radiation for example, like X-rays or gamma rays. Let's assume that each unit of exposure to X-ray radiation has the form of a needle. The diameter of the needle is the radiation strength or intensity. Let's visualize these needles spreading outward from the source, like the rays of a sun. The closer you are to the core, the more needles per square inch you're going to get. Let's assume you have a man exposed to these needles. If he's far away, and the needles are thin and far apart from one another, he might get a couple of pinpricks, but overall, he'll be fine. If he stays in the radioactive area for longer, he'll take more needles in full. At some point in time, there could be too many. That's why we measure radiation exposure levels in millirads per hour."

"Ah, I see," Alex said, "you've made it very clear."

"There's more. If the radioactive source in our example is small, the needles are really thin and don't fly too far, like the case with modern, safer imaging equipment. Note I said safer, not safe. Regardless of how thin and small these needles can be, if you are exposed to too many of them, over time, your body will suffer health consequences. Radiation accumulates in the body in the vital organs. Unlike with real needles, if exposure to even trace levels is prolonged, radiation triggers mutations in the individual's DNA. Building on existing genetic predispositions, it leads to higher cancer risk."

"I see," she said, her frown reappearing. "Then it's okay to say five minutes at ten units equals one minute at fifty units?"

"Simplistically yes, considering all needles are precisely the same size and speed. We didn't even discuss the effects of specific isotopes or half times. In case the needle is larger, like the size of a hatchet, you will only take one, maybe two, before you're dead."

"Got it," she said. "Then what does *trace levels* really mean for these people?"

"Most of them will be unaffected for the remainder of their natural lifespan. There are higher risk classes, like pregnant women, who will be affected. There is proven, documented correlation between heightened radiation exposure levels and birth defects."

"Oh, my God . . . How about the cancer risk for the four million people living in this area?"

"We will probably be able to measure a heightened cancer rate in the area for the next few years. Not by much, though. That's what trace amounts of radiation really means."

"Not by much, but even the smallest increase in these rates, applied to a population of more than four million people, that means something. Something awful."

"Yes," he replied somberly. "Yes, it does."

"And yet, for me, it doesn't make much sense," Alex mumbled.

She thought of V's motivations. For V, this was too small scale, too insignificant, despite the 20,000 lives he had ended. She couldn't picture him satisfied with reading about increases in cancer rates fifteen years later. No, this had to be part of something else, something bigger.

"What doesn't make sense?"

"You know the radioactive material was Russian, right?"

His eyebrows shot up.

"Yes, I do, but we just found that out ourselves, only a couple of hours ago. I'm surprised you knew."

"Let's talk scenarios. What kind of device could have been responsible for dissipating this minute amount of radioactive contamination inside the ash cloud?"

Eddie rubbed his nape again, thinking, keeping his eyes riveted to the ceiling, as if the answer hid there somewhere, in the hangar's metallic structure.

"We thought of a few scenarios. One was that the flow of lava might have hit a buried device, a leftover from the Cold War. Theirs or ours."

Her mouth gaped open.

"The signature was Russian, why are you thinking ours?"

"It was the Cold War, remember? We did all kinds of weird things, just to have them handy in case things went a certain way. It's not unheard of, you know."

"I see."

"The problem with this scenario is that if the flow of lava had unearthed a nuclear device, we can't model the outcome. We don't have data, or the data doesn't jive. In theory it would detonate; it would trigger the nuclear reaction. However, we can't model it to validate the scenario. Not yet. It depends on too many factors."

"Such as what?"

"Technically and traditionally, when we have a detonation, regardless of method, we are able to pinpoint the precise ground zero with extreme accuracy. The detonation has a certain behavior. Take the mushroom cloud, for example. That's typical, it will happen with every nuclear detonation, and will always leave a certain pattern in dissipating radioactivity at the site of the explosion. Do you remember the radioactive sun in my earlier example? We can't find it, not by measurement. We always find it. You understand why, don't you?"

"Yes, trace the needles, where they come from, where they are denser, and where they are more rarefied. That's how you find the sun."

"Exactly. However, this radiation has a flattened, almost circular pattern instead of spherical. It's centered on the volcano crater itself. That challenges my Cold War leftover scenario. The device would have had to be buried in the volcano to generate that flattened pattern of radioactivity. Who would have buried a nuclear device inside a volcano?"

She felt her blood turn to ice. *I can think of someone*, she thought.

"Did you know there were no warning signs before this eruption?" Alex asked.

"Yes, I heard. I also heard that could sometimes happen in extremely rare cases of explosive eruptions, where magma chambers become pressurized too fast."

She scoffed; the volcanologists had figured out a way to rationalize and call natural an event that was definitely not natural. It was to be expected. Not everyone stared into the abyss the whole day long, like she did.

"Then tell me, is it possible, for the sake of scientific argument, that a nuclear device of small yield was used to detonate the volcano's caldera and initiate an eruption?"

Eddie's eyes bulged open.

Several of his colleagues gathered closer to them, listening in.

"I—I guess so, but I can't be sure though."

"What do you need to be sure? Run a different type of model?"

"No, I need to discuss things with volcanologists."

"Great," Alex replied. "They're my next stop. If I hit the road now, I can make it to Stanford University tonight. I'll catch a flight from Portland. The best volcanologist in the country teaches there."

"I'm coming with," Eddie offered, and rushed to gather some things for the road in a small laptop bag.

"I was hoping you'd say that," Alex replied. "Having you both in the same room will work wonders. Hurry up though; we have a long drive."

"No, we don't. We have helicopters. We fly directly from here."

"Awesome. One more thing: I need to get into more appropriate attire; I think you might agree. Can I do that here somewhere? I'd appreciate it."

He made an inviting gesture with his arm, then went outside to get the helicopter ready. A minute later, Alex emerged from the hangar, dressed in jeans, a sweatshirt, and sneakers. The wig was gone too, making Eddie give her an astounded look when she climbed aboard.

"What's going on with you?" he said loudly to cover the whirring rotor blades.

"Oh, well . . . It's a—"

"A long story," he said, chuckling. "Heard that before."

He handed her a headset and plugged the jack in the dashboard.

"Hear me okay?" he asked.

"Yeah, crystal clear."

"All right, hang on. We'll be flying relatively low, in case the engine stalls. But don't worry," he added quickly, seeing how petrified she looked. "They fitted this helo with extra air filters; it works fine."

That was going to be interesting.

Alex kept her eyes fixated on the horizon line, where the sky lit up, clear of the ash cloud. A few more minutes, and they should be safe from the risk of a stalled engine in midflight. She shot Eddie a quick glance and wondered how they did it. How do these people do what they do? They go to the most dangerous places on earth, where terrorists and lunatics of all flavors threatened the very existence of humankind, and somehow make it better.

"How do you do what you do?"

"Huh?"

"Yeah, how does one do what you do?"

"Um . . . there's a lot of procedure written for all kinds of situations," Eddie replied. "We have protocols we follow; it removes most of the guesswork from what we do. We also have these," he pointed at several screens installed on the helo's dashboard. "Our helicopters have state-of-the-art detection equipment, and we see instant results here. This monitor displays radiation levels in a visual manner, so we can fly toward ground zero and identify it, and measure intensity at the core of the event."

"Aren't you afraid?"

"Of what? Of radiation? We take precautions. We have levels of protective gear, and most of the time we wear it."

"No, I mean of being wrong, of making a mistake."

Eddie shot her a quick, inquisitive glance.

"The scariest thing for me is the blackmailing madman scenario. The callers who say they will blow up such-and-such nuclear device, contaminate the water, and so on, unless we do what they want. They want money, most of the time. That's what used to scare me a lot; it still does sometimes."

"Why?"

"Because we screen the area, searching for trace amounts of radiation to support the terrorist's claim. We find nothing, so at some point we have to call it a hoax. Other agencies take care of finding the guy, but for me there's always that anxiety: what if we missed something? What if it wasn't a hoax? What if this time they had better shielding and the bomb didn't leak radiation into the atmosphere? What if my judgment call will cost people's lives? Radioactivity is a ghastly thing to make a mistake about."

He paused. "It used to keep me up at night, you know."

Alex smiled faintly, thinking how much the two of them had in common.

"What did you do to make it better?" she asked. "Can you share?"

"It was mostly technology that helped make it better. We have traps now; sensing equipment placed in all major cities, in places of strategic interest for terrorists. Subways, airports, railway stations, major malls, any place like that. Our equipment is so sensitive it can pick up even medical radiation. A few years back, when we didn't do a good job distinguishing between types of manmade radiation, we picked up and interrogated several people who were undergoing radioactive therapies of all sorts, because they tripped our alarms. Then we learned to differentiate. That's what made it better for me; that, and getting used to being right, building my self-confidence, my experience."

"So this radiation you're seeing in the ash cloud, your sensors didn't pick that up before the eruption?"

"Nope. It just materialized out of thin air. It's frustrating as hell. Normally, the moment something emitting the slightest amount of non-natural radiation comes into play, not only our sensors pick it up immediately, but with such accuracy that we can pinpoint the exact individual who carries the radioactive material out of the masses of people using the subway, for example."

"That's impressive," she said. "How do you explain this radiation source then? How did it happen to appear here, at Mount Rainier, without leaving any trail?"

"I don't, that's just it," he admitted with a grimace of frustration. "Scientists hate unexplainable events, you know."

She pulled her phone out of her pocket, thinking of a dozen questions she had for Sam.

"Can I call someone from here?"

"Yes, sure, just hook up your phone to that jack over there. It will put it through your headset. This button allows you to share the audio with me, if you'd like."

She dialed Sam's number after she launched her encryption app.

"Hey, Sam."

"Hey kiddo, whereabouts are you?"

"I'm flying south with a new friend; we're going to Stanford."

"What's at Stanford?"

"The School of Earth, Energy, and Environmental Sciences. In other words, that's where the best volcanologist in the country can be found."

"Oh, I see. Good luck!"

She flipped the switch to let Eddie listen.

"Sam, I put you on speaker. Eddie is a scientist with NEST."

"Eddie," Sam greeted him.

"Hi," Eddie replied.

"Sam, can you tell me if the Russians used to bury small nukes back in the days of the Cold War?"

"No. Nukes weren't small back then. The small nuke is a modern invention."

"Ah . . . I see. So this isn't, in any way, a leftover from the pre-glasnost era?"

"No," Sam replied, "absolutely not. Suitcase nukes have only been made in the past twenty-five years. We had them first. The Russians came later with their version; I'd say only in the past ten to fifteen years. I'm sure Eddie knows more than I do about the subject."

She looked sheepishly at Eddie, who nodded a few times, with a hint of a smile in his eyes.

She hung up the phone.

"Sorry, Eddie, I didn't think—"

"It's all right, no need to apologize. Yes, I could have told you all that and more. I can tell you that there is literally no evidence supporting any Cold War leftover theory. Ours or theirs. I checked and rechecked. It doesn't add up. I wish it did, because then I wouldn't have an unexplained appearance of nuclear material that we can't account for to keep me up at night. You do realize, until now we thought we had it under control. We thought no one could move radioactive material anywhere in the United States without us knowing about it. Now that certainty is gone."

She remained silent for a while. The helicopter had cleared the ash cloud completely, and Eddie flew higher and faster, heading south along the Pacific coast. The beauty of the rugged Golden Coast landscape registered in a remote corner of her mind, but not enough to distract her from her dark thoughts.

If V was behind this, and she believed more and more that he was, how did he pull it off? How did he get nuclear material near Mount Rainier? More important even, what was his end game?

What was it that Eddie had said? Yes, radioactivity is a ghastly thing to make a mistake about. He was right about that, for sure. Alex needed to be sure she understood V's next steps, his final agenda, and she didn't. Not yet, not fully. It made her angry, clouded her judgment, it made her fearful and hesitant. She hated that more than anything. Right now, she needed to be clinically rational, cold and lucid, so she could extract information and construct scenarios that made sense, that were realistic, doable, regardless of how bold and unprecedented.

Her first question in dire need of answer was how did V do it? How did he cause Mount Rainier's eruption? Because there was no doubt in her mind that he had, somehow, pulled that off. Then the second mystery and the most unsettling one was his end game. She couldn't explain why, but she believed 20,000 victims weren't enough for V. It was an appalling death toll for a terrorist attack; it was the biggest one in history. Yet somehow, she knew V wanted more, much more. What did he want in the end? Could this have been a mistake? Maybe he had planned for a much worse outcome, or denser, stronger radioactive fallout and something just went wrong.

"Son of a bitch," she mumbled, forgetting the sensitive headset mic picked up the tiniest sound.

"Excuse me?"

"Ah . . . nothing," she replied hastily. "My apologies. Sometimes I do that."

"What? Curse? We all do that. What's on your mind? Please don't say long story."

"Huh," she chuckled quietly, and then turned somber, grim. "I need to understand if Mount Rainier's eruption was triggered by a terrorist. I desperately need to have this theory validated, or invalidated, to understand if and where he strikes again. Because not knowing is the worst. I can't foresee what he's going to do if—"

"A terrorist . . . whoa . . . wait, that means you have someone specific in mind for this?"

"Yeah, I do," she admitted reluctantly, "a Russian, a brilliant mastermind."

"Then let me ask you, no disrespect intended, why isn't the entire FBI here with you? Why isn't every agent fully immersed in this investigation?"

"My theory is just a theory for now, which no one really believes. I've been allowed to investigate, but—"

"But FBI and CIA think you're nuts, and they decided to discard your theory and pursue traditional investigative channels, right?"

She nodded, her lips pursed with frustration. "Pretty much."

"I get that sometimes. If that's what they believe, and you're here on your own, what are the rest of the feds working on? What scenarios?"

"Beats me," she said with a shrug, limited somewhat by her harness. "I'm more of an external contractor, you know. They didn't bother to tell me."

"I don't get it. Don't you guys work together?"

Great question, she thought bitterly. It took an organized, keenly analytical mind like Eddie's to ask the most important, yet simple question in modern counterterrorism.

"Think of me as an alternate channel of sorts," she sighed, frustrated to see how difficult it was to explain what she did, and how she worked. "I work in parallel with them. My theories are somewhat different from what they're used to. I test the ideas and if they are valid, then I get the fed's attention."

They flew silently for a few minutes. She recognized the Golden Gate Bridge;

they were getting close.

"Eddie, what kind of long-term consequences will this radioactive cloud have? Where will all this ash go?"

"Long-term effects? Almost none. It's too small to cause significant contamination to soil or water. It will disperse by wind and be washed away by rain. Most of it will probably end in the Pacific as part of the cleanup."

"When will you notify the population?"

He looked down for a moment, embarrassed.

"Probably never. We have protocols for that. Can you imagine the panic?"

"Oh, my God . . . these people will never know?"

"No. Again, the measured radioactivity is at trace levels. Our protocols dictate we do not disclose trace levels to the public, just as we don't disclose the bomb threats that we receive."

She remained silent, mulling over what she'd just heard. There were many things she didn't agree with, but she didn't want to take it out on Eddie either. He seemed equally uncomfortable with that policy of silence, and it obviously wasn't his say.

"Are we landing in San Carlos?" she finally asked, changing the subject.

"No, we land directly at Stanford, on campus." He was descending slowly, flying lower as they approached the university grounds.

"You can do that?"

"Yes. We're under FLYNET authorization; we get to fly when everyone else is grounded. We also get to land wherever we need and where we can fit. It will save us time. Which building is it?"

An elderly man holding a briefcase stood in the doorway of the building, watching the helicopter land on a small patch of green. He had a distinguished air about him, but carried around him a shroud of sadness. There was a somber kindness in his faint smile and maybe a hint of understandable curiosity. His eyes were the most telling, surrounded by deep black circles and shaded by slanted eyebrows.

He lifted his arm to shield his face from the strong airflow coming from the helicopter's rotor and waited patiently for Alex and Eddie to approach the building.

"Miss Hoffmann? Walter Tedford," he said, giving her a strong handshake. "I was about to give up on you."

"We were delayed, professor, my apologies."

"Not to worry, you're here now."

He showed them to his office, a rather small room, filled to the brim on one wall with books and with electronic equipment on the other wall. His desk, old-fashioned and also small, took the center of the room.

"Professor," Eddie said, extending his hand. "Eddie Zoller."

"A pleasure. Take a seat, please," he invited them. "Now, what can I do for you?"

"Thank you," Alex replied. "Professor, we need to understand how volcanoes work."

"My students call me Dr. Ted; it's less ceremonial. You two are about their age," he smiled faintly, unable to remove the sadness from his face. "You see, some people study volcanoes for years and still don't know everything there is to know about what goes on underneath the surface of the earth. How much time do you have?"

"We don't have anywhere near that much time. Just a few minutes, that's all," Alex clarified.

"Oh . . ." He seemed disappointed. "Then what specific questions do you have for me?"

"I've read up a little, on the flight over," Alex said, aware she was blushing. "Now I have more questions than answers. For example, the caldera, how does it get formed?"

"Did you know the word *caldera* is based on the Latin word for cauldron?" Dr. Ted explained, powering up a laptop and lowering a projection screen from the ceiling. "As you can see here, the moment an eruption runs its course, the magma chamber underneath it is emptied, and it collapses. The roof of the chamber collapses, becoming the future caldera's bottom. That can happen two ways; either through an explosive eruption, or more gradually, through what we call effusive eruptions. Those are smaller-scale eruptions, sometimes taking place at a distance from the magma chamber."

"Which type of eruption was Mount Rainier's?"

"Explosive. If you imagine the mountain erupting explosively, literally blowing its top off, the resulting shape is a truncated cone. That's what we have at Rainier today."

"What causes an eruption, typically?"

"Like with every other type of explosion, the accumulation of pressure inside becomes stronger than the resistance posed by the hardened caldera bottom, or the earth's crust, if we're talking about the birth of a new volcano. Mount Rainier's eruption was what we call a magmatic eruption. The mountain spewed jets of molten rock, or magma, into the atmosphere. The pressure inside that magma chamber must have been tremendous."

"Didn't you know that was going to happen?" Alex asked. "Aren't scientists these days able to foresee such events?"

"We definitely can, or so we thought until last week." He removed his glasses and wiped them before continuing. "Your question has two parts; I'll start with the first. Magma chambers are hard to detect or predict. We can barely detect the very superficial ones, typically those at less than 10 kilometers from the surface. That, by the way, is very superficial for a magma chamber.

"I won't go into the dynamics of magma flows in much detail. All I will tell you is that the rivers of molten rock that form magma rise toward the surface and pool into magma chambers. Pressure in those chambers increases gradually, as new magma rises from beneath. Eventually, when that pressure becomes too strong for the caldera bottom or the hardened crust to withstand, it erupts, most of the time explosively. Again, this only applies to magmatic eruptions like Mount Rainier's, not phreatic, or phreatomagmatic eruptions, although similarities do exist."

"How about predicting these eruptions?"

The professor removed his thin-rimmed glasses again and rubbed the base of his nose.

"We didn't think people could die from volcanic eruptions in this day and age," he said, speaking with sad inflexions in his voice. "We thought science was past that. For the past fifty years, almost no one had died at the site of volcanic eruptions. Well, some still do; fifty-seven people died when Mount St. Helens erupted in 1980, but we can prevent most potential deaths. Magmatic chamber pressure builds slowly, over time, and, as it does, small earthquakes start happening. We have deployed seismometers and tiltmeters around each volcano. We record all earthquakes, and triangulate their epicenter precisely. We measure their intensity, and we can see how that intensity climbs, predicting a future eruption. We also watch for other signs of pressure buildup in the chamber. We could see small steam-blast eruptions, generated by the rising magma levels heating and vaporizing the aquifer. Alternatively, we could see leaks of gasses in the aquifer. We test the aquifer periodically and take samples from nearby water sources: water wells, rivers, lakes, and springs. Any change in the chemistry of the water is indicative of an approaching eruption. We watch active volcanoes particularly closely."

"Was Mount Rainier classified as active before last week?" Eddie asked.

"Yes, and it was considered very dangerous. Mount Rainier had its own place on what we call Decade Volcanoes list. Sixteen volcanoes have been identified as being the world's most dangerous, most active volcanoes. Mount Rainier is one of them."

"That means you were watching it closely, right?" Alex asked.

"Absolutely, for many years. That list was built in the 1990s. We have deployed our most sophisticated monitoring equipment around Rainier's caldera. Every year, there are at least two research grants going toward understanding and predicting Rainier's future behavior. Scientists camp on the mountain and study in detail every bit of information the mountain is giving out, from water chemistry to earthquake frequency, intensity, depth, and duration. This eruption was not supposed to happen."

Dr. Ted shook his head, the sadness in his eyes telling of his internal turmoil.

"You see, the entire region counted on us, volcanologists, to keep them safe. We failed, and what makes it worse, we don't know why or how."

"Someone mentioned a press release quoting, um, pressurized magma chambers building pressure too fast," Alex probed. "Do you think that's what happened?"

The professor sighed, hunching his shoulders.

"No. Neither do the other volcanologists. But you have to understand something. Theoretically, this would be the only logical explanation for the mountain to blow up without any warning. Something caused a brutal buildup in magma chamber pressure. But what? We don't know. Nor have we ever seen anything like that before. Yet we had to make a statement, and very few scientists were comfortable with that statement, because it wasn't validated by measurements of any kind. But when 20,000 people die on your watch, and so many people are affected by this disaster, we have to issue a statement, and 'we don't know' was not the best option either."

"You're saying you don't believe that's what happened?"

"I'm saying in practical reality, I don't think that's possible. Magma chamber pressure builds slowly, not brutally fast. Everything we believe in as scientists, and everything we worked on for decades supports this statement. Yet what happened with Rainier can't be explained, and that makes all of us doubt everything we thought we knew or believed. One unforeseeable eruption and our life's work was annihilated, together with the lives of the people who died on our watch."

He lifted his eyes and looked at Alex, then at Eddie, his unguarded look showing the depths of his turmoil. Then he hunched his shoulders a little more, burdened.

"However, science doesn't care about what a bunch of useless volcanologists might think and neither does nature. There is an explanation out there, and we will find it, eventually." He sighed and then continued, "What else can I answer for you?"

Alex shot Eddie a quick look.

"Let's think outside the box, Dr. Ted, really outside the box."

He looked at her, intrigued.

"I'm listening."

"If magma pressure didn't build, because otherwise you would have known about it, why did Rainier erupt?"

"That's exactly the problem. I don't know what else could have happened. It makes no sense. Think of it logically. To form an explosion, you have to have explosive pressures building. Whether combustive or of any other nature, that's the textbook definition of an explosion: a sudden, violent release of mechanical, chemical, or nuclear energy. I know it by heart because I've been looking at it from all angles during the past few days. An eruption is nothing but an outward explosion that decompresses gasses and magma into the atmosphere."

"Exactly," Alex replied, and Dr. Ted frowned. "What if the caldera was blown up?"

"Huh? How, exactly?"

"Your textbook definition applied exactly by a small nuclear device, say, two or three kilotons; that's 15 to 20 percent of Hiroshima."

"You mean to say you found radioactivity at the site?" the professor asked. "Oh, my God . . . Do you realize what that means? How the hell did we miss it? My colleagues ran detailed analyses of everything: ash, dust, gasses, water, and lahars."

"It's trace amounts, present in the ash cloud," Eddie clarified. It puzzles us too.

"Us, who?"

"Um . . . I'm with NEST, professor. We're deployed near the site."

The professor's mouth gaped. He ran his fingers through his hair as he walked toward the blackboard on the wall. He picked up a piece of chalk, getting ready to write. "Let's run this."

He drew the conical trunk shape of a volcano, and superimposed on it the shape of the caldera, a rectangle drawn in dotted line.

"Let's see; if you place the device here," he said, marking the spot with a small x on the bottom of the caldera, "the force of the explosion would head outward. Path of least resistance, right? The explosion has no reason to go downward, all the way down to the magma chamber. It will choose to dissipate its energy into the atmosphere." He drew the contour of a mushroom cloud on top of the mountain. "No . . . unfortunately, I don't think this scenario would work," he concluded.

"The radioactive particle distribution doesn't match this scenario either," Eddie said, approaching the blackboard. "Allow me," he said, reaching for the chalk.

Eddie drew a flattened shape on top of the volcano and a funnel shape above it.

"This," he pointed at the funnel, "was what we believe was the original distribution of radioactivity. By the time we deployed, most of it was gone. The flattened sphere, the one that makes no sense, is the current distribution of the radioactive particles."

"I'll be damned . . ." the professor exclaimed. "Do you know what that is? Do you know what you just drew? A collapsed plume."

"What's that?" Alex asked.

"The eruption column, what gets thrown into the atmosphere, is called a plume. It's made of ash, gasses, steam, and so on. Some plumes can rise all the way into the stratosphere, but not all of them. If the eruption column is too dense, too heavy to be lifted by the eruptive force and convection, the plume collapses. It falls back on the volcano's flanks, where it forms pyroclastic flows; lava flows. Its shape at particle level looks just like that, a flattened sphere. While the heaviest particles fall back on the ground, the remaining airborne particles of dust and ash crown the mountain just like in your drawing."

"So it's possible, right?" Alex asked excitedly.

"I don't see how," the professor replied. "The only way that could happen is if the nuclear device was buried, deep enough to find a path of least or equal resistance toward the magma chamber."

"Yes, exactly, that's what we thought of," she blurted. "Why is it impossible?"

"Let's say, in theory, that a nuclear device can be lowered into the ground enough to destabilize the magma chamber. Being that the nuclear explosion is a thermo-generating event of immense power, at first it would push downward. It would force the magma down, but then, the reaction would come. Magma would fly high, and you'd see a strong, violent eruption. It would also explain why we didn't see any warning signs."

"But?" Alex asked.

"There's no feasible way to bury a nuclear device in the caldera of Mount Rainier without us knowing about it. Absolutely no way. This is no longer the 1900s, you see. Our equipment is so sensitive, that we sense people *walking* on the edge of the caldera if they stomp their feet a little. That's why I am saying that it's impossible someone buried the device in the mountain. If anyone would have drilled in that mountain for even a single second, we would have picked it up."

Alex rubbed her hands, frustrated. The moment she felt she made any progress, something happened to eliminate all hope. If there were a single shred of logical, natural explanation to Rainier's eruption, she would have given up her quest by now. However, V's recognizable brand had always been apparently unexplainable events, hiding strategic-level terrorist plots. As crazy as she knew that sounded, even to herself, she still believed V had pulled it off somehow. She just had to find out how.

"Let's say, for the sake of argument, that someone managed to drill in that mountain unnoticed. How deep would he have to go?"

Eddie exchanged glances with the professor.

"I'd say at least 200 feet," the professor said. "There is no precedent, you see. No one has done that before, not even on a computerized model."

"We've done underground nuclear explosion modeling for fallout and effect," Eddie said. "For nukes buried in the ground, solid ground, not in volcanoes. If buried deeper than 150 feet, a 3-kiloton detonation would be contained under the ground's surface."

"That might generate enough disruptive energy to crack the bottom of the caldera and push it against the magma, initiating the eruption," the professor added. "Again, *if* you can drill down to 200 feet unheard, unseen, undetected. That's a big if."

"That works for me, though," Alex said. "One more question, Dr. Ted."

"Go ahead."

"What would happen if the nuclear device were bigger?"

"How much bigger?"

"Seriously bigger. Give me worst-case scenarios."

Both Eddie and the professor gazed at her in disbelief.

"Absolute worst-case scenario? It could split the planet in half."

LESLIE WOLFE   111

She crinkled her nose. Not even V could possibly want that; he wasn't suicidal.

"Second worst then?"

"If the explosion was strong enough, it would put enormous pressure on the tectonic plates and could destabilize the San Andreas Fault."

That sounded more like something V would want. Such a plan would be worthy of his end game. It could mean endless, high-magnitude earthquakes with months of aftershocks, tens of millions dead, decades of aftermath.

"Whoa . . ." Eddie said quietly.

The professor rubbed his forehead, thinking.

"I will run some simulations with the new data you gave me to see what that could look like. I'll share my results as soon as I have them. What will you do next, if I may ask?"

"Oh, we'll solve the problem you gave us: how to bury a nuke undetected," Alex replied. "I'm willing to bet good money against peanut chaff that it has a solution."

Five was sleeping when the ship's loud horn woke him. The vessel was approaching the Port of Long Beach, his point of entry into the continental United States. He'd been lucky so far. His intermodal container carried furniture items from China. He had shifted things around a little, rearranging the items in the container, and gained himself decent rest space on a sofa. The three hours it took the CSCL *Bao Chang* to get to destination since he'd made it inside the cargo container had passed quickly, with him sound asleep.

Now he was wide awake, a wave of excitement pumping adrenaline through his body and getting him ready for the next phase of his mission. Within twenty-four hours, his mission should be complete, and he should be on his way to the five million dollars' worth of freedom and easy living waiting for him on his return. There was magic in numbers; he strongly believed that there was. His call sign was Number Five, the five million dollars were waiting for him to get the job done, and he'd been the fifth in line departing the *Admiral Yankulov* by chopper, although they hadn't departed in order of their assigned numbers. The Chinese had placed him in a container five levels up from the deck of their vessel. It was definitely a good sign; it had to be.

The Chinese had set him up inside a container at the highest level, among the first ones to be unloaded after arrival. He didn't have much time to get ready. He peered outside through the tiny hole he bored in the container door and saw the port lights closing fast. The *Bao Chang* was already maneuvering, well underway with its docking procedures.

Five covered the peephole with a bit of chewing gum and turned on his flashlight. Then he unzipped his backpack and extracted the lead blanket. He moved the furniture around some more, making sure it remained stable for the unloading process, and found a good place for him to crouch and cover himself with the X-ray shielding material.

Within minutes, he heard the crane mechanism whirring above his head. A loud bang, followed by several metallic creaks, and he felt the container move. The crane had latched onto his container, and was whisking him into the air.

Five fought a strong wave of motion sickness and leaned his head against the container wall to steady himself. He took deep breaths, fighting it off, and telling himself it wasn't going to last long. He felt the container descending already. Within seconds, the container had landed and was secured in place onto a platform. He could hear locking latches slam into place, and people chatting casually nearby. He was loaded onto something; he couldn't tell whether it was a truck or a railway car.

The container was set in motion with a distinguishable whistle of compressed air brakes being released, and he knew he was on a truck. By the looks of it, he'd been lucky yet again; the truck was gaining speed, most likely getting ready to leave the port, without passing through the dreaded X-ray machine.

Then the truck slowed and came to a full stop. He heard a crane whirring again and felt the same bout of nausea as the crane lifted the container and then lowered it again. It made a loud thud as it landed on a new surface, which sounded hollow and resonating.

One by one, latches snapped into place, in all four corners of the container. Then silence, stillness, and darkness.

He waited for a while, then emerged from underneath the lead blanket and looked outside. He was on a railroad car, double-stacked, and his container was on the upper level. There was no X-ray gate in sight, just railroad cars loaded with containers, and some empty platforms, awaiting their loads. Trucks maneuvered in and out of the loading zone, bringing intermodal containers to be loaded on railroad cars. There was no way he could leave his container while in the loading area. He had to wait.

He curled up under the lead blanket again, just in case, and dozed off. He took pride in his ability to sleep whenever he had a chance, resourcing his system and getting ready for when the opportunity presented itself. When he woke, the train had set in motion with a long, loud screech. He'd been waiting for that exact moment.

He checked his GPS and saw that the train was leaving the port area. He'd made it. Now he had to get off the train, and that wasn't going to be easy. He was stacked up high, behind bolted metallic doors; he had to get busy.

Five turned on his flashlight and localized the locking bars placement, the precise spot where they extended past the length of the door and into the upper and lower frames of the container. That's where he had to cut. He lit his blowtorch and got to work, after cutting through the rubber door seals to expose the bars.

"Come on, already," he mumbled, fearing that the blowtorch wouldn't last as long as he needed to cut all four bars.

He finished working on the fourth point and kicked the door vigorously. The door resisted. He grunted and kicked it again, more forcefully that time. The door gave and swung open, then bounced right back after hitting its maximum range of motion. He pushed it open again and looked outside. He was high above the ground, but he could make it. The railroad car had a small platform at the end, enough for him to gain footing and a good place to drop his backpack. The train headed into a wooded area, offering him some natural cover. It was still dark; no one was going to see him hop off that train.

He packed his lead blanket and then lowered his backpack onto the railroad car's platform, using a looped piece of climbing rope. Then he let himself slide down and landed in one piece next to his backpack. The only issue was he couldn't secure the container door back shut. It flung open, bouncing back and forth as the train moved.

Jumping from a moving train with a backpack weighing more than seventy pounds was not easy, even if the train moved slowly, at about twenty miles per hour. It could break his back. He weighed his options; he decided to lower the backpack onto the ground with climbing rope and ease it onto the ground. Then he could easily hop off and walk back to retrieve it.

As he jumped off, the train came out of the forest and entered a well-lit, suburban area, blowing its horn repeatedly.

The train continued on its tracks for hours before anyone noticed and reported a container with a swinging door.

Fate had given Number Three the privilege to make port aboard a Russian cargo vessel. That came with several perks. He enjoyed a hot cup of soup before entering his container, and he didn't have to enter it until the ship was close to port. The merchandise in the container had been rearranged to make enough room for him. Finally, the workers had rigged a system to allow him to control the door from inside, after the container was unloaded. *Creative*, Three had to admit.

A couple of hours later, Three's container was deposited on the ground, inside the Port of San Diego. Happy to feel solid ground under his feet, Three didn't have the patience to wait and see how long the container was going to sit there before being loaded on a truck and hauled somewhere. He only waited half an hour or so, enough time for other containers to be stacked around his. That gave him enough cover to move.

When he felt safe enough, he released the improvised wire that unlatched the locking bars, left unsecured by his fellow shipmates. Then he snuck out of the container and carefully locked the door behind him.

Before proceeding, he stopped and scanned the area for video surveillance cameras. There were plenty, but he mapped himself a course most likely to keep him hidden from view behind the thousands of containers awaiting processing in the port.

The early light of dawn greeted Three as he exited the port area, smiling and walking briskly toward the city. It was going to be a beautiful day.

Summer sunrise lit up the San Francisco skyline with hues of reds and yellows buried in the night's dense fog. Only the tips of the Golden Gate Bridge emerged from the fog, offering a visual feast for anyone watching.

In the Port of San Francisco, no one had the time to watch the sunrise. *Nand Rani*, sailing under India's pavilion, lined up for unloading, as the morning shift crane operators took their positions. The ground teams were in positions, wearing hard hats and heavy clothing to shield them from the bitter, humid cold of the San Francisco summer morning.

Trucks lined up to get their loads, and, as soon as the Indian vessel was securely docked, the unloading procedure started on all crane lines. One by one, cargo containers were lifted from the stack onboard the vessel, then moved toward the land and lowered onto trucks. Routine, plain routine, in every single aspect.

Only until it stopped being routine. Crane #4 latched poorly onto a container, but the operator failed to notice that only three of the four latching points were securely clamped. He started the lifting and transfer maneuver, and the additional strain given by the inertia of the swing caused the third latch point to give. The container swung violently and hit the crane pillar before dropping from twelve stories high and smashing into bits. It fell against the ship's edge first, crashing against other containers still onboard, then it hit the dock's concrete edge. Most of the debris fell in the water, through the few feet of open space between the ship and the dock.

An alarm sounded, and all the cranes came to a screeching halt automatically, some swinging their containers midway between ship and shore.

On the ground, workers gathered, slowly approaching the debris.

"Whew, that was close," one of them said, removing his hard hat and wiping the sweat off his brow.

"Yup, you can say that again," a second man replied. "Good thing no one died here today."

"I think someone did," said another, looking intently at the water between the vessel and the dock, where small pieces of debris still floated.

"What do you mean? Who?"

"Don't know, but I could have sworn I saw a guy fall in the water when the container smashed. I ain't seein' him come up though," he said, continuing to stare at the dark blue water.

"Are you sure?" a supervisor asked.

"Yeah, boss, I know what I saw. A guy fell in there."

"Where the hell did he come from? The ship?"

"I could have sworn he came from the container. He fell from high up, when the container smashed against the crane. That's what I saw."

The supervisor pulled out his radio and called it in. Seconds later, a different pitch of alarm resounded in the Port of San Francisco.

Alex released the harness buckle and hopped off the Black Hawk, inhaling the salty San Diego morning air. She felt a sting in her ribs but ignored it. It was good to be able to fly straight to where she needed to be; it saved a lot of time, and she felt she was in a hair-raising race against time, against V, against all odds. She needed all the help she could get. She'd almost felt comfortable flying on the helicopter that morning, although her first helicopter flight, threatened by ash-clogged intakes and an imminent engine stall had terrified her.

Her muscles were sore and her back hurt, after catching only a couple of hours of shuteye in the helicopter seat. Her healing cracked ribs hurt worse that morning, with every breath. Her stomach growled loudly, and she was starting to feel drained. There wasn't any time for rest nor for sustenance. Eddie and she had rummaged through Professor Tedford's office fridge and cleaned out everything they found in there. That had to keep them going for at least a few more hours. Having the helo saved lots of time, but they couldn't exactly stop at a gas station and buy snacks.

She waited for Eddie to finish securing the aircraft and checked her messages. A new message had come in from Sam, probably when they were in midflight and she couldn't hear the chime. Frowning, she opened the encrypted message.

It read, "Forensics expert now sure. Material came from the third reactor within the Rostov power plant. Rostov 3 is new, been operational for less than a year. Whatever that is you're tracking, it's brand new."

"Eddie," she called, but noticed he was on the phone. He hadn't heard her. As soon as he hung up, she grabbed his sleeve.

"Eddie, I just learned—"

"The source of the radioactive material?"

"Yeah. Definitely no leftovers. This is brand new stuff we're dealing with."

"How does this new piece of information play with your theories?"

"Quite well, I think," she replied. "I'm not sure it changes anything though. It doesn't validate nor invalidate my theory. It helps eliminate some options, but that's about it."

"Are you going to tell me your theory? What do you think your terrorist wants to do?"

"Maybe later. I still need to figure some things out. Let's see how this meeting goes."

They had landed with special permission at the Naval Amphibious Base Coronado, the home of SEAL Team 1. Their explosives expert, Lieutenant Duggan, waited for them in a small conference room.

He hopped to his feet at attention when they entered. He shook their hands firmly and invited them to take seats. His upper arms tensed the sleeves of his uniform, stretching the fabric with every move. He gave them a scrutinizing look, measuring them up, and then frowned almost imperceptibly.

Duggan smiled briefly as a courtesy, then asked coolly, "What can I do for you?"

"Um . . . We have a problem to solve, and I need your help," Alex said.

"Shoot," he said.

"Let's say you want to detonate this nuke 200 feet into the ground. It's a small one. No one can see or feel you dig. What would you do?"

"No one can feel me dig? What do you mean by that?"

"The ground where you need to bury your nuke is equipped with all sorts of sensors. The moment you trip a sensor, they come and get you. No joy."

"Got it." He scratched his buzz-cut head, then looked at them intently, his frown more visible. "I was ordered to offer full cooperation," he said, "and I will, although you two are asking a disturbing question. This is what I'd do: I'd set up a directional plastic explosive charge, positioned right under the nuke. I'd separate the two devices with a shock-absorbing plate, carbon fiber based most likely, to insulate and protect the nuke from the plastic's blast. Then I'd set this package on the ground. When the plastic detonates, it creates a vertical tunnel in which the nuke drops under its own weight. When the nuke is low enough, I'd detonate it."

"Wouldn't the nuke's detonation take the path of least resistance and blow upwards, back through the hole?"

"Sure, there's least resistance above, but not enough to channel *all* the explosive force of a thermonuclear, no matter how small. Most of the energy would still dissipate underground."

"So it could work," Alex said, sounding almost excited.

Duggan gazed at her for a fraction of a second, inquisitively.

"It's still a long shot. There are many factors to consider. What if the well so created collapses before the nuke can fully descend? You'd have to be very precise. You'd have to run tests. Lots of tests."

"But it can be done, at least in theory?" she asked again.

"In more than just theory. In the oil industry, shaped charges or directional explosives are used to complete oil wells for production. The shaped charges model the well and the bottom, getting it ready for whatever next steps are needed to take to get that well into production."

"Have you seen it work? Two separate charges, as you described, even if not paired up with a nuke?"

"I've seen the *combination* of two sequential charges work. Combat engineers use the *sandwich*, as they call it, to bore holes for cratering charges. It's a three-step process, although in most cases it's not automated."

"What do you mean?" Eddie asked.

"I mean explosion one, the one that bores the well, takes place first. The second charge is dropped and then detonated remotely to obtain the crater. I've never heard of it done deeper than 50 feet though. Never."

"Interesting choice of words, cratering," she said and glanced quickly at Eddie.

Duggan shrugged. "That's what it's called."

"Why would anyone need craters?"

"Demolitions, mainly. Remediations too."

Alex stood and looked at Eddie, to see if he had any other questions. He remained quiet, but stood as well, getting ready to leave.

"I think we're good, lieutenant. Thank you for your help."

"You're welcome, ma'am," he said, shaking her hand. "What are you guys trying to blow up, if I may ask?"

"We? We're not trying to blow anything up," she replied quickly. "Trust me."

He scoffed and tilted his head a bit, in a clear expression of "Yeah, right, are you kidding me?" conveyed silently and with all due respect.

As she left the pavilion, her mind played with scenarios, repeating key points of information Duggan had shared. *You'd have to run tests. Lots of tests,* he had said. Suddenly, she knew, at least in part, what Mount Rainier had been about. The thought had been in her mind before, but now it made sense, because now she'd found V's motive.

"You seem preoccupied," Eddie said, holding the helicopter door for her. "Where to?"

"Not sure yet. Let me make a couple of calls first."

"Sure, go ahead. You need some privacy?"

"Quite the opposite, Eddie, I need you to listen in, at least on the second call."

He circled the helo and climbed into his seat. He pressed a few buttons and powered up the dashboard, then hooked up their headsets and her phone.

"Don't you think it's about time you told me what you're thinking?"

"I need a little more time," she replied sheepishly, seeing how frustrated he looked. "I know how awful this sounds, but please bear with me."

"Listen, I've been more or less your air taxi driver for the past few hours. I believe you're onto something, but my team is in Olympia, and I'm needed there. This can't go on forever, you know. You need to tell me what this is about. All of it. We're on the same side, goddamn it! I thought we were a team!"

She bit her lip, thinking whether to share an incomplete theory and waste time defending it, or delay some more in the hope more data would bring more clarity.

"Two more calls, then I promise I'll share."

"Okay, fair enough," he agreed, punctuating with a sigh and a quick headshake.

Alex dialed Marino first. She picked up at the first ring.

"Hey, I know what Mount Rainier was about. It was a test."

"What? For what?" Marino asked, her high-pitched voice showing her surprise.

"I don't know yet, but I'm about to find out."

"Oh, God . . . You are crazy. You know that, right?" Marino asked, then hung up.

"And that was the CIA for you," she quipped, then dialed another number.

Number Seven drew in a long, calming breath as he approached the car rental desk. He was minutes away from disappearing into the great expanse of the United States.

His backpack was heavy and he'd carried it for almost two hours, making his way out of the port and through the city. He was starting to feel the strain, but his instructions were clear: do not stop until you leave the city.

He followed the instructions to the letter. He was told to rent a car from a remote, isolated location, nowhere near the port or the airport. He was to avoid crowded places, where he could trip radiation sensors. Finally, he was told to act naturally, blend in, imitating and emulating the behaviors of normal American tourists visiting San Diego.

"Can I help you?" the car rental employee greeted him without intonation, displaying an automatic, absentminded smile. She was young, too young and pretty to be so jaded.

"I thought I could do this on foot," he said in perfect English. "Visit San Diego, that is. I thought I wasn't going to need a car, but I do. Anything available?"

"Sure, what would you prefer? Compact, midsized sedan, or an SUV maybe?"

"An SUV would be nice," he answered, taking off his backpack slowly and easing it onto the ground, so the attendant wouldn't notice how heavy it was.

"For how long?"

"Six days should do it, a week at the most," he replied. If everything went well, in three days he'd be long gone.

"I'll need a credit card and driver's license, please."

He opened his wallet and extracted the two pieces of plastic without any hesitation.

The attendant swiped them through a machine, then handed them right back. He let out a long, relaxing breath. He was going to make it just fine.

"If you don't mind me asking, Mr. Patterson, I'm detecting a slight accent. Are you British?"

His hands turned cold. He focused.

"No, I'm American," he forced himself to laugh, hoping he didn't sound too nervous. "My wife is Swedish though, and, after a while, her accent rubbed off on me."

"Oh, how funny," she chirped, then handed him the keys. "You're in slot nineteen, a white Ford Expedition. Someone will be there shortly to give you the tour. Enjoy your stay!"

Alex retrieved the professor's number from her phone's memory, but Eddie touched her arm before she could hit dial.

"Talk to me," he said. "No more waiting, no more phone calls, no more bullshit. Talk to me now. Please."

She looked at him and saw a powerful ally she had been ignoring. A man willing to be open-minded about her theories, willing to give her a chance. A nuclear engineer whose expertise could make the difference between figuring this out and failing miserably, leaving V with virtually no opponents in his deadly game. An ally she was about to lose if she didn't come clean.

She sighed, then hesitated a second, not sure how much information to share.

"Remember you asked for it," she said, hiding her hesitation under the guise of humor.

He didn't even blink.

"All right, so what do you do? You're NEST; you find, measure, and contain radiation, right? You guys investigate any nuclear threat and somehow manage to keep us radiation-free."

He frowned. "Yeah, that's about right, but weren't we going to talk about you?"

"Precisely. You see, unlike you, I don't have a clear job description. I'm not with any official government entity. The FBI ID I showed around is from an older case I worked on, as a contractor. It probably should have been canceled, but that got overlooked."

"Huh?" Eddie's eyebrows shot up, ridging his tall forehead with several deep lines.

"Yeah . . . I'm a corporate investigator, working for a small undercover investigations company called The Agency."

"Great name . . . it just creates confusion with the CIA."

"I'll be happy to pass on your feedback to my boss and company founder, Tom Isaac. Until now, we've never crossed paths with the CIA. The name was never an issue. We just stuck to our corporate stuff."

"What exactly do you normally investigate?"

"Fraud cases, hostile takeovers, theft of client data, money, that kind of thing."

"How come you're here, then?"

"The past three cases I've worked on led back to this one individual, a Russian terrorist of whom we only know one initial, V. All my recent cases had the following parameters in common: plans of monumental reach, unlimited resources, and the uncanny ability to disguise the terrorist plot under the ruse of an apparently natural or coincidental occurrence."

"So, you believe this fits?"

"I *know* this fits. I still had some doubts before finding out if one could detonate a nuke deep inside the caldera with a dual explosion. When I learned there was a way it could be done, my suspicions turned to certainty. It's him; it's V."

"Then what are you still looking for here? Why not turn everything you know over to your contacts with the CIA and let them take it from there?"

"Because I don't think this is over. Not yet."

"I picked up on that from your call with them. Why do you believe that?"

"For the past couple of years I've been trying to understand how this man thinks. Without even knowing his name, I know what he wants and just how far he's willing to go to get it. He's extremely talented in getting other people signed up to do his bidding, regardless of how well off or powerful they are. He's got unlimited resources; he's a special breed of psychopath."

"Special? How?"

"The typical psychopath's victim body count doesn't satisfy him. His dreams are big, majestic even. He wants to control the world and all his personal enemies, to the point of being in absolute power over hundreds of millions. From that perspective, he's amazing. Fantastic."

"Sheesh . . . You almost sound like you're in love with the guy," Eddie blurted, taken aback.

"I'm in *hate* with the guy," she replied with a bitter chuckle. "It's equally powerful. Know your enemy and all that. Make no mistake, Eddie, if I could kill him right now with my own two hands, I would, without *any* hesitation, and then I'd order pizza."

His mouth gaped. "Huh?"

"To celebrate . . . I'm also hungry, you know. I'm dreaming of a triple-topping, extra cheese . . ." She saw the effect her words had on him and circled back. "If anyone deserves to be put down for the sake of humankind, it's V. He's done despicable things that I wish I could share with you, but I can't, regardless of how high your clearance is. This is the moment I have to ask you to trust me."

She smiled shyly. Eddie nodded once, absorbed.

"You don't work for the CIA?" Eddie asked.

"Nope."

"The FBI?"

"Nope."

"Yet the CIA called ahead, announced your visit, and asked us to cooperate in any way we could. How did you pull that off?"

"Per my CIA contact, I have statistics on my side," she replied, smiling widely. She saw how confused he looked. "I haven't ever been proven wrong.. Never. Not yet, anyway," she added with a shrug.

"Well, you should have started with *that* statement, you know," Eddie stated with a faint smile contradicted by a deep frown. "You were *never* wrong, and you think this guy's not done yet?"

"Yup," she replied, then remained silent, giving Eddie the time to think through the implications.

"Holy shit . . ." he whispered, his eyes fixated on one of the Naval Air Station buildings in the distance. "Does this have anything to do with the wig and ridiculous clothes you were wearing?"

"Yup," she repeated. "I believe he might try to kill me. He knows who I am, knows what I look like. If he finds me, I'm dead."

"How? Have you met him?"

"No. Satellites . . . damn satellites and video surveillance systems. He's into that, you know. At least I believe he is. He has to be, knowing what he does every day."

Eddie let out a long breath and leaned back against his seat.

"What's he up to next? What do you think?"

"I think Rainier was a test. Hearing Duggan's advice, to run multiple tests to get it right, made me think V might have done just that: he ran a test. The type of test he couldn't have run in his own country; the nuclear type."

"For what?"

"Like I told my skeptical CIA contact, I don't know yet. But I think we have a shot at finding out," she added, pointing at her phone.

"What are your theories?"

"I *know* Rainier was too small for him; I feel that in my gut."

He glanced quickly at her, amazed, but didn't say anything.

"I know how that sounds; let's move past it, please," she said, suddenly feeling sad and weary.

He nodded, clasping his hands together nervously.

"Let's assume I'm right, and Rainier was indeed too small for him. In that case, he could be looking for one of two things: a bigger eruption, to destabilize San Andreas, for example, or another event of bigger fallout consequences.

Bigger nuke maybe, yielding more radiation."

"Whew," he whistled, "he's one hell of a fanatic, huh?"

"Um . . . not really. Hungry for power at an unprecedented scale, yes. But fanatic? Not in the traditional sense. I can't picture him embracing someone else's ideals. Not him."

He gazed at her for a few seconds, apparently weighing his options.

"All right, then, what next?"

"Let's validate that two sequential explosions actually happened at Rainier. After all, Duggan's theory is nothing more than a theory at this point, if the data doesn't support it. Then we'll see."

She hit the call button and flipped the switch opening access for Eddie to participate in the call.

"Dr. Ted? It's Alex Hoffmann and Eddie, um . . . Zoller," she said, shooting Eddie an apologetic glance. "Do you have some time for us?"

"Yes, absolutely, go right ahead."

"We might have found a way to detonate the nuke underground, buried in the caldera. If the theory we found were accurate, you would have seen on the seismometers two explosions—two shocks, not one. The second shock coming within seconds of the first."

"That's exactly what we've seen, Miss Hoffmann. Three shocks, actually. Let me give you specifics."

The sound of rustling papers and fingers tapping on a keyboard ensued.

"Uh-huh . . ." the professor mumbled. "Found it. The first shock was recorded at precisely 12:54:12PM, and the shock wave is consistent with an artificial explosion. The peak of the wave was not preceded by any smaller amplitude oscillations. Then the oscillations decreased, reverberating for almost seven seconds, when the second shock came, more than ten times stronger than the first. It happened at 12:54:19PM, and lasted, at peak levels, for fifteen full seconds. The intensity of the shocks decreased again, and then the final, most devastating one came, the eruption *per se*."

"It fits," Alex replied. "Excellent."

She explained Duggan's method of burying the nuke. The professor fell silent, not saying anything.

"Professor? You still there?"

"Yes . . . I am just at a loss for words."

"We have more questions, because we—I don't think this is over. What would be, in your opinion, the most devastating eruption you could set up?"

"Well, now that we know you *can* set one up, there are—" he started, but then changed directions with his train of thought. "What kind of devastation are you talking about?"

"I mean, like hurting this country for generations to come," she said, feeling a chill in her bones as she spoke.

"Yellowstone, definitely Yellowstone, but that's not really active. There's activity at Yellowstone, but the volcano hasn't erupted in 630,000 years."

"What would set it off?"

"Like with any volcano, the buildup of pressure, of magma in the chamber. Yellowstone is such a hotspot."

"How big?" Eddie asked.

"The eruption? It could get up to 2,500 times bigger what we've seen in Rainier's case."

Silence fell heavy on both ends of the conversation.

"What kind of consequences are we talking about?" Alex asked in a sobering tone, aware her voice was trembling.

"We're talking about volcanic winter for years, maybe decades. The United States would take the brunt of it, but it would be a global volcanic winter."

She struggled wrapping her mind around such a devastating event. Would any human being, even V, be willing to trigger such devastation on earth? Was she losing it? Was she going down a rabbit hole, in direct communication with the wildest, deepest abyss in human history? Could anyone conceive, plan, and execute such an unprecedented attack? There were no words to describe it. The word *genocide* seemed too pale, too weak, not able to encompass the dimensions of such devastation. Add radiation on top of that and . . .

She let out a shuddering breath of air and tried to refocus, suddenly aware of the minutes of silence that had passed. She felt sick, nauseated, and she fought the urge to jump off the helo and unload her unsettled stomach somewhere near its right wheel.

"Talk to me about Yellowstone, professor," she managed to articulate.

"Yellowstone is a supervolcano," the professor replied, his words choked and faint. "It has been slowly waking up. We're seeing small earthquakes become more frequent, slightly stronger. It's not at worrisome levels. We're not predicting an eruption in the next few thousand years, but we're closely monitoring its activity."

"But in case it blows?" Eddie asked.

"It has a huge magma chamber. It's fifty miles long by twelve miles wide. If that blows up, simply put, the United States as we know it would cease to exist; parts of Canada too. The best part of North America would just disappear, covered under a thick layer of volcanic ash, and would stay frozen for years, even decades. Nothing would grow and no one would breathe. All dead. Ah, you might find interesting to know that the hotspot is moving, and has been, from Idaho toward northwestern Wyoming. It's on track to be positioned under the main caldera."

"Huh? How fast is it moving?" Alex asked with panic in her voice, shooting

Eddie a surprised glance.

"It will cross Idaho in about eleven million years," the professor replied.

She let out a sigh of relief.

"Oh, I'm not worried about that," she said.

"You should be," the professor replied dryly. "We are. That means the volcano is waking up, getting primed for the next cataclysmic eruption."

She rubbed her forehead spasmodically, trying to calm the wave of paralyzing, nauseating fear she felt. What could *she* do? *Think! Think!*

"That caldera, you have equipment on it, right? Seismometers?"

"Correct. We have a lot of equipment in place and a research facility nearby."

"Then we can keep an eye on it, guard it closely, and make sure no one sets foot near that caldera, right? We could even fence it out, I'm thinking," Alex said, with a shred of hope in her voice. "It can't be that big. It's just a—a caldera, isn't it? How big can it be?"

Silence took over the communications line, amplified in their headsets.

Then the professor finally spoke, crushing all hope.

"You've never been to Yellowstone, have you? It's about 1,500 square miles."

"The caldera?" Alex asked in disbelief.

"Yes, the caldera. It's bigger than the size of Rhode Island."

She retched spasmodically, dry heaving, holding on to the helicopter's wheel. Her stomach, mostly empty, didn't have much to give, and that made it worse. Her hands shook, and her throat constricted in the grasp of unspeakable terror.

Her knees gave and she let herself drop into a crouch next to the wheel. That was not the time to fall apart, but she did, anyway. Her mind kept going over the information she'd received, trying to find any piece that didn't fit, any bit that was illogical, that didn't belong. Nothing felt out of place; Yellowstone sounded like an end game worthy of V's strategic capabilities. Yet she hadn't pegged him for the hateful maniac that would do all that just out of pure hatred. He had to have other motives, motives she couldn't yet grasp, not completely.

She felt Eddie's hand on her shoulder.

"Are you okay? Should I call someone? I'm sure they have medics here on base."

"No, I'm fine," she mumbled, wiping her mouth with the tissue he offered.

He extended his hand.

"Want to get up then?"

She got back on her feet, unsure of her ability to stand, weak at the knees.

"We need help," she said weakly. "We need to call everybody. Even if they're going to think I'm crazy."

"How sure are you anyway?" Eddie asked.

She shot him a glare filled with disappointment.

"Out of all people, I'd expected you to have the most confidence in what I'm saying. You've been with me through the entire—"

"But you have to admit," Eddie interrupted, "it's really far-fetched. Blowing up Yellowstone? Seriously? What kind of man would do that?"

"Precisely," she replied, her voice still weak. "I can't blame you though. You're just the first in what will be a long, long list of people who will tell me I'm crazy. Been there, done that, you know," she chuckled bitterly. "Can't say that I like it though. Can't say that I can get used to it either. It's just a terrible waste of time. So I'll just . . ."

Her words trailed off. She didn't know yet what she was going to do. Why would anyone believe her, even Marino? But they had to . . . She couldn't possibly try to do this alone or with her team. What would Lou, Steve, and Tom do? Grab their rifles and keep watch over 1,500 square miles? It wasn't going to work. She needed to call them though; she needed their wisdom and their resourcefulness. She needed them by her side. Then she needed to call anyone else who wouldn't slam the phone in her face. She needed to think lucidly, clearly.

A familiar sound disrupted her thoughts. Her phone was ringing. She reached out inside the helicopter and saw the display reading, "No caller ID." She frowned, then picked up the call.

"Hello," she said, then put the call on hands-free, detaching the phone from the dashboard.

"Alex Hoffmann?" The caller's voice had a thick, Russian accent. She instantly became alert, hypervigilant, her brain switching to overdrive.

"Yes, that's me," she replied, then touched the phone's screen a couple of times to start call recording.

Eddie approached her with an inquisitive look, but she held her index finger to her lips, urging him to remain silent.

"You are Alex Hoffmann, da?" the man asked again.

"Yes, I am. Who is this?"

"Um . . . you have no reason to believe me, but something terrible is about to happen to your country," the man spouted. "I—I have a son; he's in Canada, he goes to school there. Please . . . please help me."

She clenched her jaws, thinking hard. If this man was from V's entourage, this was her shot. She'd always hoped she'd catch a break one day and find out the bastard's name. But she couldn't exactly ask . . . she risked scaring off the caller, who obviously knew of her. He probably assumed she knew a lot more than she did about V.

She took a deep breath. This is your chance, let's go for it, she encouraged herself. May the gods of bluffing be on your side today.

"I see . . ." she replied somberly. "So what's V planning to do this time?"

There was silence on the line, and her heart froze. She waited a few seconds, afraid to breathe, afraid to speak. She might have screwed it up after all, royally.

"You still there?" she finally asked. "Hello?"

She heard a worried chuckle on the line.

"Only his close foreign friends call him V," he eventually said, "mostly Americans who can't pronounce Vitaliy."

Alex closed her eyes and gestured thumbs-up with her left hand, while silently mouthing, "Yes!" She finally had a first name. She needed the last name, too. *Focus!*

"Don't worry," she replied with a quick laugh, "I'm definitely not a close friend."

"I know you're not," the man laughed.

"What do you call him?" she ventured to ask.

"I call him sir, most of the time. Sometimes boss. Lately I try not to be near him as much."

She frowned. No luck with the last name yet, but the man was still on the phone. She still had hope.

"So tell me, what's Vitaliy planning to do this time?"

"He sent fourteen people into the United States, all packing small nuclear bombs. At least twelve of them should make it to Yellowstone—"

"To blow up the caldera," she blurted, then bit her lip. Never interrupt the man who calls in with a tip. It's basic.

"You knew?" the man asked, clearly surprised.

"We just found out, earlier today. When are the fourteen men arriving?"

"They already arrived," the caller replied. "Today."

Both Eddie and Alex were perplexed. There were already fourteen Russian nuclear bombs in play in the country? How the hell did that happen? Eddie paced nervously, shaking his head and pointing at his phone. He mouthed, "It's urgent."

She gestured with her hand, trying to quiet him. She needed to focus on the caller and the information he was willing to share.

"When are they planning to blow it up?"

"As soon as they're ready, I believe," the man replied. "I know he wants to detonate himself, by satellite. I'm sorry I don't know more."

"I will take care of it, dear friend, and I'll make sure your son will live a long and healthy life."

"Spasiba," the man replied quietly, almost whispering.

"You're welcome," she replied, unsure how to proceed. "He keeps satellite eyes on the operation, right?"

"All the time."

She crinkled her nose, and shot a critical glare toward the beautiful blue sky of southern California.

"You didn't tell me your name," she said.

"I—I can't."

"Then what should I call you? How will you tell me it's you, if we ever meet?"

"We probably won't. If there's anything Myatlev really fears, it's crossing paths with you."

She gestured thumbs-up again, a wide smile spreading on her lips. She got him! She got the bastard's identity. Yes! The rest was going to be easy. Routine.

"Why is he afraid to cross paths with me?"

"He can't understand why you're hurting him. He doesn't know whom you work for, and that makes him angry, nervous."

She hadn't anticipated that. She thought he just wanted her dead, punished for foiling his best plans.

"But still, I need to call you something," she insisted, putting a little smile in her voice to encourage him.

He paused.

"Call me *chelovek chesti*," he replied hesitantly.

"What's that? What does that mean?"

"It means man of honor. Honest man."

"An honorable man, that indeed you are, chelovek chesti. Tell me please, why am I still alive?"

"He wanted to see you defeated before killing you. Now he's afraid of you again, and he's got a cleanup team on the ground, looking for you. Be careful."

She mouthed, "Oh, shit," and clenched her jaws.

"Until last week, if he'd told me to, I would have killed you myself," the man continued, embarrassment and guilt tinting his voice. "Not anymore, I promise."

"Spasiba, chelovek chesti," she replied. "Good to know."

"Good luck," he said. "Don't let him ruin our future. Or Abramovich."

"What? What do you mean?" she blurted. The Russian president was in on the plan to blow up Yellowstone? That meant way more than a terrorist act . . . That was a declaration of war. The United States was at war with Russia and didn't even know it. It hadn't received the memo.

She exchanged quick glances with Eddie, seeing her own state of shock reflected in his wide-opened eyes.

"Um, Abramovich started this. He has been pushing Myatlev for a nuclear attack for a couple of years now. Since Crimea."

...Chapter 32: Rear-Ended
...Wednesday, June 14, 2:12PM Local Time (UTC-8:00 hours)
...Interstate 15 North
...Near Primm, Nevada

Number Seven enjoyed the drive more than he anticipated. He'd been apprehensive, frightened out of his mind while locked inside the cargo container, afraid he'd get caught or buried alive in a humongous pile of containers. Then he nearly choked when the chick at the car rental place commented on his accent. However, as soon as he got behind the wheel of his rental car, things changed for the better. He felt much safer, despite the weapon of mass destruction stored in his cargo area.

Seven had never been to America before; he'd only seen it in movies and experienced the lifestyle during training, in the mock village buried deep in remote, rural Russia. Passionate about everything Hollywood touched, he binge-watched whatever he could get his hands on, from old Westerns to modern soaps. When he had given the car rental employee his ID, he was James Bond in *Tomorrow Never Dies*. He even accepted with a smile all types of insurance coverage offered, because that's what 007 had done in the movie. He would have preferred a BMW, of course, but the real-life Russian special operations agent had to settle for an upgraded Ford Expedition.

The driving route from San Diego to Yellowstone came within fifty miles of Hollywood, and he just couldn't resist the temptation. Without hesitation, he abandoned I-215 and took CA-210 West, going straight to Hollywood. As he drove, fear and guilt prickled his scalp with tiny beads of sweat. He rehearsed the excuse he was going to give Myatlev for the delay. Traffic jam on I-215 North. Detour due to road construction. Or something. He thought about it some more, then decided he was going to go with traffic jam and mandatory detour dictated by local police, if Myatlev would ever bother to ask. Seven *hoped* Myatlev would ask. Knowing Myatlev, he'd shoot him where he stood for breaking mission protocol. Seven shuddered, then pushed the thought aside and enjoyed his drive through Tinseltown.

He didn't dare to stop in Hollywood. He just slowed down to take a quick picture of the Hollywood sign with his phone camera and moved on. He didn't want to fall further behind schedule, and he knew that if he'd stop anywhere, he'd be tempted to wander about a little more, exploring, enjoying, and putting the timeline of his mission at risk.

With a sigh of regret, he turned around and left Hollywood in his rearview mirror. Too bad the five million dollars Myatlev had promised wouldn't buy him a life here in California. If he and the other thirteen agents fulfilled their missions, there was no telling what it could mean for his favorite city in the world. Yet he felt no remorse. The mission was the mission, and he had taken an oath of allegiance. He was in the service of his country, and that was that.

He drove north, excitedly anticipating the ride through Las Vegas, another cornerstone of the American culture he had absorbed through movies. Another wonderful place he couldn't stop to admire, not even for a minute. He could plan it so that he'd need to gas up the car in Sin City, but that was going to be the extent of his Vegas sojourn.

He turned the volume up on his satellite radio and relished the sound quality in his Ford Expedition. Yes, he was digging the ride, a lot. It made him feel twenty years old again, although that stage of his life was more than a decade past. The road curved gently as it started sloping, gradually steeper, as I-15 climbed up and then down the barren mountains of the Mojave. Traffic seemed to pick up, turning heavy at times, even if the Interstate had added an additional lane for slower trucks.

He had to hit the brakes more and more, and that ruined his driving experience. He wanted to go the full seventy miles per hour, to feel the road swoosh past under his wheels and to take in the power of the vehicle he was driving. His native Russia didn't have roads like that, with smooth, wide lanes and considerate traffic partners. Well, *some* were considerate, not all.

He started humming along with a catchy tune on satellite radio. A band of youngsters rapped something about being overly stressed out. *How fitting*, he thought. The sky was blue, the road ahead was awesome, his car was excellent, but he still carried a nuclear weapon in his trunk. There was a hard limit to his ability to relax.

A few honks got his attention. A black Mustang convertible with midnight blue accents and rims slalomed on the highway, honking everyone who stood in its path. The Mustang caught up with Seven's car, driving in parallel for a while, held behind by an unyielding truck. Seven admired the custom job on the Mustang. It had a blue-rimmed grille with assorted blue LEDs. The seat covers and headrests matched the metallic blue color of its rims and rearview mirror. Nice.

The Mustang's driver blared his horn again, twice, trying to get the truck in front of him to pull to the side. The truck's driver flipped him through the open window, and that made the Mustang driver curse wildly, screaming, transfigured. Seven observed the exchange with amusement. The fiery Mustang was boxed in with nowhere to go. The lane closest to the median was fast traffic, but moved bumper to bumper. The next lane had the flipping truck lined up behind another truck, and the slow lane was reserved for heavier vehicles and was a solid row of trucks as far as the eye could see.

Seven studied the occupants of the Mustang. From his elevated position in his SUV, he could see them clearly. They were kids, young kids, probably not a day older than seventeen or eighteen, but they must have been loaded to drive that beauty. The driver's shoulder-length hair was oily and unkempt, and he kept wiping his nose with the back of his hand, with the typical gesture of snorting drug addicts. He had teenage acne, and Seven thought he'd seen drool dripping at the corner of his mouth. The tattoo of a large spider adorned his neck, and the spider's hairy legs extended all the way to his left cheek. When he honked, he used his fist, slamming it against the steering wheel in disfiguring rage.

The front-seat passenger was a boy who wore big headphones and had wrapped his head in a white scarf, covering his eyes. He seemed out of it completely. Two young girls took up the back seat of the speeding convertible. One wore a sleeveless, black, mini-dress that had ridden up, almost to her panties. Tears smudged her heavy evening makeup. Her left eye showed signs of recent swelling; she was probably recovering from a bruised eye and had covered it with plenty of makeup. The other girl was on her phone, texting, while her long blonde hair flew entangled in the wind, wrapping around her sad, immobile face. Her jeans were shredded badly, all the way up her thighs and between her legs.

Junkies, Seven concluded. Both countries had them everywhere. Whether American or Russian, they all looked and acted the same. He turned his attention away from them and observed the approaching buildings. As he was nearing Vegas, advertisement banners and thousand-light signs grew more frequent. A road sign signaled he was approaching Primm, a small resort only an hour away from Vegas.

He turned his head to see what glimmered in the distance, tucked under the hills. It was like a sea of mirrors, changing its point of reflectivity as he drove by. He looked at the shimmering sea of mirrors puzzled, not knowing what to make of it. Then he remembered he'd seen something like that in a Matthew McConaughey movie, *Sahara*. It was a solar power plant.

Satisfied, he turned his attention back to the heavy traffic ahead, just in time to see the car in front of him hit the brakes hard. He slammed his foot on the brakes, and the Expedition managed to stop within inches of the car in front of him, a Toyota sedan.

He almost breathed, but then a loud thump erupted at the back of his car, slamming him forward forcefully into the Toyota. The airbags deployed, slamming him in the chest. Or was that the seatbelt, restraining him from bouncing forward? He heard himself scream.

He breathed in the smell of smoke, of gunpowder.

"Bozhe moi, the bomb!" he muttered, feeling numb and dizzy from shock.

The airbags deflated as he struggled to get a grip and understand what was going on. Someone had rear-ended him; he looked in the mirror and saw what was left of the custom Mustang. *Motherfuckers,* he thought, *damn, stupid, junkie motherfuckers!*

Then he focused on the car in front of him. His massive SUV had obliterated the Toyota's trunk. The driver and passenger were opening the doors, trying to get out.

Someone appeared out of nowhere, a bald, chubby man in a sweaty, wife-beater T-shirt. He banged furiously on his window.

"Are you all right in there?"

He made an effort to nod, but felt a jolt of pain shoot up his nape as he did. He opened the door and unhooked his seatbelt, fumbling with it for a while. His numb fingers, unfamiliar with the Ford's clasp, struggled to apply the right amount of pressure to release the buckle. Or maybe it was stuck?

After a minute, Seven got free of the seatbelt and went to the back of his car, afraid to look and see what was left of his baggage. Was the bomb exposed? Was it the end of the journey for him?

Someone touched his arm, and he turned, jolted. The Mustang's driver, wiping blood off his face with his hand, laughed hysterically.

"Dude . . . Oh, my God, dude! I'm so sorry!" he said, laughing and throwing droplets of blood and spittle in Seven's face. "This is so seriously fucked, man! Just wait 'til all my friends see this, dude!"

To Seven's shock, the kid took selfies with both cars in the background, continuing to laugh out of his mind.

His passenger had lifted the scarf off his eyes but kept his headphones on. He looked dazed, but otherwise unharmed. The girls were mostly okay too. The one in the black dress cussed incessantly, and the other one cried softly, texting and taking pictures.

Seven turned his attention toward the back of his Expedition. The Mustang had rammed it really hard, but the massive frame of the SUV and its trailer hitch had deflected the brunt of the damage back onto the Mustang. His rear storage area was now half its original size, and Seven was unable to open the hatchback door.

The junkie clung to his sleeve like a leech.

"So what do you wanna do now, man? We do the insurance shit? Or do you want some real money instead? Huh? What d'ya say?"

Seven stared into the glazed, blue eyes of the junkie, unsure what to do. No one had bothered to train or prepare him what to do in case of an accident. He knew enough about it to know he should use insurance, especially since he'd bought every type available at the car rental place. But insurance meant cops, and cops were the last thing he needed right now. He needed to get away. He needed to grab that backpack and run with it, as far and as fast as he could. He had no idea whether the seals were still intact, or if the bomb had lost containment and was leaking radioactive emissions into the atmosphere, leading everyone to him.

He looked at the front of his car, wondering if it could be driven anymore. It looked bad . . . Even if the SUV started, it probably wouldn't make it too far. The first cop to see him would probably end up chasing him.

The junkie was trying to shove cash into his pocket. He looked at him in a daze.

"You boys weren't planning to leave this party before I arrived, now were you?" a man's threatening, raspy voice startled him.

He turned and saw a cop, dressed in a navy blue uniform, staring at them intently.

"Driver's license, registration, and proof of insurance, both of you jokers."

The junkie's eyes rounded up and bulged out. His mouth gaped open, allowing a tiny bit of saliva to come out and make its way toward his chin.

Seven was still in shock. He couldn't grasp what was happening, not fast enough, so he did exactly as he was told. He extracted the fake driver's license from his wallet, remembering how Myatlev's man had sworn these would go undetected even if screened by police, hoping that it was true. Then he tried to figure out what else he needed to show.

"It's a rental," he muttered quietly.

"Rental contract should do it. You have that, don't you?" the cop insisted, seeing him hesitate.

"Yes . . ."

He went to his car and opened the center storage compartment, where he'd shoved the pink copy of the car rental contract. He took it to the cop, who grunted and snatched it out of his hands.

"Wait here," the cop told both drivers, "don't get any funny ideas." He went to speak with the Toyota's driver next, then went to his police car, marked with the insignia of the Nevada Highway Patrol. The front side panel of his car had the words "State Trooper" marked in gold lettering.

The trooper spoke into his radio, then lowered his window and asked, "Is any one of you in need of medical attention?"

No one replied. The cop didn't seem to care or mind. He resumed his radio conversation, asking for backgrounds on both drivers and their vehicles.

A few minutes later, the cop got out of his car and came straight toward Seven.

"Call your car rental company. They'll take it from here. They'll bring you a replacement vehicle and send you on your way."

Then the trooper circled his SUV and looked inside.

"Going backpacking? Where? Vegas?"

"Yeah," Seven managed, fighting the choking fear in his throat.

The cop extended him his driver's license, and Seven stared at his hand in disbelief. The cop withdrew his hand.

"Anything the matter?"

"Um, just the shock, I guess," he uttered. "From the crash, you know."

The trooper scoffed and offered him the driver's license again. This time he took it.

Myatlev heard the sound of his phone ringing, but sleep clung to his brain like chunks of mud, not letting him wake up. He dreamt he was taking the call, but the phone went on ringing. Eventually, he pulled himself out of the depths of his restful trance and picked up the call, making the dreaded sound go away.

"Hello," he said in a raspy voice.

"Hello sir, it's Davydova," a woman's voice said.

He woke up instantly, fully alert and lucid. He jumped out of bed, and turned on the bedside table lamp.

"Yes, what do you have?"

"I found her!" Davydova announced cheerfully. "She passed in front of an ATM just minutes ago, and my software picked her up."

He felt a surge of excited optimism swell his heart. Things were finally going his way.

"Where is she?"

"That's the problem, sir, and maybe that's why we lost her for a while. She's on a Naval Air Base in California."

"California? When the hell did that happen? How? You lost her in Washington!"

"Yes, sir. She might have boarded a military flight or something. There are no surveillance cameras on military flights, so I couldn't trace her. Even so, I got lucky. I only caught her now because of that ATM in the Navy base cafeteria. Otherwise—"

"Where's the ground team?"

"Washington."

"Ah, fuck . . . it will take them hours to get there! Keep an eye on her, and don't lose her again, you hear me?"

"I—I will try, sir. There aren't any cameras on that base, and satellite didn't pick her up either. For all I know, she could still be on that base, or she could have long gone on another military flight. She hasn't used her credit cards in a while, sir."

"Well, keep trying, goddamn it! Send two people to her last location in California. And, Davydova?"

"Yes, sir?"

"You better not let me down, you hear me?"

The moment she ended the call, the helicopter rotor started to spin. Eddie, already strapped in, had put his headset on and was talking into it, probably on a patched cellular call. He shot her a glance pleading urgency, then covered the mic and yelled.

"Get in here, pronto!"

Still unsure on her feet, she climbed into the helicopter and he lifted it off the ground before she had a chance to lock the door and buckle her harness.

He gained altitude quickly, to about 1,000 feet, then accelerated, almost brutally, pushing the Black Hawk to give all it had. Then he turned on his radiation detection equipment, and all screens came to life.

She put on her headset and caught the end of a conversation between Eddie and NEST, where he had advised them of the fourteen nuclear devices in play. NEST was scrambling, deploying all their contingents to search for radiation leaks. They discussed grid-pattern searches, parameters, numbers, and measurement units she didn't understand.

Alex connected her phone to the dashboard and waited for Eddie to end his call.

"Jeez, woman, you're full of surprises!" he snapped at her, as soon as he got off the phone with NEST. "There's never a moment of boredom with you!"

She shot him a sheepish look, then dialed Marino and flipped the communications channel open.

"Hoffmann," Marino answered in a frustrated tone. "Just when my day was starting to look up."

"Good to hear you too," Alex replied sarcastically. "Got news. I know what the test was for."

"What test?"

"Argh," she groaned, frustrated as hell. Marino had dismissed the information she'd previously given her, even forgotten everything about it. "Didn't I call you and tell you that Mount Rainier was a test? Remember that?"

"Yeah, I remember."

"Yeah, *that* test. He's planning to blow up a Yellowstone volcano. That's what the test was for, to see if he could pull it off. To see if he could cause a volcanic eruption using thermonuclear weapons."

Marino paused. Alex could hear her breathing heavily into the phone.

"I swear to God, Hoffmann, if this is one of your—"

"One of my what, huh? *You* said I have statistics on my side," Alex snapped, aggravated. "There's no time for this bullshit. We need to act. Now!"

"Wait a minute," Marino pushed back. "I can't just go into Seiden's office and tell him you believe that a mysterious man plans to blow up Yellowstone. Just can't. What do the volcanologists say?"

"They agree it's possible. They confirmed the theory with the seismological profile of the Rainier eruption."

"How about NEST?"

"I have NEST on this call. Henri, meet Eddie Zoller, NEST. Eddie, meet Henri Marino, CIA."

Eddie didn't have time to say hello before Marino spoke again.

"Hoffmann," Marino barked. "Did no one ever tell you that you're supposed to announce all parties on a call before they start talking? I thought you had *some* shred of business manners."

"Special circumstances, Marino, get over it," she said, feeling better just for putting Marino in her place for once.

"Okay, whatever . . ." Marino conceded, sounding resigned. "I'll send—"

"No! Don't send anyone in daylight! He'll have eyes via satellite. He might even have people on the ground already."

"What people? Who?"

"He sent fourteen Russians with small-sized nukes to detonate the Yellowstone caldera. They're already here. Passed through our border security like it was nothing, nukes and all."

Marino fell silent.

"Do you hear the monstrosity of what you've just said?" Marino asked in a menacing voice riddled with sarcasm. "Where the hell do you come up with this shit? How can you be sure? If this is a wild goose chase, you will never live to see the end of it, I promise you."

"Oh, I'm very sure this time, very sure."

"How? Spill it!"

Alex bit her lip, cringing in anticipation of what would follow, but she had no choice.

"I—I have a source," she finally said.

"You lying bitch! Can't believe that! You swore to me you didn't have a Russian source!" Marino was fuming.

"No, I didn't, I'm not lying!"

"The hell you're not!"

"Source just happened, minutes ago, I swear. Eddie was here when the call came in, he can tell you," Alex said, angry with herself and Marino for having to invoke a third party to establish her credibility.

"That is true," Eddie's voice sounded through her headset.

Marino paused again.

"Spill it. Everything," Marino asked after a second of silence.

"Source is close to the man. By the way, I finally have a name, can you believe it?"

"Give," Marino prompted.

"Vitaliy Myatlev."

"Whew," Marino whistled. "He's third in power in Russia. Oligarch, billionaire, global footprint, immense power. He's a lifelong friend of President Abramovich. I'll have my analysts look into him."

"That sounds good. It fits."

"No, it doesn't! What motivation could someone so rich and powerful have to get involved in terrorism? This identity doesn't fit the typical terrorist profile."

"He's not at all typical, but he fits. The profile fits the other cases. Remember? Unlimited resources, great strategic planning. It fits," Alex insisted.

"I'm still not 100 percent convinced. Not until we understand his motivations."

"My source is close to him, so I'm confident he was telling me the truth."

"Did you take notes during the call?" Marino asked. "Please tell me you did."

"No, I don't do that," Alex replied and heard Marino's frustrated groan before she could continue. "I *record* all my important calls."

"In my inbox, now!"

"Yes, yes, it's on its way already! Look who's talking about manners, Marino!"

"You need to debrief with Homeland Security. Where the hell are you?"

"Just left Coronado, heading back to Olympia," Eddie intervened. "We're about five hours out. We'll need to stop on the way to refuel."

"We need to talk response strategy," Marino said. "Have you considered your so-called source might be a trap? A setup?"

"Yes, but it didn't sound like one. You'll see for yourself when you listen to the call."

Marino sighed.

"All right, let's say that it's for real. How much time do we have?"

"Not sure. He said that as soon as all the players are in place, he'll detonate, but he wasn't sure. If they passed through border control so swiftly, they could make it there in no time. They could be already there by now, for all we know."

"All right, we need to talk response," Marino repeated, all business, not a shred of frustration left in her voice. "Here's what we're going to do. I'll brief Seiden. You two plan on stopping in San Francisco, I'll let you know where. I'll have Homeland meet you there. It will take us some time to scramble, so you might as well close some distance until then."

She looked at Eddie for a second. He nodded.

"Sounds good," she confirmed.

"What else do you need?" Marino asked.

Alex thought for a second.

"Cloud cover."

"What?"

"There's an awesome weather forecast for the next few days in Yellowstone. Great for camping, they said. The problem is that if we can see the clear blue sky, Myatlev can see every move we make via satellite. He can even see our flashlights at night."

"So what the hell do you want me to do?" Marino asked in a high-pitched voice.

"Listen, if we don't get clouds, we're screwed. I know it's going to be hard, but don't make a single move on the ground until we cover that damn sky."

"And how exactly are you planning to cover it?" Marino asked in disbelief.

"Not sure yet, but I'll think of something."

Eddie gazed at her with a half-smile.

"You're unbelievable, did you know that?" he muttered after the call had disconnected.

Alex turned to Eddie and studied him for a little while. He was tense, hunched forward as he kept a white-knuckled fist wrapped around the helo's cyclic pitch control. He had an expression of determination carved in his rigid, taut facial muscles. His eyes, fixated ahead, checked the monitors every few seconds.

"What?" he asked, aware she was staring.

"C'mon, Zoller, give me clouds," she replied. "Someone must have figured out by now how to make the damn things, right?"

He chuckled and shook his head.

"I've heard of something; I think I read an article or saw it on the news. It's called cloud seeding, but it's controversial as far as I know."

"It's a start," she said, "I'll take it." Then she speed-dialed Lou on conference mode.

"Hey, boss," he said in a chipper voice. "Rumor has it around here you don't need us anymore."

"Hey, Lou. Rumors are typically wrong; you know better than that. Case in point, I have an assignment for you. Find out everything there is to know about cloud seeding. I need the ability to generate cloud cover over a large surface."

"Clouds? That's a new one. Okay, I'll look into it. How large of a surface needs to have miserable weather?"

"Think Rhode Island. I need 1,500 square miles covered with thick, gray clouds, completely impenetrable to satellite imaging."

"Ah . . . I understand. Located where?"

"Yellowstone."

There was a moment of silence.

"How soon do you need the info?" Lou's voice was suddenly somber and tense.

"You have one hour. I need contact names, locations, numbers, efficiency of cloud seeding in terms of duration, reliability, and effect—the whole shebang."

"You got it."

She disconnected the call and rubbed her nape. She felt stiff and her back hurt, shooting pain up her neck and into her skull, threatening her with a migraine. Her stomach growled, and jets of burning gastric acid resounded up her esophagus.

"Who was that?" Eddie asked.

"Lou. He works with me," she replied. A brief smile of parental pride fluttered on her lips. "He's awesome. They all are."

"Sure sounded like it. He didn't need a lot of explanation to understand the situation," Eddie said. "*They*, as in your corporate investigations team?"

"Yeah."

"It's one hell of a job you got going there," he chuckled. His smile died when he checked the time. "It's getting late. Who knows how many of those Russians are already there, in position around Yellowstone."

"We'll get them, you'll see. We got you and all yours looking for them. That makes me feel confident we're in good hands. You said your equipment can pick up the tiniest traces of radioactive material, even for individual medical use, correct?"

"That's correct, or at least we thought so. However, if what that Russian said is true, we missed quite a few nukes, and I can't figure out why. Everything we thought we controlled is gone; procedures, alert levels, frequency and sensitivity of radiation sensors, everything. If we find a single active nuke, or if that mountain blows up, we'll know we have made a horrifying mistake somewhere. We have to rethink everything we thought we knew about radiation detection and safeguards."

"Hang in there, Eddie. I'm confident you'll figure it out."

"That makes one of us," he replied bitterly. "How the hell did it happen? How did they manage to blow Rainier up with a nuke, without us knowing anything? How the hell did fourteen more nukes make it inside this country?"

She thought for a few minutes. That was a good question. Maybe the answer was simpler than she and Eddie believed. Maybe it was right in front of them, staring them in the face.

"It was him, Eddie. It was Myatlev, that's how."

He gazed at her as if she'd gone mad.

"I don't get it," he said.

"It's the way he operates, with redundancies on top of redundancies. We had a case where we discovered he was running networks of intelligence assets on a rotational basis. Not one or two, but he had figured out how to turn anyone into a spy. Hundreds, maybe even thousands."

"So?"

"The way he thinks is simple in essence. He takes double or triple the normal precautions. If he wanted to bring nukes into this country, at first he must have had agents studying all the fail-safes you had in place. Maybe one or two of your latest bogus alerts were his doing, to test response times, procedures, everything."

"You mean he's been working on this for a long time?"

"Yes. If anything, my dear old V is patient, like a spider weaving an intricate, yet deadly web. He doesn't leave a single corner uncovered, and the fly has no escape when he's done weaving. I guess we'll never know for sure, but—"

"The hell we won't! The last hoax nuclear threat we had was a call claiming that a nuke was being shipped into the country via a cargo container vessel, making port in Long Beach. We were frantic. That place is huge! We couldn't find anything, and for days we almost paralyzed the port by forcing X-rays and air sampling on all cargo containers. We didn't find anything; we had to give up eventually."

"That's exactly how they got in!" Alex exclaimed. "First, they tested procedures, response times, and the most stringent security measures a port could have. Then they prepared for it really well, and went right through, undetected."

"I guess you can shield a nuke well enough to make it past our sensors, if you put your mind to it. Especially if you know the screening procedures beforehand and you're preparing for it. No matter how thick your armor is, there's always someone inventing a bigger, faster, armor-penetrating bullet." He sighed, venting his frustration. "Sometimes I hate my job."

"Don't. Hate him if you'd like, although that's my job," she smiled sadly. "Soon he'll be history, I promise you that. I have a name now. There's nowhere on earth he can hide."

He turned and stared at her, his entire face expressing the utmost surprise.

"You? You mean, the CIA will send someone? I can't imagine you—"

She nodded in an exaggerated, almost humorous fashion, keeping her eyes fixated into his.

"He's mine, this one. I've earned it. CIA can try if it wants, but I'll get to him first."

"Corporate investigator, vigilante justice, and now assassin? Who the hell have I been flying around with since yesterday?"

"Don't forget head barfer," she quipped, still embarrassed by her earlier demonstration of poor stomach control. "It's nothing like that, you know. I'm no assassin. I'm just a past-due cleanup crew of one. Maybe a crew of two or three, if my team wants to help."

"I'm starting to see why you believe so strongly this man needs to be taken out. I've known of him for a day and I want him gone too."

She checked the time and frowned.

"How much longer to San Francisco?"

"Maybe an hour, not more. Any news on where to land?"

"Not yet."

"I'll come with you," Eddie offered, "to the DHS briefing."

She shot him a thankful glance.

"Thanks, I appreciate it. How about the helo? Doesn't it need to fly searching for radiation traces?"

"It does now, and it will. My gut tells me from San Fran we'll be heading straight to Yellowstone."

"Probably," she agreed, then let her mind wander.

What could they do? In harsh reality, over such an immense expanse, what could they do? If they managed to generate a cloud cover, Myatlev wouldn't see them from the satellite, but they'd also lose access to their own satellite imaging searches. Tradeoffs . . . they sucked.

If the cloud cover was thick enough, they could fly choppers low, in a grid pattern, searching and stopping any human being they encountered. Probably that was the only solution they had, if NEST couldn't pick up radiation traces from the air and find the nukes, like sniffing dogs set on a scent.

Would they have enough time to find all fourteen Russians? Was it possible that some of them went in, left their packages buried in the bushes, then left already? In that case, they were seriously screwed.

What did the honorable man say, exactly? That Myatlev wanted to detonate the weapons himself? That meant satellite receivers on each detonator, and probably network capabilities. The Russian mules wouldn't necessarily need to be there all at the same time. It could be an in-and-out job for them. Get into Yellowstone, position the cargo, then get out, possibly even out of the country. *Yep, seriously screwed,* she thought. *We won't find them in time, we just won't. There's no way.*

She felt another wave of fear grip her stomach again and twist it hard, making it heave. She put her hand over her mouth, breathing deeply, trying to settle her betraying gut. *Hold it together, for Chrissake,* she encouraged herself. *Get the job done, then you can puke all you want. I promise.*

Her phone rang, and she picked it up immediately.

"Lou."

"Yes, it's me. So . . . clouds. You were right; we could seed them, at least in theory. So far, several companies have been successful seeding already existing clouds, making them rain-rich, to ease the southern California drought, for example. They used cloud seeding to make clouds dump their rain potential sooner, like they did in Beijing a few years ago, to ensure the Olympic games had good weather. So far, everyone's been really reluctant to make commitments to seeding clouds on a perfectly blue sky, but they're willing to try."

"Excellent," she said excitedly, forgetting her stomach. "How long will it take?"

"They can seed from ground-based machines or from planes, and they will start seeding in multiple places, to ensure faster coverage. But it will take hours. A day, even."

"We don't have a day, Lou. They need to make it work faster. How does this seeding work?"

"The pilots spray dry ice or silver iodide from planes. Or it can be blown into the air from ground machines. I could explain how the chemistry works. It has to do with the condensation of water . . . Never mind. If he's watching, how can you start flying planes left and right and not get his attention?"

"Right . . . he could detonate if he feels he's cornered, even if not all devices are in place. What if we contract with all Cessnas out there and spray paint on them something like "Sightseeing Tours"? He'd ignore those if he sees them. We could also get up high, in a 747 or something, and dissipate seeding at a higher rate. Check if it's possible, will you?"

"Sure. I guess that could work."

"How about ground equipment? Can people have those working from cars?"

"I don't see why not," Lou replied. "What do you want me to do next?"

"Send all this info to Marino at the CIA, and tell her to start seeding the clouds discreetly, but fast. She needs to throw her weight around to get this to happen as fast as we need it to. Thanks, Lou! You're a lifesaver."

"And rainmaker too!"

He hung up, bringing silence to her headset. They had a chance, a small one, but they were running out of time at an incredible rate. There was no way of knowing how much time they had left, and that single fact drove her insane with fear and anguish. That fear was mixed with anger, a devastating, all-consuming rage against her enemy who now had a name and a face.

She'd looked him up on the Internet and had stared for minutes into that face. A chubby man in his fifties, banal, there was nothing worth noticing about him. Wrinkled and swollen, his face showed signs of alcohol abuse and unhealthy living. Most of all, he was Mr. Nobody. She could have passed him fifty thousand times on the street and not noticed him at all. This was the man who had been trying to rule the world and cause so much harm? Why? What was hidden behind those pale brown, bloodshot eyes that could explain the man's extreme lust for blood and power? Was there a physical indication, any visual hint to the monster lying curled inside? Apparently, none she could identify from a photo, but it had to be there. All she could see was the face of the man who, with the push of a button, could erase everything. An entire country, hundreds of millions of innocent people, their entire future, for generations to come.

She couldn't bear to think about that scenario. That's why it couldn't happen. She couldn't let him win. No matter what, she could not let him win. She needed to think.

"Eddie," she eventually said, feeling her jaws tense and painful, "I need to know how these radioactivity sensors work. Can you deploy more?"

"Sure we can. They're already doing that. What are you thinking?"

"Something you said, about armor, or shielding was it? And bullets. What if we increased the sensitivity of your devices? Maybe he insulated the nukes more, but not completely, not 100 percent. Maybe they're insulated just enough to make it undetected at current levels of detection. Can you increase sensitivity? Can it be done fast?"

"To some extent yes, by altering the threshold we set in configuring the sensors. I thought of that. Remember the case of the radiology patients we used to harass a few years back? To avoid such incidents, we set a higher threshold for what we consider worrisome radiation, and we got smarter about the types of isotopes we're tracking. We can lower those thresholds for a short while, until we contain this mess. It could work."

She smiled through clenched jaws. I'm coming to get you, she thought. Almost there, you bastard, almost there.

A chime alerted her that she had a message. It was from Marino. It read, "Meet DHS on San Carlos airport. Will make clouds as instructed. You ARE crazy."

A surge of adrenaline invigorated her body. They had a fighting chance, and she was going to make the most out of it.

Number Ten checked his GPS, then looked at the sky. Shades of yellow, orange, and red tinted the translucent wisps of clouds scattered on the blue. The sun was about to set, and he still needed to drive for about another thirty miles.

He clenched his fist angrily. It wasn't an easy choice, but Myatlev had been clear. The safety of the mission came first. If he pressed on, by the time he'd reach the point where he had to leave his car it would be almost completely dark. From that point, he estimated he had to hike for a couple of hours before reaching his target coordinates. In complete darkness, hiking with his heavy backpack would be difficult and unnecessarily risky. If he used his flashlight, he could be seen from afar. Park rangers patrolled the area back and forth; he didn't want any attention from them.

It was hard for Ten to accept the delay imposed by reason and mission protocol. More than anything else, he wanted to get there first, to distinguish himself among the fourteen agents trusted with this charge and to impress Myatlev. He wanted a career under Myatlev's command. Being selected for this particular mission was the break that Ten had been waiting for and preparing for his entire life. He really wanted to get there first, but had no choice but to stop for the night.

He slowed as he entered a small settlement and looked around for lodging options. It was the sensible thing to do, although he also wanted to be as far away from other people as possible. He pulled up in front of a small inn, named aptly Timberlodge.

He got out of the car, stretching his stiff back and shaking his legs to restore blood flow. His shirt, damp with sweat, made him shiver in the cool evening breeze. He breathed in the fresh mountain air and took in the scenery without any emotion. Quiet. Not a lot of traffic; cars rarely stopped there. Perfect.

He went through the door, marked "Reception" with hand-painted white letters on a piece of lumber hanging from the roof ledge. Above the door, perched on the slated roof, a red sign indicated vacancies were available. Inside, no one waited at the desk, but another handwritten sign encouraged him to ring for service.

"Be right with you," a raspy, heavy-smoking man's voice replied from the back room, followed by a loud groan. "What can I do for ya?"

The man wore a checkered shirt in red and black and cargo pants that had seen better days, days from before his belly had added its most recent inches in girth. Long, yellowish salt-and-pepper hair, and an almost entirely white beard, spotted with brown stains around the mouth, left little facial skin visible. Whatever skin showed was wrinkled and lined like crumpled, stained brown paper.

Ten made a note of the shotgun leaning against the wall. Probably that mountain man hunted for a living, to put food on the table in days when tourism income disappointed.

"I need a room for the night," he said.

"Just you?"

"Yes."

"That'll be $49.99. It's got a TV, hot shower, the works. I need your license too."

Ten extracted his driver's license and credit card and put them on the counter.

"Nah, we don't take this fancy plastic here; just cash, check, or Visa," the man said, then turned his head slightly and spat loudly, sending a flying projectile of chewed tobacco into the general area of a trash can.

The door hinges squealed behind Number Ten as he was busy extracting cash from his wallet.

"Oh, hey, Billy," Mountain Man said, then cleared his throat.

"Jack," he heard a man's voice respond to the greeting.

Ten turned to see who walked in and froze. A park ranger, armed, stood in the doorway. He touched his hat with two fingers in a sketched salute.

"That Altima out there yours?" the ranger asked.

Ten didn't reply. He didn't understand the question, and he hoped the officer asked Mountain Man, not him.

The ranger took a step closer to him. The door closed with a long, rusty creak.

"Yeah, you, sir, that thing yours?"

"The blue car?" Ten asked. "Yeah, it's mine. It's a rental. I don't know—"

"Going camping or something?" the ranger pressed on.

Ten frowned, unsure. "Who, me?"

The ranger nodded, pursing his lips. "See anyone else here?"

"Yes," Ten replied. Sweat broke on his forehead, but he refrained from wiping it. "Going camping."

"Alone?"

"Yes." He held his breath.

The ranger frowned, then turned his head and looked outside at Ten's car.

"I need the peace and quiet," Ten offered, hoping he'd just go away.

The ranger measured him from head to toe, his frown persisting.

"Uh-huh," he eventually muttered, then touched his hat with two fingers, like before. "Have yourself a nice stay."

The ranger turned and left. Seconds later, Ten heard his car leave, throwing tiny pebbles against the inn's wooden wall. Through the dirty window, he watched him disappear after turning the corner.

"Mr. Harris?" Jack called. Ten didn't react. The man whistled, then called louder. "Mr. Harris!"

"Yes?" Ten replied serenely.

"Here's your receipt and driver's license. You're in room four. Have a good night!"

Ten reached out and collected his key, then turned to leave. As he did, he locked eyes with the man behind the reception desk. The man's eyes were frozen cold, scrutinizing. Dangerous.

Alex was happy to feel terra firma under her feet again, although her knees still felt weak and shaky. She waited for Eddie to secure the helo and then walked with him toward the terminal, visually searching for video cameras. It was almost completely dark, but she still needed to be careful.

The terminal door opened and a man, dressed in a charcoal suit and light blue shirt held the door for them. She sped up her pace and entered the terminal panting, her hands shaking badly, worse than her knees.

"Miss . . . Hoffmann?" he asked dryly.

"Yes," she replied with a timid smile.

The man gave them both a frigid look and then showed them the way.

"We're in the conference room, over there. Follow me, please."

In passing through the lobby and then a corridor, she noticed several surveillance cameras. She swallowed a curse and tried to cover her face with her hand. The wig and the sunglasses were back in the helo, and she wasn't going to go back for them.

The man held open another door. The conference room was small and poorly lit. Two men and a woman sat at the table. Her heart swelled when she recognized one of the agents.

"Weber! What the hell are you doing here? I thought I was meeting Homeland."

Jeremy Weber approached her and they exchanged a quick hug.

"Good to see you," she continued.

"I saw your name on an interagency memo and I couldn't resist," Weber said, grinning widely. "I was in the area, so I *volunteered* for this joint task force, can you believe it? As you might remember, I'm self-destructive," he chuckled.

"Yeah, I know," she laughed. "Eddie, this is Jeremy Weber, FBI. He and I worked together on a case, eons ago."

She turned toward the other agents. Her smile froze under their glares. She bowed her head in a silent greeting.

"I'm Special Agent Olvera with Homeland Security," the man who'd shown them the way introduced himself. He spoke with a hint of a Spanish accent.

Alex shook his hand.

"Alex Hoffmann, and this is Eddie Zoller with NEST."

"Special Agent Sauli, Homeland," said the woman. Her handshake was cold to the touch and unenergetic, limp. She looked more like an accountant than a Homeland agent.

"Special Agent Barnett, Homeland, leader of this joint task force," the third DHS agent said in a somber tone of voice. He smiled politely as they shook hands, but the smile didn't touch his eyes. His high forehead showed two parallel lines of tension that refused to disappear. "Let's get started."

Everyone took their seats and fidgeted a little, waiting for Barnett to start the meeting.

"Let's start with the recording of the call, then I'll answer questions and we can discuss options," Alex spoke first, aware she was stepping on several toes. She didn't have time to waste either. Screw the politics.

She started the playback of the call, then whispered in Eddie's ear asking to borrow his phone. She typed quickly for a couple of minutes and showed the screen to Eddie. He nodded his approval.

The call recording ended. Alex retrieved her phone from the table and looked at her audience. Olvera frowned, pursed his lips, and scribbled something on a small notepad. Sauli had an incredulous look on her face. Barnett seemed dark, bothered, and concerned. Weber's was the only look to convey any confidence, although it also conveyed worry in the highest degree.

"You've been tracking this Russian for how long?" Barnett finally asked.

"A couple of years, give or take," she replied firmly.

"Who are you?"

"Just a . . . civilian contractor."

"Can you provide us with some reference for your work, your credibility?" Barnett continued. "Why should we believe any of this?"

Alex felt the blood rush to her head. Sometimes people simply refused to think, preferring instead to waste valuable time. She took a deep breath, calming herself. Biting their heads off would probably not work very well. She needed them cohesive, committed, and filled with a sense of urgency, not doubting every word she spoke.

"You're here because CIA called you, right? With Director Seiden's approval, I believe?" Alex asked with a pacifying smile. "That's reference number one."

"Huh . . ." Barnett muttered, unconvinced. "Our director hasn't endorsed it though."

"Agent Weber, here, is reference two," she added, and Jeremy nodded. "We've worked—"

"Yeah, I heard you before, you worked together on a case," Barnett cut her off impatiently. "What kind of case was that? What kind of work do you normally do for the CIA or the FBI?"

"I—I'm afraid I can't disclose any particulars."

"We all have top secret clearance here," Olvera said in a patronizing tone, shooting her a dismissive look.

"Not for this stuff you don't," she pushed back, raising her left eyebrow.

"Miss Hoffmann," Barnett said somberly, "you're asking us, you and your CIA pal, to throw millions of dollars on the weirdest cockamamie idea I have ever heard in my career. You're not asking us to secure a warehouse. You're talking about thousands of square miles. Do you know what that means? You'll have to do better than that, or we all go home right now."

She bit her lip angrily. They gave her no choice.

"All right, suit yourself," she replied coolly. "Call the White House. Ask to speak with President Krassner. He probably won't be sitting by the phone expecting your call, so the operators will try to send you away. Mention my name and voice your concerns. It's almost midnight on the East Coast, but I think you'll still be able to . . . check my references."

Barnett glared at her fiercely. She held his glare patiently, yet firmly.

He pushed away from the table. "Have it your way," he said, then walked toward the door. "Fucking unbelievable nerve," he muttered under his breath as he left the room.

Silence fell heavy after the door closed behind Barnett.

"Hey, Jer, can you see if pizza's here?" she asked.

A minute later, Alex was working though her second slice, and Eddie kept up. She felt the trembling in her legs subside.

The Homeland agents refused the invitation to partake and stared at her in disbelief.

"We haven't eaten anything since yesterday morning, guys, that's all," she explained, after washing down a mouthful with some Perrier water. "There hasn't been any time."

Barnett opened the door quietly and came in, walking slowly and staring at the carpet. He looked scolded, humiliated. He took his seat, then asked, "All right, Miss Hoffmann, what would you like us to do?"

Agent Sauli's mouth gaped open, and she covered it quickly with her hand.

"Wait . . . So this is true? All this is real? Someone's trying to blow up nukes at Yellowstone?" she asked in a weak voice. She turned pale, grabbed the Perrier bottle in front of her, and gulped down some water.

Barnett deferred to Alex with a hand gesture.

"Yes," Alex replied, "every bit of it. We're the only ones who can stop it, so let's get to work. I understand this will be very hard to do, but there can't be any action before we have cloud cover over Yellowstone."

She explained everything, and they took plenty of notes.

"Until cloud cover sets in, restrict access to the park in two layers. No one goes in, and anyone looking to go in should be screened, tested for explosive residue and radiation. Ditto for anyone coming out. All good so far?"

"Yes, go on."

"NEST will set up sensors. Eddie's team is already setting them. His people are dressed in park ranger uniforms, and, from satellite, it will appear they're checking something near a bush or a tree, then moving on. These sensors are rather small."

"Will it work?" Olvera's Spanish accent was more discernible.

"We hope so," Eddie replied. "We have increased the sensitivity of our sensors to the max, and we'll be screening for all known isotopes."

"What are you planning to do if we find one, if those clouds are not there yet?" Barnett asked. "How should we handle it?"

"Mark the location on your maps, but don't remove the device. Don't go near it. We have to be able to examine the device in place, where it was set," Eddie explained. "Until we see one, there's no way of telling how they're rigged. There's a risk you could trigger an explosion if you tamper with it. We have to wait for the damn clouds."

"How long? I've never heard of making clouds," Sauli asked. "How long until they are thick enough?"

"At least twelve hours," Alex replied. "Maybe twenty-four, we can't be sure. The surface is huge, and this type of cloud seeding has never been attempted before."

"What?" Barnett snapped, springing to his feet. "You don't even know if it's going to work, and you just want us to sit and wait? This is insane!"

"It *will* work," Alex replied calmly. "Trust me on this one. Please."

Barnett sat back on his chair, rubbing his forehead forcefully and shaking his head.

"All right," Alex continued. "As soon as the clouds set, start sweeping the park. Eddie will be your NEST liaison, and he'll dispatch as many helicopters as possible, with radiation detection equipment onboard. Any other available helicopters should fly low and grid-search the area. Agent Barnett, you'll determine who will be in charge of the search grid."

"Got it," Barnett confirmed.

"When you search the grid, please be aware that the cloud-seeding machines are set up in cars and SUVs scattered throughout the park. Each cloud-seeding car has an agent watching it, dressed like a tourist. You'll find them everywhere."

"How much time do we have?" Olvera asked. "Before they blow up?"

Alex exchanged a quick glance with Eddie.

"We don't know, unfortunately."

"What? Then how can you ask us to wait for the weather to change? They could go up any minute!" Sauli's high-pitched voice was tinted with panic.

"Make no mistake," Alex said gravely, "if this man, Myatlev, sees you tamper with any of his devices, he will detonate. If he catches you arresting any of his people, he will push the button, no matter *where* the bombs are. We have strong reasons to believe the bombs are fitted with satellite receivers. You all heard the call."

Alex saw the expressions on their faces, and dropped the pressure down a notch. "I know it will be difficult, guys, but you have to be patient, and hope cloud seeding will work fast enough. We believe there's still time. Our source said they entered this country earlier today, so there must be some time provisioned for them to make it to their designated locations at the park. There's still time, there has to be," she repeated encouragingly, hoping she was right.

"Got it," Barnett said. "Wait for cloud cover, grid search, air and ground. Until then, we stop traffic both ways, and instruct the rangers."

"Perfect," Alex confirmed. "Find these bastards; make them pay. We'll work together through every tactical aspect of this deployment. One more thing; you might draw attention doing so many searches, and you might get one of the Russians edgy enough to call home. Post an amber alert. If anyone asks, you're looking for a missing kid. That should help set their minds at ease."

"Where will you be?"

"This is where real team work comes into play. You guys keep Yellowstone intact, while I'm going hunting. I've got me a Russian terrorist to take down, and hopefully I will find him before he pushes that damn button."

Barnett's jaw fell.

"In what capacity?" he asked. "Is this sanctioned?"

Alex looked at him and smiled dryly. He didn't ask again.

"By yourself?" Jeremy prompted.

"Thanks for the offer, cowboy," she said, "but you're needed here. Text me for anything you need."

"You shouldn't go alone," Jeremy insisted.

"I probably won't," she replied. "Surely I can sign up some friends to help." She winked at Jeremy. "Now can anyone get me on the next flight to Santa Ana?"

Myatlev jumped to his feet at the first ring of his phone. Maybe it was news. Maybe the bitch was finally gone. That would be the perfect start to a perfect day. It was a day that held immense promise, the promise of a new future, a new world, and all his to own and rule.

He remembered hearing someone say, "The power to destroy a thing is the absolute control over it." Or did he read that somewhere? Oh, yes, it was *Dune*, the most amazing work of strategy and leadership ever written. How true it rang today, when he was close to proving his absolute control over the entire world.

He grabbed the phone and smiled in anticipation, recognizing Davydova's number.

"Da?"

"We found her again. In San Carlos this time, at the airport." Davydova said.

"Where's that?"

"Some 500 miles north from where she was when I lost her last time."

Myatlev ran his hand through his thinning hair, pulling it back angrily.

"How the hell is she moving so fast? Where are our people?"

"They're on a flight to San Diego. They should arrive in a few hours."

"Goddamn it!" he bellowed.

"One more thing, boss," Davydova spoke timidly. "She knows we're on to her."

"What? How?"

"I'll text you a picture. She covers her face when she passes by a surveillance camera. She knows we're hacking into their systems. Or she assumes we are."

"Damn it, she's good! Get this finished already, taken care of, you hear me?"

Alex sensed someone moving near her and struggled to wake up. Her brain, foggy with heavy sleep, refused to function. Then she heard chatter, too close to her to be any good, and she startled, half awake and confused.

"Whoa, easy, it's just me," she heard a familiar voice speak gently. "It's me, don't worry."

Steve held her hand and looked at her with kind, protective eyes. It felt good to have him near. She breathed deeply and made an effort to sit up, feeling sore, and stiff. Almost fully awake, she took in her surroundings.

The small conference room at Santa Ana airport had little to offer in terms of comfort, but it had offered some privacy. She'd curled up on the table and fell asleep instantly, exhausted after almost forty-eight hours of being on the road. Her joints were stiff and painful after resting on the hard surface, but the power nap she'd managed to squeeze in had worked wonders.

She hopped to her feet and wiped her eyes.

"Good morning, guys," she said with a quick smile that disappeared instantly, replaced by a deep frown. "Thanks for meeting me here on such short notice."

"Anytime," Blake replied.

"Sure," Lou said.

"I'm not sure how much you know already—" Alex started to say, but Lou chimed in.

"I filled them in on the way over."

"Great," she said. "I've also found out who V is. I have his identity."

"What?" Steve reacted. "Are you sure?"

"Yes, I am. I need you to help me profile him. I want to understand everything: motivations, weaknesses, everything."

Lou set up his laptop on the table, getting ready to dig for information.

"What's the name of this walking carcass?" Lou asked.

"Vitaliy Myatlev," Alex replied. "He's a powerful magnate in Russia."

"Yes, I've heard of him," Blake replied. "He's been the kingpin of Russian armament, oil, and energy for years now."

"Yes, and that's where I struggle," Alex said. "Why would someone like that become a terrorist? What more is there to gain that he couldn't get speculating oil prices? Why is this man's finger on the button that could destroy America?"

Lou typed quickly, his tapping on the laptop's keyboard were the only sound for a few seconds.

"All right, here goes," Lou said. "Born in 1957, KGB officer in his young days, then disappeared off the radar for a couple of years after KGB imploded. He reappeared as an investor and businessman when he was thirty-six years old, in 1993, bringing hordes of Western stores into Russia. Then he moved into financial products and banking, then oil and energy. Before he turned forty, he had his first armament manufacturing facility. His main client was the Russian government."

"Interesting," Alex said. "Weapons, huh? Who else did he sell them to?"

"Everyone who had money, really. African conflict regions, dictators, you name it. He continued to amass weapons manufacturing facilities and became one of the biggest weapons dealer in the world. Says here he's number two currently."

"Where can we find him?" Alex asked. "I think it's about time we met in person, don't you think?"

"Alex, no," Steve said in a soft voice.

She turned to him ready to blow up, but then met his concerned eyes. "I have to, Steve. I just have to," she replied. "Trust me on this one."

"Ahem," Lou said, "he's everywhere, all over the place. He has homes in Moscow, Kiev, near the Black Sea, Austria, France, England, and the United States. His business empire has locations in more than thirty countries."

"Damn it," Alex said. "Let's track financials next. Credit cards, spending, anything you can figure out."

"He probably has a personal jet," Blake offered. "You can easily track those through flight plans and refueling orders associated with his tail number. If you can find where the plane is, he probably isn't very far."

Lou nodded appreciatively.

"Good idea. I'll remember this one. Wait for it," he said, typing fast. "Found it! It's in Kiev."

He tapped on his keyboard a little longer and then added, "It's been there since Tuesday, flown in from Moscow."

Alex pursed her lips nervously.

"We still don't understand what makes him tick. Why does someone who has it all risk everything on becoming a terrorist?"

"His personality is not compatible with devotion to a cause," Steve said. "Let's pick up where we left off with his profile, if you insist he's the same man we've been talking about."

Alex nodded, and Steve continued, his voice calm and professional.

"He's most definitely a psychopath, a narcissistic psychopath. This type of individual will align himself with others just as long as his interests dictate it. Alex, you're right when you say it doesn't make sense that someone like him becomes a terrorist. It doesn't make sense, unless one of two things is happening. One, we have the wrong person."

"No, we don't. I'm 100 percent positive," Alex said. "You'll see, when you listen to the call I received."

She'd deliberately decided not to play the call to her team, afraid the references to her being on Myatlev's kill list would paralyze them, and make them become overprotective instead of bold. She needed them to be bold.

"What call?" Steve asked, a wave of suspicion washing over his face.

She hated lying to him; he was, out of them all, the most qualified to catch her. Sometimes she wished he were an engineer or an analyst, rather than a shrink.

"Someone in his inner circle would prefer to not live through a nuclear winter, so he warned us. During this call, he spilled his name."

"And you didn't think of mentioning this earlier? We need to listen to that call," Steve said firmly. "I can profile him more accurately."

"We will, I promise. We'll have time, later. For now, let's just focus on why someone like Myatlev turns to terrorism. What's your second theory?"

"By orchestrating these terrorist acts he stands to gain something of massive importance to him, enough to compensate for the risk," Steve replied. "Or maybe the risk is lower for him than we anticipate."

Alex paced the room slowly, thinking. *How did a man like that think?* She stared into the abyss, but this time the abyss was too dark; she didn't see anything yet.

"Let's continue with the profile," she said, checking the time. "It's getting late."

Steve sighed and looked at her quietly for a long second.

"He's definitely aggressive, greedy, and unscrupulous. Remember, psychopaths don't have a conscience to hold them back. If they want something, they do it, regardless of consequences."

"I think we got that part, Steve, right about where we learned about his plan to blow up Yellowstone," Blake said bitterly. "He has no conscience and doesn't care what happens to hundreds of millions."

"Yes, but what does he *gain* from a nuclear attack on the United States?" Alex asked. "If he's not a slave to ideology, and we can say with certainty he's not, then what's in it for him?"

"His profile doesn't align with any ideology other than his own greed and self-interest," Steve confirmed. "A patriot sacrifices, even if for the wrong ideology. That even applies to other terrorists. They strongly believe in something and they sacrifice for it. Some even sacrifice their lives, like suicide bombers, for example. But this man is a predator. It simply doesn't fit."

"He's a business predator," Blake said, thinking out loud. "Let's just follow this for a minute. His only motivators are money and power. That's very common to most business people," he added, blushing slightly. "Out of all business people motivated by money and power, the psychopaths are the most aggressive, due to their lack of conscience, and the most successful."

"So what do you think he's gaining from the attack, ego points?" Steve asked.

"No. Money and power, beyond your wildest dreams," Blake replied.

"What do you mean?" Alex asked, confused.

"Just think what knowing about such a holocaust in advance could do for him. He can position very solidly for food futures, clean food sources, agricultural land investments, and so on. That's only what he could do *knowing* about such a holocaust. But he also *controls* it, and he's careful and thoughtful. He doesn't just dump some nukes here and there, in our major cities, on the surface, risking the contamination of the entire planet. No. His plan is to have enough radiation and ash to eliminate most of *our* food sources, and make the survivors pay fortunes for the clean food that *he* will own. He wants to control the world. That's his motivator," Blake said with a long sigh.

Alex looked at Blake, shocked, unable to speak. They fell silent, the only sound in the room being Lou's typing. The abyss had opened and looked back into her weary soul. Alex felt her skin cover with goose bumps, and another wave of nausea hit her.

"It fits," she said quietly.

"Yes, it does," Lou added, continuing work on his laptop. "His coffers are seriously depleted. His business empire is leveraged to the bone, because he bought hundreds of millions of acres of agricultural land in Asia, even some portions of Africa. All in the past few months, all under various corporation names."

Alex nodded a few times, absorbed in her thoughts. It was time for action.

"How do we lure this bastard?" she asked, swallowing with difficulty.

"What do you want to do?" Steve asked, frowning.

"Lure him out of hiding. Kiev is probably his stronghold; I don't want to risk going there. I want to lure him and take him out."

"You?" Steve asked in a high-pitched voice. "Why can't the CIA agents handle it? You're serving them everything they need to know on a silver platter, for Chrissake. Why you?"

She sighed.

"Everyone asks me that . . . We're faster. I'm faster. I want this, badly," she said, her eyes pleading with him. "He killed 20,000 people this past week, just to run a damn test. He's planning to kill millions more, and our future will be destroyed along with them. I need to look him in the eye, to get that closure. It's become personal."

"I was hoping you'd say that, boss," Lou replied, gaining himself a glare from Steve. "I'm in."

"So am I," Blake added. "I have a personal debt to settle with this bastard."

"So, how do we lure him? How do we make someone like that change his day's agenda? What do we offer to someone who's about to own the world?"

"We just established that," Blake replied. "Money. He's cash strained. He probably hates the thought of not having plenty of cash flow."

"Money won't be enough," Lou said. "Here's what I found. Out of his many business ventures, he cares the most about his military investments. That's where his heart is."

"Why?" Steve asked.

"He only spoke in person at a handful of company inaugurations. He doesn't do that stuff; his people do it for him. Out of the total of three public speeches, two were for weapons factories, and the third was for a helicopter manufacturer he'd acquired. The man just loves his guns."

"Then let's buy us some guns," Alex said.

She sent a text message to Sam. "I know you're still recovering, but we're going V hunting. Wanna come?"

A minute later, his reply hit her inbox. "Wouldn't miss it for the world. I'm on the next flight out."

...Chapter 40: Setting Up
...Thursday, June 15, 12:42PM Local Time (UTC-7:00 hours)
...Yellowstone National Park
...Northwestern Wyoming

Number Ten hiked steadily, taking deep breaths of fresh mountain air every few steps and watching the screen on his handheld GPS. Vigilant, he scrutinized the area for signs of anyone nearby and saw nothing, not a soul. It was as if the entire world was his, peaceful, serene.

He was more afraid of bears or wolves than people in these parts of the park, though. He'd seen bison from a distance, and that meant their natural predators weren't far behind. Out of reflex, he touched the Beretta tucked in his belt.

A mix of sun and clouds kept the temperature moderate and his hike pleasant, despite the heavy backpack he was hauling. Toward the southeast, the clouds seemed thicker, darker. Probably it would rain in a few hours, but he was almost there. He'd left the beaten path behind a while ago, heading straight through the tall grasses, in the direction indicated on his GPS. He followed a winding river for a while, then found a place where the river was shallow and narrow, and crossed it, getting only his feet wet. It didn't matter; soon the two dots on his screen, the blue one showing his position and the red one indicating his destination, would overlap perfectly, and he'd set up camp.

He checked his GPS again and stopped, releasing the backpack's buckle and easing it onto the ground, breathing with ease. He had arrived. Satisfied, he looked around, searching for the best place to set up. He was in the middle of a picturesque clearing, where tall grasses met coniferous thickets in a harmonious blending of seasonal with evergreen. A rivulet with crystal clear water ran through the pasture, reflecting the darkening colors of the moody sky.

Instructions allowed him to set up camp a few yards off the precise GPS coordinates, but not more than fifty feet. He saw a cluster of firs a few yards north of his location, with some thicker bush around their roots. He chose a place carefully, where his tent could be pitched without showing from a distance, hidden by tree trunks and shrubbery. Then he carried his backpack to that spot and started unpacking.

He took out his tent first and pitched it quickly. It was olive green, modern, with feather-light, carbon fiber structure. The color was an almost perfect match with his surroundings, and that simple fact reasserted in Ten's mind the respect he held for the great strategist who was Myatlev. Once the tent was up, Ten anchored it firmly with several stakes he drove into the ground with the help of a rock. Satisfied, Ten walked a few yards away and inspected his work. The tent was barely visible, perfectly camouflaged in the brush.

He unzipped the entrance and crawled inside, dragging his backpack with him. Once inside the tent, he unzipped the tent floor and removed it completely, exposing the ground underneath it. He tested the earth; it was dense, solidly packed, and hard to scratch. But he had time.

He took out more items from his backpack, placing them carefully around him. First, he removed the lead blanket he'd used to wrap himself in as the container made its way through port. On one side, the heavy plastic blanket had the same olive green color and a small camouflage pattern. Then he removed the corrugated steel plate from the backpack's lining, and set it on the ground. Finally, he removed the two main components of the bomb, both sealed in layers of protective sheathing.

Ten followed the instructions to the letter. He had everything memorized and recited it quietly as he worked. First, he was to remove the sheathing from the plastic explosive charge. He did that carefully, surprised to find that the explosive charge had been vacuum-sealed in heavy-duty plastic foil with built-in air cushions. When he pierced the wrapper at one corner, it leaked air and hissed loudly, startling him. He cussed under his breath, then finished peeling the wrapper off the charge and set it aside.

Finally, he unwrapped the first protective layer of the nuclear device, studying it with curiosity. It was a strange, gel-like material that felt heavy and warm to the touch. He checked the dosimeter hidden in his backpack and stared at it for a good, long minute. The dosimeter showed the same reassuring shade of light gray. He wasn't supposed to touch the second layer of protective sheathing on the nuclear device, and he had no intention to.

Next, he needed to scratch a hole in the ground only deep enough to allow the two bombs to sit in there without being visible from a few feet away. He couldn't dig forcefully; he wasn't supposed to make any noise, or generate any vibrations. The only sounds he could make were those compatible with animals burrowing, or campers setting up tents. Armed with a knife and a tent anchor, he started scratching the surface, pulling out the tall grasses, moving slowly, patiently.

He checked his time and started digging. With a little bit of luck, he could still be the first to finish setting up.

Number Five felt his good fortune draw closer and closer with each minute. He obsessed somewhat, trying to decide between Thailand and the Bahamas as his retirement destination. Would the fallout affect the Bahamas? Probably yes, he concluded, shifting the scale permanently to Thailand's favor. A land of picturesque emerald beaches and low cost of living, Thailand offered the newly made millionaire a world of opportunity. A house worthy of a king, built directly on the lavish, golden sand beaches. Young girls, eager to please, who'd do anything to make him happy, famous for their skill in satisfying a man's wildest fantasies. Yes, he could definitely settle for Thailand; no doubt about that.

He inspected his work carefully. His tent had been pitched on a hard, uneven surface, making it impossible for him to scratch more than an inch of dirt off the ground. However, the terrain was rugged, providing natural cover for the device, so all was good. He inspected the directional charge carefully, and made sure the wiring was properly connected. Both devices had satellite receivers, and, once armed, the receivers would detonate the charges in sequence.

He carefully positioned the devices as briefed. At first, he set down the directional plastic explosive charge; he placed it face down, per the markings on its frame. Then he set the shock absorbing plate on top of the plastic explosive, making sure it was aligned properly. He clamped it down and checked to see if the wiring was still protected, while giving him access to the timer. Then he positioned the nuclear device on top of the corrugated plate, clamping it in place. Finally, he connected the wiring of the two explosive devices together, hooking the custom-made serial ports and screwing them tightly together. The detonating signal of the directional charge would also send a timer code of ten seconds, arming the nuclear device. One receiver, one timer, two detonations. Brilliantly simple.

He was ready to notify home base he was done. He took his encrypted satellite phone, and texted, "Number Five in position and ready." Seconds later, he received his instructions. "Start the timer."

He took one last look at the devices assembled neatly on the ground. He turned on the timer, and the red LED numbers started counting down. There were 32 hours, 21 minutes, and 19 seconds left. Plenty of time to get to safety.

He covered the device ensemble carefully with the lead blanket folded in four, paying attention to leave the satellite receiver antenna extension uncovered. The lead blanket was meant to further reduce radiation leaks into the atmosphere, and its camouflage pattern kept it invisible to the naked eye. Then he zipped the tent floor back into place. With a sigh of relief, he crawled out of the tent and sat on a boulder, absently staring at the clouds scattered on the blue sky.

He'd never tasted Thai food. Would he like it? What if he didn't like it? Where would he go?

Vitaliy Myatlev experienced a forgotten, worrisome feeling that the entire world, nature, and God were working against him. It made him feel angry, as he always felt when he was powerless. Someone addicted to power and thriving on challenge as he was couldn't take defeat easily. Yet defeat came to him that day in the form of shitty weather, covering with a nasty layer of gray clouds what should have been his window into the execution of his plan.

He wanted to see it all. He wanted to watch from the sky how each one of his agents pitched his tent and set up the charges. He wanted to see all those nukes blow up, when he pushed the button. None of that was going to happen anymore, because clouds just kept pouring in, appearing out of thin air. Where the hell were they coming from?

His office, set up in a large room at his Kiev villa, was furnished and equipped for the occasion. On his desk, six monitors showed various satellite feeds from above the Yellowstone caldera. The same six monitors promised to show the most colossal, most devastating volcanic eruption known to humankind, captured live and in high resolution. For now, the six monitors only showed a thick, solid cloud cover, spanning the entire region.

Myatlev had ordered another desk to be brought in, so he could oversee the progress of his agents via GPS tracking. Every explosive package was fitted with its own tracking device, so Myatlev could take one look at a digital map and see where his agents were. A huge LED screen took up most of the auxiliary desk, displaying a digital map with several overlaid types of feeds. Red dots marked the target locations for all devices, where they needed to be placed to achieve the maximum destructive effect on the caldera. Blue dots marked the actual devices and most of them still moved, in transit anywhere from the seaboard to Yellowstone Park. Finally, green dots marked the devices that had been delivered to the target locations, set up, and armed. Only two green dots showed on Myatlev's digital map.

If he could take a look via satellite, he'd see what the holdup was with the rest of the men. But no, weather had to play against him. He slammed his fist down, making the huge monitor shake and flicker.

"Goddamn it! Didn't you check the long-term forecast?" he asked Ivan, who waited at attention.

"Yes, boss, I did. It was supposed to be clear for at least ten days."

"Then what the hell happened?"

"Um . . . it's weather, sir. It's got a mind of its own. No one can control it. I'm sorry, sir . . . There's nothing anyone can do about weather."

Myatlev stared at the monitor, counting the blue dots, checking to see how long it would take the farthest one to reach its destination.

"This one," Myatlev said, pointing at a certain blue dot, "Seems to be stuck there. It hasn't moved. Where is it exactly?"

"It's in the Port of San Francisco. The fog's been heavy there, and I can't zoom in to see where exactly it got stuck. It hasn't moved since the cargo vessel docked yesterday."

"What do you think happened with it?"

"I can't be sure until the fog lifts. He could be stuck inside the container, trapped in a pile of intermodals, or awaiting processing. He could have been unable to break free from the container. He could have been injured during transport. There's no way—"

"Yeah, I got that," Myatlev replied impatiently. "We have enough explosive power without it; we don't need to wait for that one. When the rest are in position, we'll blow this shit up, and Port of San Francisco will blow up too—as a bonus."

He paced slowly, pensively, running his hand through his hair every few minutes. He wanted to see Yellowstone blow up with his own eyes. He wanted it so badly, he was inclined to postpone the light show until the weather cleared. However, he knew he ran a huge risk by doing that. More time for the devices to be in place, more time in which they could be discovered, by accident, or because of traces of radiation leaks. Was it really worth it? This was the masterpiece of his existence; he deserved to see it.

He'd built in some options for himself, when he had the bombs made. Once armed, they were on a centralized timer that he controlled from his own office in Kiev. He could modify the timer any way he pleased, to suit his changing needs. He also had a central command console, fitted in a titanium briefcase. It sent a signal via satellite to initiate detonation on all devices, regardless of their locations, and regardless of the status of the timer. The briefcase sat open right there, on his desk, equipped with an access key, fingerprint scanner, and numeric access code dial pad. Just looking at that briefcase made his heart swell with pride, with the sense of immense power he held. Only presidents had such devices under their control. Only presidents and him.

The agents had been instructed to remain with their respective packages until the timer dropped under six hours, to ensure the nukes remained undisturbed. He knew which agents stayed put as instructed. GPS trackers were hidden in the heels of their boots. These trackers lit up purple on his screen the moment a man put more than twenty yards of distance between himself and the nuclear device in his ward.

Yeah . . . he had options. At some point, Myatlev had been inspired to add poetry to his plan. He thought of detonating the devices at the precise moment the sun set at Yellowstone Park. It was, after all, going to be America's last sunset for many years to come; the moment deserved being suitably celebrated. But who would ever know?

He gave up the poetic approach in favor of the pragmatic one. Everyone's demons are larger and scarier in the dark, so he decided for the midnight hour instead. There was also a little poetry in the choice of the midnight hour, but of a different nature. The new day, marked by the passing of midnight, was not going to be a day anymore; just darkness: perpetual, suffocating, and deadly. Perfect.

The timer had been set for midnight, local time, Friday night. Of course, he could push that back, if he decided he wanted to see the fireworks via satellite and had to wait for the sky to clear. Alternatively, he could push that forward, if he had the tiniest reason for concern or anxiety.

A chime disrupted his almost obsessive thinking. He turned to his laptop, where a new email had dropped in his inbox. Tired of staring into screens, he waved Ivan over.

"Read it for me."

"It's a request for a weapons deal, boss. Says, 'Dear V, we've crossed paths before, in the States, when you helped me, and I helped you. Here I am, seeking your help once more. I have interests demanding immediate protection, in Sierra Leone and Liberia. Your vast weapons portfolio came to mind. I am, as always, willing to pay premium for expedited delivery at destination. Let's meet in person to discuss. I'll bring cash. How's Vienna airport, tomorrow night?' Signed, Otto W. Dreiers," Ivan finished reading.

"Ugh . . ." Myatlev sighed. "Do you remember this guy, Ivan?"

"The name sounds familiar, but I can't be sure. You met a lot of Americans."

"This guy isn't American. His name is German or something, maybe Dutch. Look him up," he said, leaning back into his leather chair.

Cash . . . this Otto whoever the fuck he was, had just spoken the right words for his ears. He'd never before in his life been able to turn his back on a good arms deal; there was something about weapons changing hands that was almost arousing to him. The schedule was tight though; a meeting in Vienna the night he was supposed to watch Yellowstone from the sky, with his hand on the button that would change history? Maybe it wasn't such a great idea. Could he suggest another time? Most likely. Of course, he could postpone the detonation a couple of hours, or leave it to the timer to handle. He had options.

"This guy's big in diamonds, boss," Ivan said, reading from the screen. "He's got several diamond mines in Sierra Leone, Liberia—"

"I could have told you that from his email, Ivan, what the hell . . . anything else interesting?"

"South Africa, and Zimbabwe," Ivan continued, unperturbed. "He has warrants for his arrest in several places, including the States. That's new . . . He's probably moving his business to Africa permanently. I can find citations for him to appear and testify under United Nations Security Council Resolutions 1173, 1295, and some others. That's about trafficking blood diamonds. Divorced, no kids, ex-wife is in rehab on the Côte d'Azur in France."

"I still can't remember him . . . Do you have a picture?"

Ivan turned the monitor toward Myatlev. The screen displayed the picture of a man in his fifties, who looked vaguely familiar. His wavy, combed-back hair was almost entirely raven- black, only touched here and there by a gray strand. He wore a closely trimmed beard and dark shades, hiding his eyes.

"Yeah, I think I know this guy. His timing is bad, though. I'll need to think about this."

At dusk, the inn's dark red roof and the yellow lights that lit its porch reflected in the lake's waters, on a backdrop drawn with shades of deep red and yellow coloring the gathering clouds. From a distance, it looked like one of those fancy mountain retreats one sees in lifestyle magazines; from up close, Jack had an entirely different perspective.

His legacy and livelihood, Timberlodge was also Jack's biggest pain in the rear. He didn't make enough money to hire the help he needed, but couldn't bring himself to close it down either. He just hoped that tourists would someday start flocking in, bringing high-limit credit cards and poor shopping impulse control on their way to Grand Teton National Park. Everyone in the small town shared that hope, some clinging to it more than others, like Jack was. Even if one day he'd give up hope, he wouldn't know what else to do, or where else to go. Timberlodge, Snow Springs, and its dwellers were his home, his family, his entire world.

Jack's days were all the same. He wasn't really busy, but he wasn't free either. He spent his days and nights in the little room in the back, buried in a busted recliner worn out to the thread, with his feet up on a tree trunk, watching TV shows on an old tube that still worked after twenty years of faithful service. He was there every day and every night, seven days a week, waiting for the next tourist to check in. He couldn't leave Timberlodge; he couldn't take days off or leave for a vacation. No one would be there to greet the occasional tourist, and he needed that tourist to stay at Timberlodge. He couldn't afford to close shop either. The dismal revenue the inn brought barely kept the lights on, and he couldn't give any part of that up.

The only times when he closed that reception office was when he went hunting. He relied on his shooting skills to put meat on the table, and he was good at it too. That was his life, all in all: Timberlodge (where he was the owner, front desk clerk, accountant, and janitor) and hunting.

The door creaked open, then slammed shut. He groaned and put his feet down, then slipped his old boots on.

"Be right with ya!" he called.

"Hey, Jack," a familiar voice answered.

"Billy," he replied, then shook the ranger's hand. "What can I do for ya?"

Billy took off his wide-brimmed hat and scratched the receding line of his sandy hair.

"We got a situation, a nasty one, bombs and stuff. Seen anyone suspicious or anything unusual?"

Jack's eyes bulged out a little, pushing his bushy eyebrows up high.

"You askin' me?" he scoffed. "You seen him too!"

"Who?"

"The fellow yesterday. Remember him?"

"Yeah, the one with the Altima, I remember him. He was a little strange, I give you that."

"A little? The man didn't even know his own name! I called him twice before he realized I was talking to him. That's plenty strange by my book."

Billy jotted a few notes in his notepad.

"Any idea where he went?"

"Nah . . . Yellowstone somewhere, camping. He had a mighty heavy backpack. Strong, young feller like him and grunted when he picked that up from his trunk. The car bounced up a couple of inches."

Billy shook his head, pursing his lips.

"Damn it to hell, I was right here! Who knows where he went . . . why the hell didn't you call me?"

"I figured you seen him and you know people better than me," Jack replied. "I have his name, if that's his real name, anyway. That car was blue, right? He said it was one of them rentals."

"I'll keep an eye out for that car. Got the license plate, by any chance?"

"You know me, Billy, course I do," Jack replied, and laughed, his harsh husky voice sounding more like a cough than laughter. He copied the car's plate from his guest registry and handed it to the ranger.

"Next time call me, all right?" Billy said, thanking him with a nod of his head. "Who knows where he's at by now?"

"Well . . ." Jack said, scratching his head, "if you find that car, why don't you take a dog to it? I ain't cleaned up his room yet. You can get the dog to sniff the sheets 'n' towels. The dog will find him."

By the time Jack finished talking, Billy had already started his engine. The reception office door finally closed, just as his wheels furiously threw a bunch of white pebbles against the inn's wall.

Jack grabbed his shotgun and stuffed his pockets with a couple fistfuls of shells, then grabbed the box too. He slammed the door on his way out, then hung from the door's handle a sign that read, "Gone hunting. Make yourself at home."

He hurried inside room four, where the stranger had stayed the night before, and came out with the used sheets and towels in a large trashcan liner. Then he hopped in his ratty old Chevy truck and sped away, trying to catch up with Billy. Those young kids needed help.

People poured in from everywhere, under the solid cover of thick clouds. They started flowing in after midnight, when the sky was more than 90 percent cloudy. Endless rows of Humvees loaded with Marines and infantry took positions around the park, then unloaded their passengers. Infantry men and women, armed with M4s, deployed to their respectively assigned locations. National Guard deployed in the remote areas of the park's periphery. Snipers took vantage points and set up their M24s, getting ready to fire, and scrutinized the area through powerful scopes. Marines patrolled in teams of two.

A couple of MRAP vehicles deployed next, getting ready to clear explosives as soon as they were found. Support vehicles and tactical trucks weren't that far behind, and rumors spread that a fleet of helicopters and unmanned aerial vehicles (UAVs) were assembling and getting ready to deploy just a few miles away, where the noise they made didn't pose a problem. The leaders didn't want to risk alerting any of the terrorists of their arrival, so they kept a polite distance for the time being.

Separate teams, consisting of rangers, local police, and infantry, had set up roadblocks on any road that led into the park. They stopped everyone, going in or coming out. They showed everyone a picture of a missing seven-year-old girl, the same picture that had been stapled to tree trunks here and there. Roadblock teams took positions in multiple points on Highway 191, north of Grand Teton, and on the stretch from west Yellowstone. They were on Highway 14, coming from Pahaska Tepee, and on 89, from Gardiner. So far, no luck, and very little traffic had moved on those highways at night. With the crack of dawn, things were about to change.

The task force team had requisitioned Old Faithful Lodge, built in front of the most predictable eruption geyser known. Every 30 to 120 minutes, Old Faithful spewed boiling water high in the air, for the enjoyment of tourists who flocked in from far away to see it erupt.

The task force closed off the lodge's cafeteria, placing armed guards at the entrances. They covered all windows with tarps, ensuring complete privacy, and deployed maps, computers, field-tracking equipment, and communications in the improvised space. A new landscape awaited the lodge guests in the morning: a parking lot filled with military vehicles, and a morning that seemed taken from a military drama. That landscape would most likely scare some tourists and drive them away. It couldn't be helped.

There had been discussions of an evacuation of the park, but that idea had soon fallen off the agenda. Time spent trying to save a few hundred people scattered everywhere took resources away from finding the nuclear devices and saving millions. Special Agent Barnett from Homeland and Jeremy Weber agreed for a change, marking a first in a tense, complicated working relationship.

Henri Marino had flown in and arrived a few minutes after 4:00AM. Cranky and impatient, Marino's presence confused things further for the joint task force. Although the task force was technically under Barnett's command, there was no precedent to guide anyone on how operations should be handled in a case like this, and fierce arguments erupted more frequently than Old Faithful Geyser.

Marino noticed immediately that Barnett was somewhat overwhelmed and unable to organize. She swallowed her comments and decided to assign areas of responsibility instead.

"All right, Weber, you take interrogations. Sauli, you take all database searches and inter-agency communications. Olvera, grid searches."

"Got it," Weber confirmed.

The two named DHS agents froze and searched the eyes of their task force leader, Barnett.

"You heard her, let's go," he said frowning, as his face turned a dark red.

Eddie Zoller took a table in a remote corner of the cafeteria, and spent most of the time on the phone or on his computer, in touch with the NEST team conducting radiation searches. He had increased the sensitivity of the sensors to the maximum possible, and still he couldn't get enough trace information to allow him to find a source. There was slightly more radiation than normal, and manmade isotopes were present, but very scarce. They were so scarce, they could very well have been carried by the winds from Mount Rainier's eruption, just 800 miles west north west. The same readings came from all equipment deployed, whether on helicopters or ground sensors. They had nothing they could use.

Twenty-something miles north, Jack and Billy stared at the trunk of a blue Nissan Altima, parked in a small quarry off of Norris Canyon Road. They'd requested K9 support for some time, and after a couple of hours of waiting, Billy finally lost his patience and escalated the situation. After numerous attempts, he left Jack and his shotgun to keep watch over the Altima, drove off to Old

Faithful Cafeteria, and demanded to speak with the man in charge. Forty-five minutes after speaking with the irritated and reluctantly helpful Agent Barnett, a K9 unit was inbound by chopper. Billy had instructions on how to approach the individual, and a radio to speak directly with Barnett when he found him.

The German Shepherd sniffed the towels enthusiastically and whimpered quietly, signaling he had the scent. Then he took off, pulling hard against the leash, straight across the fields. An officer stayed behind with the car, to make sure he caught the man if he returned to his vehicle. Jack and Billy followed the dog and his handler as fast as they could, but Jack started panting heavily, falling behind. He waved Billy off.

"Go ahead, I'll be fine. Just a sack of old bones . . ." he muttered between raspy, shallow breaths.

The dog led them along Gibson River for a while, through fields of shrubbery and tall grasses, then across fallen tree trunks through a thickening forest. Then the dog stopped and sniffed the air, whimpering a little.

"What's going on?" Billy asked. "He lost the track?"

"He's still working, give him time," the K9 handler replied.

The dog sniffed in the wind a little more, then barked once, sounding cheerful, and pulled everyone across the river, to a place where a sandy bank made the crossing easy.

Billy looked behind, where Jack was coming as fast as he could, but had started dragging his left leg.

They continued to follow the tireless Shepherd and soon came to a clearing. The dog whimpered quietly, and the officer touched his nose with his hand. The dog fell silent.

"Found him," the officer said. "There, between those trees, there's a tent."

Billy nodded, then took out the radio.

"This is Billy Burton, calling for Special Agent Barnett, over," he whispered in his radio.

"Come in for Barnett," the radio crackled, the sound seeming thunderous against the stillness of the forest.

"We found the suspect's tent. Do we approach?"

"Negative. Confirm, over."

"Confirmed. We do not approach. Over."

He shrugged and took off his hat to wipe the sweat from his forehead. They withdrew a few yards behind the tree line, and soon Jack caught up with them, breathing heavily and coughing every few minutes.

It didn't take long for a Humvee to reach their location. Agent Barnett and three of his armed Marines disembarked, followed at a distance by Edward Zoller and his inseparable laptop bag filled with equipment. He introduced himself to Billy and Jack, and shook their hands.

"Eddie Zoller," he whispered. "Good to meet you."

"I saw you at Old Faithful. Are you an agent too?" Billy asked.

"No, just an engineer."

They took positions around the tent moving quietly, like felines, despite the paraphernalia of hardware they were hauling. Then Barnett invited Billy to approach the tent.

"You're the ranger," Barnett whispered. "He won't react as badly to you. Just tell him it's a no-camping zone or something."

Billy nodded and swallowed hard, gripping the handle of his gun with a sweaty hand. He approached the tent quietly, then listened for a few seconds. No sound came from the tent.

"Hello? This is Ranger Burton, good morning," he said, changing his typical approach.

Nothing, not a sound came from inside the tent.

He crouched and grabbed the zipper with his left hand, pulling it up gently.

He recognized the man curled on his side in a sleeping bag. The man's eyes opened widely, terrified to recognize the ranger.

"You're in a no-camping zone, sir. Please step out of your tent."

The man complied without a word. The moment he cleared the tent and stood, two Marines immobilized him, grabbing his arms and holding him still. A third Marine leaned and looked inside.

"There's nothing in here, sir, just a—"

"Don't touch anything!" Edward Zoller yelled. "Move away, slowly."

He approached the tent holding a radiation detector, and the beeps started to gain in frequency and strength. He kneeled at the tent's door and looked inside, then backed away slowly.

"You," he directed the Marine, "help me split open this tent. Let's cut it through here, at the center. Don't step on anything and move slowly. There's a bomb inside somewhere."

"Holy mother of God," Jack whispered, watching the radiation detector in Eddie's hand with transfixed eyes.

Billy pulled his knife and approached to help. The Marine had already started slicing along the top seam of the tent, from front to back. When they finished cutting, they gently set the two sides of the tent on the ground, folding them outward and exposing the tent's floor.

There wasn't anything much in there: a backpack, a sleeping bag, a flashlight, a length of climbing rope, some carabiners, a Beretta handgun, and a satellite phone. Eddie approached the backpack slowly, carefully, and registered a slight increase in ionizing radiation, very slight. A sensor just fifty yards away wouldn't have picked anything up.

He kneeled next to the backpack and gently examined it without moving it.

He opened the main flap and peered inside. Then he patted the pockets and none opposed any resistance; they were empty. All the time, his detector beeped quietly, flickering numbers on a small digital display.

He picked the backpack up, expecting it to be very heavy, but it was light and almost completely empty. He removed it from the tent floor and put it on the ground, a few feet away from the tent. Then he removed the sleeping bag carefully, and placed it on the grass, near the backpack.

"There's nothing here," Billy said.

"Yes, there is," Eddie replied, frowning into his device's display. "We just haven't found it yet."

He took several steps in all directions starting from the tent, and the radiation seemed to dissipate in all directions. No, the source had to be right there, in the tent. Then he remembered . . . *Buried* nukes . . . that was the plan. Somehow, they'd figured out how to bury them.

"This is weird," Billy said. "I've never seen this in a tent."

"What?" Eddie turned to see.

"A zipper, along the bottom. Can I?"

"No, let me do it." Eddie kneeled carefully near the tent and gently pulled the zipper along the tent's floor. Soon he had detached the floor entirely and removed it gently.

There it was, a packet of sorts, covered in what seemed to be camouflage tarp, which proved to be lead-covered shielding. He peeled that away, moving microns at a time, and uncovered the device.

The red digits of the timer display read 17 hours, 19 minutes, and 4 seconds, counting down in a hypnotizing rhythm. Eddie checked his time, then announced, "They're set to blow up at midnight tonight."

"Fuck me . . ." Jack reacted. "What do you mean, *they*? How many are there?"

No one replied.

Eddie called in the find, and the command center dispatched a team to remove and disarm the device. Then he took a few seconds to text Alex. He just wrote two words: "Found one."

His phone rang instantly.

"Don't move the nuke," Alex said, "and don't move the guy from there either, you hear me?"

"Why?"

"I'm sure V would GPS track them if I were in his shoes. Wouldn't you want to know, at all times, where your bombs and your people are?"

Eddie exhaled forcefully, feeling pressure build in his chest.

"Damn . . . But we can't stay here either. I can study the device here, but the man—"

"Strip him naked, have someone run a metal detector over every inch of his body, in case they had the GPS emitter implanted under his skin. Then you can move him."

"Got it. Any luck on your end?"

"Bait is set. Just getting ready and waiting for the son of a bitch to bite."

Within minutes, a couple of NEST choppers flew in, followed closely by another two loaded with the task force team.

Eddie and his team suited up and worked feverishly on the device, kneeled around it and conferring quietly in technical lingo no one understood. Another few minutes later, he stood and gathered everyone around him.

"It's disarmed," Eddie jumped straight to the point, "but we've let the timer run, because it's fitted with some sort of satellite transmitter. My guess is that the bomber controls and monitors these timers remotely. I've also found a GPS tracker inside the nuke's detonator unit. We will leave that behind, exactly where we found it."

"Why?" Agent Barnett asked.

"We believe the bomber has the ability to detonate remotely regardless of the timer. The detonator has an input channel from the satellite receiver that bypasses the timer altogether. I think the timer is a failsafe, nothing more."

"What do you mean, just a failsafe?" Marino asked.

"We believe, and it's just a theory at this point, that the bomber can detonate and will detonate the devices when he sees them all deployed in their pre-set positions. That's why he's tracking them, and that's why he built in the remote detonation circuit. In itself, this is the work of a top-notch professional, not some amateur with a nuke or two."

"How the hell many are there?" Billy's high-pitched voice broke the silence.

"Fourteen," Eddie replied.

"Wait a minute," Agent Barnett said, "we can't really—"

"Yes, we can," Marino replied dryly before Eddie could jump in. "The source who told us about Yellowstone said fourteen. Unless there's evidence to prove otherwise, I'll go with fourteen. So get to work, people, and let's find the rest!"

Jack whistled loudly.

"We have a problem," Eddie added hesitantly. "The insulation on this nuclear package is exceptionally good. I was right here, inches away, and my tracking device couldn't detect enough isotopes to pinpoint a location. All we've done with radiation detection so far, the sensors, the grip searches, has not yielded any results, and now we know why."

"How do you suppose we find them then?" Agent Barnett asked, doing a poor job at masking his irritation.

"We start the grid searches again, from the air, but this time we use thermal imaging. We stop everyone and test them for explosive residue. They will turn out positive; that guy did. In close proximity with them, our sensors will pick up some radioactivity."

"What if the others left already? They buried their bombs, then picked up and left?" Agent Olvera prompted. "I know I wouldn't stay, GPS monitoring or not. These are Russians, not suicide bombers."

"Good point," Eddie replied. "The nuke wasn't buried; just cradled in a shallow indent into the ground. It's obvious they know about our seismological sensors and they didn't want to trip any alarms. The nuclear device itself emits low levels of thermal radiation. We might be able to spot them from a low, slow-flying helicopter. They would appear square or rectangular, due to the lead blanket they used for radiation shielding. That warms up from the nuke and should show on the screens."

"There's no fucking time!" Barnett snapped. "What do we got left, seventeen hours? This is crazy! You scientists had better come up with something that actually works, for Chrissake! Where do we even start?"

"Hold it together, Barnett," Marino growled.

"You don't know that you have seventeen hours," Eddie replied. "The devices could blow up anytime, as far as we know. Start your grid searches at the edges of the caldera, moving inward. Break it down in sections, get organized, and deploy everything you can. Have infantry walk the perimeter, as much as it's possible. Be diligent at all points of entry. No one in, no one out, everyone swab-tested as they do at airports."

"It's a huge surface to cover! Do you realize what you're asking?"

"Yes, I do, and we're shit out of luck, I get it. However, we don't have any other choices. So let's just get going. There's no time left."

Barnett glared at Eddie for another few seconds, then turned away and left. Marino nodded in his direction, followed Barnett to the helicopter, and then flew with him back to the command center.

In a small room in the improvised command center at Old Faithful Cafeteria, Jeremy Weber had very limited success interrogating the Russian terrorist. He remained mostly silent and pale, muttering occasionally something about a number ten, whatever that meant.

Within the next hour, the joint task force got lucky, and recovered two other devices, intercepted at highway points of entry into the park.

Then their luck ran out.

Alex ended the call and slid the phone in her jeans pocket, then sat in one of the jet's leather seats, looking absently out the window.

"They found three bombs so far," she said. "I'm getting nervous. It's too slow; we're running out of time. Any reply from the bastard yet?"

"Not in the last two minutes, no," Lou replied, but hit the refresh key anyway.

Blake sat across the aisle from her, reading his email. "He'll reply, don't worry. He probably doesn't want to seem desperate, so he's stalling."

"Huh?"

"If he responded immediately, he would have lost most of his ability to negotiate the deal," Blake clarified. "Well, at least in a real business situation. In our case it doesn't matter, but he doesn't know that yet."

"Do you think he'll recognize you? Us? We sent him your cover identity, but that linked back to a real picture of you. He'd seen us by satellite last time we crossed paths. I'm getting worried. Not to mention you're a public figure, known in the business world."

"Again, don't worry. He'll be in greedy mode, looking to make a quick arms sale. He'll think I look familiar, which works perfectly with the email we sent. He'll bite. Don't second-guess yourself; there's no need."

"We got email," Lou announced excitedly. "We're set!"

Alex sprung to her feet.

"Seriously? When?"

"He'll meet us near Vienna tonight, at a small airstrip," Lou replied, then checked his time and hopped on his feet. "We should get going in a couple of hours. I'll just be forty minutes or so, doing some last minute shopping."

He winked at Alex and then disappeared off the plane, taking the stairs down two at a time.

"What do I do? Should I reply and confirm?"

"Yes, but not now. Let him sit and wait for a few hours. We mustn't seem desperate either," Blake laughed. "We lose our ability to negotiate."

"Do you plan to negotiate?" Alex wondered. "I thought we'd pull the trigger the moment we see the first opportunity, and be done with it."

"People like him travel with an entourage for such meetings. Arms trade is a dangerous line of work. I'd recommend we play along until we put his fears at ease, then pull the trigger. I'd prefer we come home afterward, if possible."

"Agreed," Sam said. "Good idea. Let's test the waters for a while, see how it goes. But remember we're pressed for time. There's a timer running."

She paced the small plane's aisle back and forth, impatient, nervous. That was it . . . her chance to get close to modern history's biggest terrorist. Most people thought of the late Osama bin Laden as the biggest terrorist ever, and that still held true by sheer terror value, although Myatlev surpassed bin Laden in number of casualties. But the same people had no idea that Mount Rainier had been an act of terror, not an act of nature. If her team were unsuccessful preventing the Yellowstone eruption tonight, Myatlev would indisputably hold the title, but then again, no one would know.

Tonight she would finally get to meet him, face to face. He was a man able to wipe off the face of the earth millions of innocent people and not break a sweat. How would their encounter go? How would it feel to stare into the eyes of pure evil? She was afraid she'd hesitate when the time came, with the gun in her hand. After all, killing a man is not easy. Maybe Lou, or Sam would be better at it. Then she recalled a time in the recent past when she didn't hesitate to take out a man who held a bunch of innocent people hostage. This wasn't going to be any different; she'd do just fine. *Some vigilante justice, some assassin,* she thought with amusement, recalling Eddie's reaction. He probably overestimated her abilities. *I guess I need to keep my day job.*

"Blake," she said with a smile, offering him her bonus check, "here's my contribution to the bait fund. I just got a sizeable bonus, if you recall."

"There's no need, I got it covered."

"Yes, I know, but it doesn't seem right. How much cash are you planning to have on hand?"

"I'd say five million dollars should establish our credibility, don't you think?"

"Whew," she whistled, "that's a lot of money!"

Dylan, Blake's pilot and personal assistant at times, came out of the cockpit.

"I've asked Dylan to make a run to the bank and get us the cash."

She turned to face Dylan, who smiled nervously. She handed him the check she was still holding.

"So, Dylan, are you up for another adventure with us?"

Dylan cleared his throat, visibly uncomfortable.

"Honestly, when I heard what you're planning to do, I considered resigning from my job."

"I'm glad you didn't," Alex replied. "I'd fly anywhere with you."

He thanked her and disappeared. While he was gone, running errands, a crew came by and covered the plane's tail number with a bogus Dutch-based tail number, and added some blue and red decals as design elements.

Alex paced the aisle every few minutes, then went on the tarmac and walked around the plane, then returned to the plane, pacing the aisle. Nervously anticipating, counting the minutes, she recited in her head the things she wanted to tell Myatlev, the questions she wanted him to answer for her before drawing his last breath. But no matter how much she rehearsed her spiel, she fell back inevitably to the anger-ridden, throat-choking question, "How could you? How could you kill so many people, and why? Why can't you realize you have enough?"

Blake had told her people like Myatlev never had enough. There was never enough money, never enough power to satisfy them. As long as a single, other human being was even remotely more powerful, or more affluent than they were, they kept on going. It was the thrill of the hunt, combined with an excessive competitive spirit. It was the nature of the malignant narcissistic psychopath, Steve had added.

"Kiddo, get in here and look out this window, discreetly," Sam said quietly, disrupting her introspection.

"What's up?"

"See those two clowns over there? Those guys aren't here for the landscape."

She saw two men, hunched forward as they were walking covertly along the wall of the terminal building, holding their handguns. She felt her blood freeze. Those were Myatlev's men, coming to get her. How the hell did they find her there?

She texted Lou and Dylan, while Blake made a quick call. Within minutes, a couple of cops came out of the terminal building, guns in hands. Sirens started blaring in the distance, approaching fast. Alex cringed . . . *Oh, no!* Two city cops didn't stand much of a chance against Myatlev's killers.

She drew her weapon and approached the plane's open door. Sam followed her, and Blake took position on the opposite side of the door.

"Drop your weapons!" one of the cops called out.

Quick as lightning, both Russians turned and discharged their weapons. One cop fell on his back and remained still. The other, hit in the leg, managed to crawl out of the Russian's line of fire, behind a concrete retaining wall.

The Russians continued to fire after the second cop. She didn't hesitate. She fired her Sig twice from the plane's door. From her side, she heard Sam's support fire. The two Russians were on the ground, lifeless.

"This is going to get interesting, guys," Blake said, "and I don't think we have the time to stick around for hours of questioning."

"Where's Dylan?" she asked. "We can't leave without him."

"He's right behind me," Lou said, popping up on the plane, dragging two duffel bags filled with gear.

Dylan showed his head hesitantly behind the terminal door, and then trotted as fast as he could with the two huge bags he was carrying. He gazed with horror at the two bodies as he walked past them, turning pale.

"So that's what five mil looks like, huh," Alex said with a chuckle.

"Power it up, Dylan, and let's hit it," Blake said. Within seconds, the jet's engines were roaring.

It was getting dark at Yellowstone, making the search even harder. The park's numerous steam jets, warm springs, and other natural sources of heat had wasted tremendous amounts of time, confusing the thermal detection sensors and the units that were grid-searching the park.

Old Faithful Cafeteria was a boiling pot of stretched nerves and panic waiting to set in. A display on the wall matched the bombs' timers counting down, showing 3 hours and 23 minutes left. Next to it, on a portable whiteboard, the number "10" was handwritten, underlined, and circled, annotated with a time code, 6:18PM. That meant the joint task force had already found ten devices, the last one located at 6:18PM. In the past two hours they'd found nada.

When a device was located, NEST moved in and dismantled it carefully. They neutralized each nuclear device and placed it in isolation, in special tanks built for nuclear material containment and removal. Then explosives experts moved in and dismantled the plastic charges, placing them in different containment units. Then they were loaded on heavy-duty M1070 equipment transports and hauled out of there.

DHS agents Barnett, Olvera, and Sauli, along with CIA agent Marino stood in front of that display, arguing bitterly.

"This is *my* task force," Barnett bellowed. "I run this search as I goddamn see fit!"

"Yeah, but you're not finding shit!" Marino snapped. "You need to think differently. You need to get over yourself and your role in this task force, and start thinking like your damn life depended on it!"

A couple of seconds of silence grabbed the room. Eddie's tapping on the laptop's keyboard was the only sound for a short while.

"What are you saying?" Barnett finally asked, his tone slightly more reasonable.

"I'm saying maybe not all the bombs made it here. Maybe they're still on the road."

"Yeah, but the timer shows less than four hours left," Olvera chimed in.

"Maybe that's why the timer can be overridden," Marino offered. "Zoller, that's what you said, right? The timer can be overridden?"

"Yeah, it can. It hasn't been, though. Not yet."

"You sure? "I remember you couldn't remove the timers from the site, right?"

"Yeah, because of the GPS trackers built in them. I have cameras set up at each location though; I can see their displays. None of them has changed."

"So isn't that telling you that the devices are all here, ready to blow?" Barnett pushed back.

"It tells me they *could* be here, nothing more."

"What else are you expecting? A handwritten note?" Barnett started raising his voice to irritating levels.

"No . . ." Marino took in a deep breath, gaining the strength to refrain from bitch-slapping the man. "It could mean that the bombs we couldn't find are close by, and they could be here in three hours. It could mean that this Myatlev character has redundancies, just like Hoffmann drove me crazy insisting. It could mean he only needs eight devices to trigger an eruption, so if ten are here already, then he's got enough and he doesn't care about the rest, or where they are. It could mean not all terrorists made it inside the country. Or it could mean the devices are stuck somewhere in transit, they'll never make it, and he knows it. He won't wait for them. He's happy blowing up whatever locations these devices might be at."

Barnett lowered his eyes and rubbed his forehead.

"It's—It's been a long couple of days," he said, in way of an apology.

"Yeah, I know. How about if someone does a thorough database search across all law enforcement agencies and looks for any unusual event in the past forty-eight?"

"I can do that," Sauli offered, then turned on her heels and disappeared. She looked more and more like an accountant. Tired and drawn, she'd tied up her hair in a loose ponytail and carried a pen behind her ear. Marino almost chuckled, wondering for a split second if anyone had ever told her.

"Um, probably only if he detonates the bombs himself," Eddie interjected.

"What do you mean?" Marino asked.

"Myatlev. You said he'd be happy to blow up whatever locations the bombs might be at. That won't happen unless he chooses to detonate them himself. From what I could tell, the timer needs to be armed manually on each device. I don't think the terrorists do that before reaching their target location. If the explosions will be initiated by the timer, only those armed will go up."

"How about later, then? Couldn't he choose to detonate those later?"

"Yes, definitely. You don't want any nukes unaccounted for, anywhere in this country."

"Nothing's changed then. Any ideas?"

No one replied; they were tapped out.

"How's Weber doing in interrogations?"

"It's . . . not going well," Olvera replied. "These bastards are fanatical."

"What percentage of the surface has been grid-searched and cleared so far?"

"About 82 percent," Olvera replied. "But it's dark now, and it's more difficult. It takes more time to clear an area. NEST's grid software helped a lot, by the way."

NEST had software that allowed the overlay of a digital grid on top of a GPS-enabled map view. Any cleared area would be marked green if cleared, yellow if in need of further searches, and so on. The system saved them tons of time and kept them organized. That way, they didn't risk missing a spot, or working through an area multiple times.

"Hey guys, come on over here," Sauli called from across the cafeteria.

They rushed to her. She covered the speaker on her phone and filled them in.

"There was an accident yesterday morning at the Port of San Francisco. A container fell off the crane while being unloaded, and there was a man inside, unidentified yet. He fell into the ocean with the container debris. They fished him out dead, broken neck."

"Why are we hearing of this now?" Marino asked angrily. "Put them on speaker."

Sauli pressed a button.

"You're on speaker," she announced.

"This is Henri Marino and Special Agent Barnett with Homeland Security," she said, purposely omitting to mention the CIA. "I need you guys to go to the bottom of the water where that man fell, and see if there's a barrel or a backpack with a nuclear device in it. If there is, don't touch it."

"Jeez . . . a what?" the man on the phone asked.

"Yeah, you heard me. Dive and find it. This man had luggage. We need all of it found."

"What, now?"

"Yeah, now! You have thirty minutes," Marino said. "We'll get NEST on standby, geared up, and ready to dive with you." Then she ended the call, wishing she'd held a receiver she could physically slam.

The Phenom turned gracefully and aligned with the runway in the shy light of dawn; they had arrived. As they were coming in for the landing, Alex and Sam spotted another light jet, a Challenger, parked on the tarmac with its lights on and door open.

"He's here, he's early," Alex said. "Let's get ready."

She checked herself in the mirror, making sure she looked the part of the decorative assistant of Mr. Otto Dreiers. She wore tight black pants, which contoured her shape, and a white silk blouse, with the top two buttons left undone, showing just a tad too much cleavage, enough to capture the interest of most warm-blooded males. Her boots hid her backup Walther on the inside of her right ankle, and a medium-sized tactical knife above her left ankle, tucked in the lining. Her Sig rested in its holster on her belt, covered by a light, black, sateen jacket she wore casually, unbuttoned.

She ruffled the black hair of her wig, and applied fresh lipstick. Then she hesitated a little, but then decided to add another couple of silver necklaces to accessorize her attire. She checked the light outside once more and grunted angrily. It was still too dark to wear her glitzy sunglasses. She rearranged her hair to fall as much as possible over her face, and checked the mirror one last time.

Sam watched her with tense amusement.

"I taught you to check your weapons before a confrontation . . . what are you doing?"

"Checking my weapons," she laughed nervously.

"Ha," Lou reacted, "Good one!"

"How about you, Sam? Are you up to it? You're still recovering, technically."

"Wouldn't miss it," he replied, pursing his lips. "I'm ready. Let's nail the bastard."

The plane stopped with its nose a few yards away from Myatlev's Challenger. The small airstrip was entirely deserted, except for the two planes. That had to be unusual. In the distance, a city's myriad lights glimmered against the dawn's early light; it was close enough to justify some traffic, some activity at the airstrip. Maybe it was just too early.

Dylan opened the plane's door and quickly stepped to the side. Blake was the first to get off, followed by Alex. Blake stopped as soon as he reached the tarmac, and she approached him, remaining politely one foot behind, just as a respectful executive assistant would do.

They waited calmly for about a minute; Myatlev finally appeared at the top of the Challenger's steps, followed by one of his goons. He descended slowly, then walked toward them. Blake took a few more steps to meet him halfway, and they shook hands.

"V," Blake said, "It's good to see you, dear friend." He shook his hand warmly and was a little surprised by Myatlev's unexpected hug, followed by the traditional three kisses on the cheek, typical for Russians who greet dear friends.

"Welcome to Vienna," Myatlev replied. "Always good to see old friends, right?"

"Yes, it is; yes, it is," Blake said, then cleared his throat a little.

Don't panic on me, Blake, Alex thought, seeing Blake clench his jaws. You're Mr. Hot Shot Banker; you close deals like this every day.

She checked discreetly to see if anyone else was visible inside the plane or nearby. She didn't see anyone, but that didn't mean much. She kept her eyes mostly lowered, avoiding Myatlev altogether. From what she could see without looking directly, Myatlev didn't even know she existed; he was focused entirely on Blake. Perfect.

"What brings you here in such a rush, my friend?" Myatlev asked, patting Blake on the shoulder and bringing their heads together.

"This," Blake replied, extracting a diamond from a small leather packet. He handed it to Myatlev.

"Ahh," he said, admiringly. "Wonderful. Eight carats?"

"Ten. Yours, by the way, for meeting me here so early in the morning."

Myatlev nodded obliquely in appreciation. He held the diamond in the dim light of the early dawn and admired it.

"You know how to get someone's attention, that's for sure. Now, what can I do for you?"

"There are fights where this came from," Blake replied serenely, "fights that impact my business, if you know what I mean. I need to win those fights and put an end to the senseless waste of time and money. I need armies, with good weapons and plenty of ammo."

Myatlev scratched his buzz-cut head.

"AKs?"

"Yes."

"RPGs?"

"Definitely."

"Fifty cal machine guns?"

"I'll take a few."

"What else?"

"A few helicopters, if you can spare them. With machine guns installed on them."

Myatlev sized Blake up, as if he was seeing him for the first time.

"I have something you'll like. Kamov KA-60. New design, great performance. Versatile and fast, perfect for your . . . hostile environment."

"All right, let's talk price."

"Let's talk volume first. That dictates the price. How much money do you want to spend?"

"About one hundred million I could spare. I came here trusting you'll give me the best deal there is to be had in this market, yes?"

Myatlev put his hand on his chest, above his heart. "Absolutely. African conflicts are the best source of repeat business I have. I won't risk sending you away unhappy, my friend."

Blake smiled and remained quiet.

"Can I see a sign of good faith?" Myatlev asked.

Blake signaled Alex with a move of his head. She nodded once and hurried back to Blake's Phenom. As she did, she crossed briefly through an area lit by the Challenger's landing lights. She muttered a curse under her breath, lowered her head, and kept on going.

A minute later, she returned followed by Lou, who carried the two duffel bags filled with cash. Lou put them on the ground and pulled the zippers, opening them wide for Myatlev to appreciate the contents.

"I hope this establishes my credibility," Blake said calmly. "There's plenty more where that came from."

"Let's discuss delivery," Myatlev said. "We can—"

His phone rang, and he interrupted himself, checked the screen, then declined the call.

"Sorry. I—"

The phone rang again. Frowning, he mumbled another apology and took the call, turning his back to them.

Alex listened intently. He spoke Russian, quietly, but she thought she heard him ask the caller, "What do you mean it's her, right there?"

She felt a rush of adrenaline hit her gut. It was not going that well . . . they didn't prepare carefully enough. They'd winged it; *she'd* winged it, placing the entire team in danger. Again. They just rushed in, pressured by the threat of fourteen nukes blowing up the Yellowstone supervolcano. Sloppy, *sloppy* work.

"I think we're blown," she whispered.

Myatlev turned to face them; he was holding a gun. He whistled loudly, and a bunch of his men jumped off his plane. A couple of them climbed aboard the Phenom and came down dragging Dylan. They must have missed Sam somehow, because she didn't see him anywhere.

Two of his men grabbed Blake and hauled him toward a hangar nearby, followed closely by two more, who held Lou tightly, despite the firm resistance he was opposing. They soon overpowered him, and a fist to his left temple put his lights out for a while.

She watched Myatlev, petrified, unable to do or say anything. He kept the muzzle of his gun inches away from her chest. In the corner of her eye, she saw his men getting ready to set the Phenom on fire. *Oh, my God . . . Sam!* He was trapped aboard the plane, hidden somewhere.

Myatlev gazed at her with ice-cold eyes, in which she thought she saw a flicker of excitement, of achievement. She stared into his eyes hypnotized, unable to react, like staring into the eyes of a deadly snake getting ready to pounce.

He touched her skin with the cold barrel of his gun, running it up and down her sternum, from her throat down to her cleavage, smiling. Then he took one more step toward her and wrapped his right hand around her throat, clutching it tightly. She choked, struggling to breathe, as her vision darkened. She kicked and flailed her arms without hitting anything. She tried to loosen his grip with both her hands, but he didn't budge. Then she felt his breath on her face and heard him speak.

"You're mine now, bitch."

The number "13" was written on the whiteboard in thick, red marker, and circled a couple of times. The time stamp next to it read 10:52PM. Technically, they'd found twelve devices in the park, but the NEST team at the Port of San Francisco confirmed the backpack recovered from the bottom of the ocean contained an identical device with those sown all over the Yellowstone supervolcano caldera.

"Come on, people," Marino called, raising her voice to cover the entire cafeteria, drowned in all sorts of noise. "Forty-three minutes left and we're still missing one nuke! Where is it?"

No one responded. Barnett clenched his jaws furiously, but chose to keep quiet.

"I thought it wouldn't blow up if the timer wasn't set, right? I thought they only set the timers if they got in position," Sauli asked, her voice trembling a little.

"Correct," Eddie replied, "but we can't be sure—"

"What do you think is gonna happen when Myatlev sees the timers go off and nothing happens at Yellowstone? Even if we have cloud cover, an explosion like that would show on satellite, would blast right through the clouds. What's the very next thing he's going to do when nothing happens, huh?"

"He'll push that button, you're right," Sauli replied.

"Damn right he will. All right, roll call, then," Marino said. "Grid search, where are we?"

"One hundred percent complete on the caldera surface. Extending search outside the caldera now," Olvera replied.

"Good, maybe the last man got lost, or put the bomb in the wrong place. Maybe he got injured along the way and never made it to the caldera." She turned to see a map pinned on the wall behind her. The contour of the caldera had been drawn on it, and red pushpins marked the locations of the nukes in an almost perfect oval, smaller than the caldera.

"What do we see here, people?" she asked, her voice adding another degree of impatient irritation as she pointed at the map. "The bombs were meant to be placed in a pattern, following the caldera's contour on the inside, several miles inward of the caldera's edge. What do we see here and here? Two gaps. I'm guessing one is where the nuke we fished out of San Francisco Bay should have been. The second must be for the nuke we're still missing. I know," she added, raising her hand to pacify a wave of indiscernible protests, "I know we don't know which is which. But if we were to focus on these two spots, how would the terrorist get there? Which roads would he take? Let's see what we find, all right? Make it happen. Now!"

Two DHS agents left the group hurriedly, heading for their workstations.

"Interrogations, any insights?"

"Very few," Jeremy Weber replied. "Two killed themselves before we could remove the cyanide capsules from their teeth."

"Cyanide? Who uses that anymore?"

"Yeah, old-style spy stuff. I've seen it before though, recently. A couple of them indicated they'd rather die than talk, because if the bombs go off, their families would be taken care of for life. Overall, nothing we can use."

"Perimeter?" she turned toward the DHS agent in charge of screenings.

"Nothing new. The park's been dead quiet in the past few hours, although it's Friday. It's gotten late."

"Unusual border incidents?"

"Nothing involving cargo containers," Agent Sauli replied. "San Francisco was the only one."

"Unusual anything? Police reports, traffic stops, anything involving rental vehicles originating on the West Coast?"

A young FBI agent came forward.

"I've searched every single traffic stop from the West Coast toward Yellowstone, on all eastbound roads. The only thing that was somewhat unusual was a rear-ended rental SUV driven by a white male. His ID checked out just fine. The police report described the driver as being deeply confused, unwilling to accept medical assistance or to leave his damaged rental car behind. Because of severe traffic jams on top of bureaucracy, the car rental company took almost twenty hours to bring him a new car. He refused to leave, waiting on the curb next to the totaled SUV."

"That's him, guys! That's why he's late! Typical case of bad luck," Marino said, sending waves of electrifying excitement in the cafeteria. "You," she said, pointing at the young fed, "find out what replacement car they gave him, and put out an APB." Then she moved to the next agent, waiting with a notepad in his hand. "You, communicate with all roadblocks what kind of car we're looking for."

The agent didn't get a chance to send in the communication; the radio crackled to life.

"Mountain Base, this is Checkpoint Bravo, come in."

"This is base, go ahead," Marino replied, snatching the radio from the agent's hand.

"A silver Jeep Compass did a 180 when he saw the roadblock, but then went off-road into the park."

"Send everyone in pursuit, but *do not* open fire! If you feel like shooting, remember what you'd be shooting at!" She handed the agent the radio, and said, "Send in air support. Tell them to block him any way they can."

She turned to the first agent, but didn't get to ask. He put the phone down and said, "Yeah, the replacement car was a silver Jeep Compass. It's him."

"We found him, guys! Let's roll!"

They stormed out of the cafeteria and took off in a swarm of Humvees and SUVs, speeding on the narrow highway, heading west toward Checkpoint Bravo. They followed 89 to the Grand Prismatic Spring, then took the back roads leading to the freight road west of Firehole River.

Marino rode in the lead Humvee, driven by a young sergeant whose uniform bore a nametag, Phillips. She held on to the handle above the door, and looked to the sky, trying to find the helicopter's searchlights.

"There," she said, pointing at the sky to their left. "Cut it through there."

"Through the forest, ma'am? It could get thicker in a—"

"We got eighteen minutes left; what do you think? Wanna take the scenic route instead?"

"No, ma'am," he replied, then veered left without hitting the brakes.

The Humvee bounced badly as the driver cut directly toward where the helicopter lit the sky, avoiding trees and hopping over fallen branches, tree trunks, and rocks. The driver soon found a wider, cleared path, probably something the loggers used. Phillips took that turn and sped up.

Marino looked behind them and saw most of the other vehicles were following closely, jouncing, hurdling, and thumping badly off-road. Then she focused on the road ahead, seeing that at times the helicopter's projectors flickered closely through the scattered trees. She could already see the headlights of the approaching cars and the red and blue flashing lights of the ranger cars in pursuit, farther behind.

"There he is, ma'am!" the young man said, hitting the brakes.

"No, don't slow down," she ordered. "Go at him; don't give him time to think. Hit him if you have to."

"Yes, ma'am," he acknowledged, giving it more gas.

The Jeep was coming at them fast, bouncing over the rugged terrain like a broken toy. At least six vehicles followed him with their flashing lights on, all in a trembling circle of light coming from the helicopter above.

He had nowhere to go, and he knew it. He grew hesitant in his driving, taking his foot off the gas, slowing.

Marino's Humvee closed most of the distance and skidded to a stop, throwing rocks and dirt everywhere. Suddenly, the Jeep surprised everyone and turned right, accelerating madly, rolling down a sloping hill. The Humvee resumed its pursuit, Phillips white-knuckled and tense.

"Six more minutes," Marino said. "Floor it, Phillips!"

They were closing in on the Jeep. The Humvee, more robust, heavier, and sturdier, had less difficulty rolling over downed tree branches and rocks. They were just a few feet away, catching up with the Jeep, when it maneuvered abruptly to avoid a tree and hit something with its front right wheel. It flipped through the air and landed on its left side, sliding to a stop against a tree trunk.

The Humvee stopped right behind it, sending a new wave of dust and small debris into the air, visible like menacing storm clouds in its headlights. Marino and Phillips jumped out, soon followed by the rest of the team as they arrived at the scene.

"Coming through, make a hole," Eddie Zoller yelled.

He approached the Jeep and tried to open the tailgate. It was damaged from the crash and wouldn't budge.

"Allow me, sir," Phillips offered, and broke the tailgate window with the stock of his gun, sending bits of glass everywhere. Then he reached in and pulled out the backpack, laying it on the ground in front of Eddie.

"Three minutes, everyone," Marino yelled.

Eddie kneeled in front of the backpack and moved fast. He'd dismantled those devices before, twelve times exactly, so he moved faster than usual.

Marino pulled a feed from one of the timer cameras on her phone, staring at it intently.

"Ninety seconds," she announced.

No one made a sound; they held their breaths, watching Eddie work diligently and calmly. Phillips was the only one who moved. He broke the Jeep's windscreen and dragged the half-unconscious driver out of there, then slammed him to the ground. Two rangers searched and disarmed him, then cuffed him and hauled him to lean against one of their cars.

"Thirty seconds," Marino's voice announced again, more somberly. "Come on, Zoller, what the hell . . ."

He worked as fast as he could, forgetting where he was. The devices had not yet been assembled into their final configuration, and that threw him off a little. He unpacked them carefully. He started with the nuke and took apart its detonator with slightly trembling fingers. He set that circuitry unit aside, and then checked to see if the nuke held any other detonation circuits hidden in its shielding.

Then he put that to rest, yelling loudly, "Nuke's clear. Everyone, get the hell out of here!"

No one moved.

"Ten seconds," Marino read off the display in her hands.

Eddie examined the plastic explosive and inspected the detonation circuits for potential trip wires or safety mechanisms.

"Five," Marino counted down.

He removed the first layer of shielding, causing everyone a start when he punctured a pressurized protective air cushion. The air hissed loudly as it came out.

"Four."

He removed the protective air cushion, peeling it off slowly, millimeter by millimeter, until he exposed the detonation circuitry and the timer.

"Three," Marino said, a slight tremble coloring her voice.

He separated the detonator from the plastic explosive packet, then yelled, "Clear," just as Marino announced only two seconds were left.

Everyone breathed a little, but remained perfectly still, listening intently, looking at the pitch-black night sky. What if there were more than fourteen nukes scattered in the park? In two seconds, they would know for sure.

"Time's up," Marino announces, holding her breath. "And . . . nothing! We're in the clear! Yeah!"

They all cheered loudly, hugging one another, dancing in place, happy to be alive, happy to know their ordeal was over.

"What do you think you have achieved?" the Russian laughed arrogantly from the car. "There are more bombs, many more, thirteen more!"

"And we have them all, you fucking dumbass," Phillips replied. Then he punched his lights out.

Alex didn't remember how she got there. Myatlev's men must have dragged her as they did the rest, after she'd passed out, almost choked to death. She tried to swallow and instantly regretted it. Her throat, swollen and painful, felt like sandpaper. She tried to loosen the ties binding her hands, but that didn't work either. She felt the sharp edge of the plastic cable tie cut into her flesh and winced.

She sat on a chair, tied with her hands behind the backrest, with little room to move. Her feet were loose, but she couldn't run anywhere. Myatlev's men were watching with cold, impersonal eyes. For them, it was probably just another normal day at work.

They were inside a hangar. A few scattered tools hung from hooks on the walls, but there wasn't any aircraft. The main hangar door was closed. The dim light came from a few electric fixtures, most of them fluorescent. Voices echoed in the hollow space surrounded by sheet-metal walls and ceilings, mounted on a metallic, open-web truss.

Dylan lay unconscious on the floor, hunched against the wall. To her left, she saw Blake, tied up on a chair just like she was. A deep cut marked his forehead, and blood still dripped from it. One of Myatlev's men approached Blake and grabbed him by the hair, lifting his head forcefully as he took a picture of his face with the phone camera. Then he slammed his fist in Blake's stomach. Blake grunted, almost in surprise, but the man stared at Blake intently. Blake lowered his eyes, cringed, and moaned. The man walked away casually, texting on his phone.

Lou was on the next chair over; tied up, constantly grunting, and struggling to free himself. He was in worse shape than Blake. His right eye was swollen shut, and his cheek was badly bruised and cut. Blood stained his shirt, but his spirit wasn't dimmed. He swore incessantly, attracting more attention than he needed from his captors. Alex silently urged him to shut up and save his energy for something useful.

Alex didn't see Sam and then remembered he had been on the plane. A moment of worry pierced her, not knowing what had happened to him. He was still weak from his injuries.

She didn't have too much time to worry. Myatlev appeared through the small hangar door and walked straight to her. He signaled with his hand, and one of his men rushed to get him a chair. He sat in front of her, examining her with curiosity, the type of excited, almost happy curiosity fueled by years of wondering what his enemy looked like, felt like, or what she had to say.

Alex shared that morbid interest and barely waited for the opportunity to satisfy it. She stared back at him, with the same kind of curiosity in her eyes. So this was what the famous V looked like, up close and personal. In pictures, she hadn't been able to sense the evil lurking inside that man. Evil was a slippery concept though. It was a religious notion, not a scientific one. But she hesitated to apply scientific labels to the man, before having had the opportunity to evaluate him.

Sure, it was easy to call him a psychopath; he was one, no argument there. But what kind of psychopath? How did he end up becoming one? Was he born like that? Or did he grow into it, in a hostile, traumatic climate of abuse and neglect? Was there an explanation for who Vitaliy Myatlev was? Or was he just a freak of nature? What fueled his lust for blood and power, his incessant ambition? What made him tick?

"Who do you work for?" he asked calmly, snapping her back to reality. His voice was low and balanced, almost friendly, as if they shared a cup of coffee together.

She felt a surge of adrenaline refocus her.

"I work for myself," she replied. Her voice sounded hoarse, and it hurt to speak. "I'm what we call in the States an independent contractor."

His blow caught her off guard; it came incredibly fast. She saw stars, and heard her teeth clatter. She heard herself make a guttural noise, the swelling in her throat affecting her vocal cords. She took a deep breath, trying to calm herself.

"Who do you work for?" Myatlev repeated his question, in the same friendly and calm manner.

"I'm in it for myself," she said, changing her tactic. "I like money, you know? I'm a gun for hire."

This time she expected the hit and didn't have to wait long for it. The sound of his hand hitting her face echoed loudly through the hangar, sending Lou in a frenzy.

"Motherfucker," he yelled. "You fucking coward! Hit a man if you have the balls for it! I'm right here, you hear me, asshole?"

The sound of a fist landing hard in Lou's stomach ended his attempt to help her. He groaned and fell silent for a while, heaving and breathing heavily.

"Do you work for Blake Bernard?" Myatlev asked.

She swallowed hard, wincing from the pain. Damn . . . they were really blown. He knew who each of them were. It was time to change strategies.

"No," she replied candidly. "He's just a friend with a plane, that's all. I, however, have a strong interest in you. I've been hunting you down for the past couple of years, you know."

"Who do you work for?"

"I just told you, I'm on my—"

He grabbed her by the hair, but ended up holding her wig. He threw it away disgusted, like it was a rat or something. He grunted and muttered a few cuss words in Russian, then slapped her again, hard.

She felt the metallic taste of blood fill her mouth. She licked her swollen lip, then raised her eyes and fixated him defiantly.

"Why don't *you* tell me why you do what you do? Is it power? More money? What is it?"

This time she screamed when the hit came. She felt tears burst out of her eyes and burn their way down her swollen cheeks. She hated herself for crying, for appearing weak, feeble in front of her enemy.

"Goddamn it!" Myatlev cursed. "I have more important things to do than waste time with this bitch. Ivan!" he called.

"Yes, boss," the man guarding Blake replied.

"It's almost time. I need to focus on what we need to do today, weather or no weather."

"Do you want to change the time—" Ivan started to ask.

"No. This was a nice surprise," he added, gesturing toward Alex, "but we have to go now. Load them on the plane. We'll continue our conversation in Kiev, later."

Myatlev walked briskly toward the hangar door and disappeared. Two of his men grabbed Lou and hauled him through the same door, kicking and screaming. Two others picked up Dylan, still unconscious, and headed out. They were probably going to come back for Blake and her, being that only one of Myatlev's goons was left.

She felt him touch her arm and flinched. The Russian had grabbed her arm and was cutting through her restraints. She winced, feeling the cold blade of the man's knife brush against her skin.

"Easy now," he said quietly, "there's no need to be afraid of a chelovek chesti."

"You?" she whispered.

He nodded, then moved over and released Blake, who watched the exchange without a word, but didn't seem too surprised.

Alex rubbed her swollen wrists and followed the man. He showed them where their weapons were piled up, near the exit, and they grabbed them immediately.

She turned to leave, but the honorable man grabbed her arm and stopped her.

"You need to kill me now, please," he said, his Russian accent thicker. "Otherwise, he will."

She looked him in the eye, gauging his determination. Everything in his being showed he was ready to die. Amazing . . . Why die, when he could fight? Why die, when he could have killed Myatlev long ago, and everyone would have been safe? Some twisted sense of honor, maybe, who knows. She shook her head and replied, "Never."

They exited the hangar carefully, watching out for Myatlev's men. They were nowhere in sight. Surprisingly, the Phenom was still there, and it seemed intact. No one else was visible though; no workers, airport personnel, or security. Then she remembered Dylan saying on their way in that the airport's lights were off, maybe too early to have them on. He also had said the tower had been unresponsive, but they assumed it was Myatlev keeping things on the quiet, maybe paying people off to get lost for a few hours. Then she finally realized, under the crisp light of day that made small details stand out and become relevant, that the airport wasn't operational anymore. The taxi and runway lights were off, and so was the rotating beacon, frozen permanently in place.

They approached Myatlev's Challenger quickly, aware that anyone could see them from the plane's windows. It was full daylight already, and they had to cross an open tarmac in plain sight. Alex was the first to climb aboard, her hand gripping her Sig, ready to fire. The moment she stepped inside, one of the Russians yelled, drawing everyone's attention. She put two bullets in his chest, and he fell with a heavy thud. Another Russian leapt from the back of the plane and pulled his gun. He fired, barely missing them and laying bullet holes in the cockpit door, just as Alex and Blake discharged their weapons. The Russian fell on his back, and the blood started pooling around him. His right foot kicked the air a couple of times. Alex rushed to the back, but Lou had already kicked the Russian's gun away. She cut Lou loose, then cut Dylan's restraints, too.

"Where's Myatlev?" she asked.

"Don't know. He was here, then he disappeared," Lou replied. "There's no way he heard gunshots and didn't come to check it out. I think he's gone, off the plane somewhere. Two of his men are gone too."

"There's no way I'm leaving here without taking care of business," she said.

"I wouldn't dream of it," Lou replied dryly.

She sensed more than heard movement behind her. She turned instantly, weapon drawn.

"Easy, now," Sam said, "it's just me."

"Sam! You're alive! Where did he go? Did you see him?"

"I saw three men head toward the terminal. Not sure if it was Myatlev or just his men. You know they rigged the Phenom to burn, right? It's soaked in gasoline."

Blake clenched his jaws. "Bastards."

"Let's move," Lou said. "I'll take Sam and we'll go check out the terminal. You should stay with the plane, in case he comes back."

"Oh, hell no," Alex replied. "He's mine. I'm coming with. Sam should stay with the plane."

Sam and Lou exchanged a quick glance, getting ready to protest.

"I'll check the hangar one more time," Blake offered.

"You guys go ahead," Alex said softly, changing her mind, seemingly preoccupied. "I'll stay here."

"What happened? What's wrong?" Sam asked.

"That," she pointed at a silver briefcase. "I'm betting that's Myatlev's, and he's not far. Good luck, you guys!"

She watched them disappear toward the terminal building, taking cover as much as they could against the surrounding buildings. For the most part, they were in the open, crossing the tarmac. She saw them make it to the door safely, and she turned her attention toward the briefcase.

She opened it carefully and examined it, intrigued. She'd never seen a remote detonator device before, anywhere but in the movies. It had a numeric keypad hooked to a computer. The small LCD screen above the keypad had flickered to life, and read, "Please enter access code." Next to it, a fingerprint scanner eliminated all hope she'd be able to somehow access the controller. She'd expected a timer on countdown, something she could attempt to neutralize, but there was nothing of the kind.

Then her phone chimed, startling her almost to death. She pulled it out, and saw a message from Eddie. It read, "All fourteen found and safe."

She cheered out loud. Yes! She checked the time. It was only a few minutes after midnight, back in Yellowstone. They'd cut it really close this time, but they were safe.

"How the hell did you get loose?" Myatlev's voice startled her, sending jolts of panic through her blood. She turned to face him and met the barrel of his pistol, aimed point blank at her chest. His eyes were fixated on the open briefcase set on a small, lacquered table next to Alex.

"You stupid bitch," he growled. "It's time for you to die. Let's finish what we started, yes?" He grabbed her throat in a strong choke, sending waves of excruciating pain to her head. She reached and grabbed him by his head, weaving her fingers behind his neck and pulling hard, resisting the temptation to fight against his choking hands. She poked his eyes with her thumbs, shoving her fingernails in as hard as she could. He continued to squeeze hard, and she felt her field of vision narrowing, as blackness closed in. With one last shred of effort, she hit him as hard as she could, sending her knee to his groin.

He grunted loudly and collapsed on top of her, in the aisle between the Challenger's leather seats. He crushed her under his weight, and only briefly released his chokehold. She saw the flicker of killing madness in his eyes, and knew she had no way out. She gasped for air, but his merciless fingers constricted her trachea, crushing it. Out of options, she quit fighting, and let the blackness take over.

He released his hold a little, letting some air get to her deprived lungs. She gasped instinctively, drawing as much as she could, then opened her eyes. Why wasn't she dead? He was still on top of her, pinning her down, and looking her in the eye with an indescribable expression. She saw hate, mixed with curiosity, with lust, with admiration even.

"You ruined everything I tried to do, everything I tried to build," he said, panting and groaning. "That makes you a formidable enemy." He stopped talking, pursing his lips, as his face reflected a wave of mixed emotions. "When you could have been a powerful ally," he continued. "Can you imagine? You working for me?"

Her eyebrows shot up. He couldn't be serious. *What the hell?*

His hand released the deadly choke a little further, and she inhaled deeply a few times, despite the pain she felt with every breath. Her sternum hurt badly, where she hadn't completely healed. His weight, crushing her, sent shots of pain where her ribs met the sternum, worse with every breath. She stirred a little, trying to release some of the pressure. She struggled to free her right leg, where her backup Walther hid in her boot. He didn't let her budge.

"Are you serious?" she asked in a hoarse, strangled voice. "How much would you pay me?"

"Twenty million dollars," he said calmly. "Per year."

"Oh, wow," she blurted, surprised. That was a lot of money. Having so much money definitely changed things in one's life. She felt flattered, intrigued. "What would I have to do?"

"I'm about to own the world, as you'll soon discover," he said, lifting his weight off her a little more. She squirmed and shifted, sending much-needed blood flow to her extremities and feeling her muscles awaken. "I need someone of your caliber to make things happen for me. I need someone with your kind of brain."

He watched her with fascinated eyes, colored by lust at times. She held his gaze and didn't even blink.

"So tell me," he asked, "Are you considering it?"

She stirred some more, freeing her left hand from underneath his bulky chest, and taking a deep breath, despite the pain in her chest. What an interesting turn of events! The man was full of surprises; she had to admit.

"Let me think for a second," she asked, almost smiling, buying herself some time, watching how his excitement grew.

"No, no more thinking," he insisted, frowning. "What's it going to be? Will you work for me?"

"Hell, no," she replied forcefully, as she stabbed him in the chest, driving her tactical knife deep between his ribs. "Take your job offer to hell with you!"

He gasped, making a gurgling sound as the air hit his pierced lung. He resumed his deathly choke on her throat, and let out an agonizing cry as her knife hit again. Then she felt his weight suddenly lift off her, and saw Lou's strong arms grab his neck in a chokehold. With a swift move, Lou broke his cervical spine and let him drop to the floor, lifeless.

Sam helped her to her feet and scrutinized her with a worried expression in her eyes.

"We done here?" she croaked. Speaking sent shots of pain in her throat. She put her hand on her throat, where it hurt the most.

"Yes, I think so," Lou replied. "How do you suggest we get home? Our plane's covered in gasoline."

"What's wrong with this one?" she asked, smiling widely. "I don't think anyone will miss it."

Roars of laughter resounded in Tom Isaac's backyard, punctuating the witty conversation of those present. Alex smiled at times, but couldn't laugh wholeheartedly yet, and when she talked, she had to speak quietly in a raspy, annoying voice. Her doctor had checked for tracheal fractures and had cleared her; all she needed was time to heal and ice cream. She agreed with the ice cream prescription; she hated she had to wait until she healed. They'd been back almost a week, but apparently, her wounds needed a little longer than that.

She wore a silk scarf loosely wrapped around her neck, to hide her bruises. Lou had said, "Battle scars you should wear with pride," something only an ex-SEAL, or a man, would say. Maybe scars looked good on him, but she preferred to have her flawless skin back.

She saw Marino lean against the wall, seeming a little out of place, as she stared absently at her almost untouched bottle of beer. She only knew Alex and Weber and had briefly met Blake and his wife, Adeline. The rest were complete strangers to her; no wonder she felt she didn't belong.

Alex went to her and raised her bottle.

"Cheers, Marino, and bottoms up!"

"I'm not that thirsty," she replied. "I normally don't—"

"Cut it off, Marino. If *I* can drink, so can you!"

She swallowed carefully a few small sips and winced as they went down her bruised throat.

"See?" she added hoarsely, "it's easy. Plus, I heard you kicked some serious ass at Yellowstone. You ruled!"

"Yes, she totally did," Jeremy said, approaching the two women. "She took over as soon as she realized Barnett wasn't up to the job."

Alex frowned.

"Why? What happened? I thought Barnett was really tough."

"He . . . just wasn't up to it, I guess," Marino replied. "He's not a bad guy . . . he's a great professional, you know. It's hard for most people not to panic when they see their entire existence threatened. He has a family, a wife and two kids.

He probably couldn't stop thinking of them. He probably thought he should have been running home to load them in a car and put as much distance between them and Yellowstone as possible, instead of being there at Old Faithful with us. It's normal."

"Yet you managed," Alex said, and raised her beer bottle again. "Cheers to the brave one, girl!"

The rest of the gang cheered loudly, raising their wine glasses and beer bottles.

Marino blushed and took a gulp of beer.

"That's why you're the best," Alex said, patting her on the shoulder. "Listen, hurry up with that beer, because I won't let you off the hook until you sing for us."

"Sing? Me? I never sing," Marino replied coldly.

"Uh-huh, you will sing with me, right here, you'll see," Alex winked. "If I can, you can."

Jeremy and Lou laughed, and Blake and Adeline joined them. Blake held Adeline's hand; they looked like newlyweds. Alex smiled, remembering a conversation they once had about soul mates. Blake had been right; he'd found his.

"I'll pay to see that, you two singing. With what voice exactly?" Jeremy asked, and Alex stuck her tongue out at him.

"I think I can get a betting pool started," Lou offered.

"Do that and you're a dead man," Marino threatened him, only half-jokingly.

The smell of burgers sizzling on the grill caught her attention, brought by a gust of early summer breeze. Alex wrinkled her nose in the wind.

"Yum, let's go see what's going on over there."

They approached the grill, where Tom and Steve talked casually, flipping burgers, and warming the buns.

"We're finally getting noticed," Tom said. "Youth is so unforgiving."

Alex reached up and placed a kiss on Tom's cheek. "Thank you," she whispered in his ear.

"What for?" he asked, surprised, still holding on to his tongs.

"For everything. You know," she said, struggling to express her gratitude to the man who had given her a purpose, a life, and a family the day he'd decided to take a chance on her and give her a job with The Agency.

He didn't need any words; he understood. He gave her a side hug. "You make me proud, Alex, every day."

She turned her head away, to hide the tears that suddenly pooled in her eyes, and took another sip of cold beer to hide her emotion. She didn't fool Tom though.

A brief smile fluttered on his lips, then he asked, "Who was the client, by the way? I need to know where to send my bill."

Everyone laughed hard.

"There's no client," Alex replied smiling, "not this time. This was pro bono, all of it. We don't have any paperwork, and no one will get paid. Not even me," she added, letting out a long sigh.

"Well then, stop working for unpaying customers," Tom joked, starting another wave of laughter around the barbecue. "We'll go broke!"

"Tell me about it," Alex said bitterly. "I lost all my money!"

"I lost my plane too, not just money," Blake chimed in. "But somehow I think we'll do okay."

"What, you didn't keep Myatlev's Challenger?" Alex asked.

"No, it wasn't mine to keep," he said smiling. "The US government seized it."

"Pfft," Alex scoffed, rolling her eyes. "Too bad. I liked that plane; it would have brought back such nice memories."

Everyone laughed again, and she raised her hand to quiet them.

"By the way, what happened to the money?" she asked. "It wasn't on the Challenger, but it wasn't on the tarmac either."

"I bet that's why two of the Russian goons disappeared," Sam said. "I bet they grabbed the money and ran."

"Chelovek chesti didn't steal it, I promise you that," Alex replied. "He's too chesti for that. He was willing to die, instead of just shooting Myatlev and doing the world a favor."

"No, I meant the two guys who hauled Lou out of the hangar. We never found those guys."

"Yeah, I never got to beat the crap out of the guy who punched me," Lou replied sadly. "I lost some ego points there, lots of ego points. Don't tell anyone . . . But your money, boss, that sucks."

"Ah, whatever . . . easy come, easy go. I guess I need to keep my job for a while longer, huh?"

Tom gave her another side hug. "Glad to hear it, my dear."

"Hey, everyone, come quickly!" Claire called to them. "You have to see this."

Claire was setting the table under the covered porch, while watching the news on the flat-screen TV hanging from the ceiling.

They approached in a hurry, and she resumed the live TV she had paused. The breaking news marquee scrolled at the bottom of the screen, as the announcer, Stephanie Wainwright, filled the screen with her perfect hairdo and impeccable face.

"We have learned that Russian President Piotr Ivanovich Abramovich has been killed in a hunting accident near Moscow earlier today. The world was stunned to hear the news. President Abramovich, the first to lead Russia for more than two mandates after the dismantling of the USSR, has—"

"Whoa . . ." Alex commented. "He must have run into the local CIA bear," she quipped, to everyone's amusement except Marino's.

"I have no knowledge of any such—" Marino said coldly, but was swiftly interrupted by another wave of laughter.

"Right," Alex said cheerfully and raised her bottle to Marino, who shook her head in disbelief, angry at first, but then burst into laughter with the rest of them. She gulped her beer down, then accepted another, quickly offered by Jeremy.

Alex raised her bottle again, toasting.

"To teamwork!"

"To teamwork," they replied merrily, clinking their bottles and gulping their beers.

"Oh, crap, the burgers," Tom jumped.

"No worries," Steve replied, approaching with two plates in his hands. "They're safe, just a little overdone."

Steve had been quieter than usual, happy to be observing the group from a distance. He set the two plates on the table, then turned and looked straight at Alex.

She blushed and looked away, finding it hard to hide her emotions. Everyone stopped laughing and talking and watched their unusual interaction.

"I have something to say to you," Steve said, looking at Alex with warm, loving eyes.

She nodded, her mouth open a little. She felt her heart beating fast and her breath caught.

"I've been thinking about things a lot, and here it is," Steve added.

He started slowly unbuttoning his shirt, one button at a time, cheered by almost everyone present. Adeline and Marino didn't dare cheer, but nevertheless smilingly watched Steve's performance. Alex rounded her eyes, unsure what to expect.

Two of the guys whistled loudly just when Steve undid the lowest button on his shirt, then removed it quickly, exposing the T-shirt underneath. It was custom printed in colorful lettering and read, "Facts of life learned the hard way: She's always right, I'm always wrong."

Alex laughed hard despite the pain in her throat, feeling tears of joy flood her eyes. Steve took her hand, kissed it gently, and whispered, "Forgive me." She hugged him, relishing his touch, and gave him a long kiss. Then she breathed in his ear, "Let's get out of here."

They turned to leave, saying goodbye to everyone.

"You're off the hook with the singing for today, Marino," Alex conceded before leaving. "Safe travels, and please stay in touch!"

"Yeah . . . right," she quipped. "I'm dreading the day I'll see your name on my caller ID again."

Alex gave Marino a long hug.

"Have fun, kids!" Tom said. "Oh, and Alex, please make sure you're in New York City on Monday morning, all right?"

She turned on her heels, surprised.

"Why?"

"One of the major credit card companies has an interesting problem. Some of their transactions are just a couple of cents off, here and there. They can't figure out why."

~~ The End ~~

Did *Operation Sunset* keep you on the edge of your seat as you raced through the pages, gasping at every twist? Meet Special Agent Tess Winnett with the FBI in another unmissable Leslie Wolfe thriller series.

Read on for an excerpt from

DAWN GIRL

A short-fused FBI Agent who hides a terrible secret. A serial
killer you won't see coming. A heart-stopping race to catch
him.

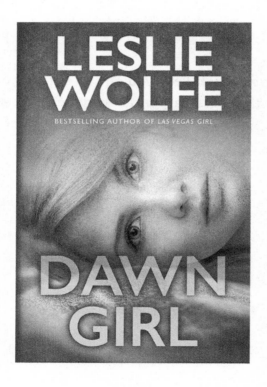

~~~~~~~~

THANK YOU!

A big, heartfelt thank you for choosing to read my book. If you enjoyed it, please take a moment to leave me a five-star review; I would be very grateful. It doesn't need to be more than a couple of words, and it makes a huge difference. This is your link: http://bit.ly/OSReview

Did you enjoy Alex Hoffmann and her team? Your thoughts and feedback are very valuable to me. Please contact me directly through one of the channels listed below. Email works best: LW@WolfeNovels.com.

CONNECT WITH ME

Email: LW@WolfeNovels.com
Facebook: https://www.facebook.com/wolfenovels
Follow Leslie on Amazon: http://bit.ly/WolfeAuthor
Follow Leslie on BookBub: http://bit.ly/wolfebb
Website: www.LeslieWolfe.com
Visit Leslie's Amazon store: http://bit.ly/WolfeAll

PREVIEW: DAWN GIRL

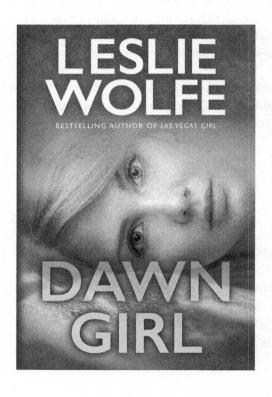

Chapter One
Ready

She made an effort to open her eyes, compelling her heavy eyelids to obey. She swallowed hard, her throat raw and dry, as she urged the wave of nausea to subside. Dizzy and confused, she struggled to gain awareness. Where was she? She felt numb and shaky, unable to move, as if awakening from a deep sleep or a coma. She tried to move her arms, but couldn't. Something kept her immobilized, but didn't hurt her. Or maybe she couldn't feel the pain, not anymore.

Her eyes started to adjust to the darkness, enough to distinguish the man moving quietly in the room. His silhouette flooded her foggy brain with a wave of memories. She gasped, feeling her throat constrict and burning tears rolling down her swollen cheeks.

Her increased awareness sent waves of adrenaline through her body, and she tried desperately to free herself from her restraints. With each useless effort, she panted harder, gasping for air, forcing it into her lungs. Fear put a strong chokehold on her throat and was gaining ground, as she rattled her restraints helplessly, growing weaker with every second. She felt a wave of darkness engulf her, this time the darkness coming from within her weary brain. She fought against that darkness, and battled her own betraying body.

The noises she made got the man's attention.

"I see you're awake. Excellent," the man said, without turning.

She watched him place a syringe on a small, metallic tray. Its handle clinked, followed by another sound, this time the raspy, telling sound of a file cutting through the neck of a glass vial. Then a pop when the man opened the vial. He grabbed the syringe and loaded the liquid from the vial, then carefully removed any air, pushing the piston until several droplets of fluid came out.

Dizziness overtook her, and she closed her eyes for a second.

"Shit," the man mumbled, then opened a drawer and went through it in a hurry.

She felt the needle poke deeply in her thigh, like it was happening to another person. She felt it, but distantly. She perceived a subdued burning sensation where he pushed the fluid into her muscle, then that went away when he pulled the needle out. She closed her weary eyes again, listless against her restraints.

The man cracked open ammonia salts under her nose, and she bounced back into reality at the speed of a lightning strike, aware, alert, and angry. For a second she fought to free herself, but froze when her eyes focused on the man in front of her.

He held a scalpel, close to her face. In itself, the small, shiny, silver object was capable of bringing formidable healing, as well as immense pain. The difference stood in the hand wielding it. She knew no healing was coming her way; only pain.

"No, no, please…" she pleaded, tears falling freely from her puffy eyes, burning as they rolled down her cheeks. "Please, no. I… I'll do anything."

"I am ready," the man said. He seemed calm, composed, and dispassionate. "Are you ready?"

"No, no, please…" she whimpered.

"Yeah," he said softly, almost whispering, inches away from her face. "Please say no to me. I love that."

She fell quiet, scared out of her mind. This time was different. He was different.

Chapter Two
Dawn

"What if we get caught?" the girl whispered, trailing behind the boy.

They walked briskly on the small residential street engulfed in darkness, keeping to the middle of the road. There were no sidewalks. High-end homes lined up both sides, most likely equipped with sensor floodlights they didn't want to trip.

She tugged at his hand, but he didn't stop. "You never care about these things, Carl, but I do. If we get caught, I'll be grounded, like, forever!"

The boy kept going, his hand firmly clasping hers.

"Carl!" she raised the pitch in her whisper, letting her anxiety show more.

He stopped and turned, facing her. He frowned a little, seeing her anguish, but then smiled and caressed a loose strand of hair rebelling from under her sweatshirt's hood.

"There's no one, Kris. No one's going to see us. See? No lights are on, nothing. Everyone's asleep. Zee-zee-zee. It's five in the morning."

"I know," she sighed, "but—"

He kissed her pouted lips gently, a little boyish hesitation and awkwardness in his move.

"We'll be okay, I promise," he said, then grabbed her hand again. "We're almost there, come on. You'll love it."

A few more steps and the small street ended into the paved

parking lot of what was going to be a future development of sorts, maybe a shopping center. From there, they had to cross Highway 1. They crouched down near the road, waiting for the light traffic to be completely clear. They couldn't afford to be seen, not even from a distance. At the right moment, they crossed the highway, hand in hand, and cut across the field toward the beach. Crossing Ocean Drive was next, then cutting through a few yards of shrubbery and trees to get to the sandy beach.

"Jeez, Carl," Kris protested, stopping in her tracks at the tree line. "Who knows what creatures live here? There could be snakes. Lizards. Gah..."

"There could be, but there aren't," Carl replied, seemingly sure of himself. "Trust me."

She held her breath and lowered her head, then clasped Carl's hand tightly. He turned on the flashlight on his phone and led the way without hesitation. A few seconds later, they reached the beach, and Kris let out a tense, long breath.

The light of the waning gibbous Moon reflected against the calm ocean waves, sending flickers of light everywhere and covering the beach in silver shadows. They were completely alone. The only creatures keeping them company were pale crabs that took bellicose stances when Kris and Carl stomped the sand around them, giggling.

"See? Told you," Carl said, "no one's going to see us out here. We can do whatever we want," he said playfully.

Kris squealed and ran toward the lifeguard tower. In daylight, the tower showed its bright yellow and orange, a splash of joyful colors on the tourist-abundant stretch of sand. At night, the structure appeared gloomy, resembling a menacing creature on tall, insect-like legs.

"It looks like one of those aliens from War of the Worlds," Kris said, then promptly started running, waving her arms up in the air, pretending she was flying.

Carl chased Kris, laughing and squealing with her, running in circles around the tower, and weaving footstep patterns between the solid wood posts.

"Phew," Carl said, stopping his chase and taking some distance. "Stinks of piss. Let's get out of here."

"Eww..." Kris replied, following him. "Why do men do that?"

"What? Pee?"

"Everybody pees, genius," Kris replied, still panting from the run. "Peeing where it stinks and bothers people, that's what I meant. Women pee in the bushes. Men should pee in the water if they don't like the bushes."

"Really? That's gross."

"Where do you think fish pee? At least the waves would wash away the pee and it wouldn't stink, to mess up our sunrise."

"Fish pee?" Carl pushed back, incredulous.

"They don't?"

They walked holding hands, putting a few more yards of distance between them and the tower. Then Carl suddenly dropped to the ground, dragging Kris with him. She squealed again, and laughed.

"Let's sit here," he said. "The show's on. Let's see if we get a good one."

The sky was starting to light up toward the east. They watched silently, hand in hand, as the dark shades of blue and gray gradually turned ablaze, mixing in dark reds and orange hues. The horizon line was clear, a sharp edge marking where ocean met sky.

"It's going to be great," Carl said. "No clouds, no haze." He kissed her lips quickly, and then turned his attention back to the celestial lightshow.

"You're a strange boy, Carl."

"Yeah? Why?"

"Other boys would have asked me to sneak out in the middle of the night to make out. With you, it's a sunrise, period. Should I worry?"

Carl smiled widely, then tickled Kris until she begged for mercy between gasps of air and bouts of uncontrollable laughter.

"Stop! Stop it already. I can't breathe!"

"I might want to get on with that make out, you know," Carl laughed.

"Nah, it's getting light. Someone could see us," Kris pushed back, unconvinced. "Someone could come by."

Carl shrugged and turned his attention to the sunrise. He grabbed her hand and held it gently, playing with her fingers.

Almost half the sky had caught fire, challenging the moonlight, and obliterating most of its reflected light against the blissful, serene, ocean waves.

Carl checked the time on his phone.

"A few more minutes until it comes out," he announced, sounding serious, as if predicting a rare and significant event. He took a few pictures of the sky, then suddenly snapped one of Kris.

"Ah… no," she reacted, "give that to me right this second, Carl." She grabbed the phone from his hand and looked at the picture he'd taken. The image showed a young girl with messy, golden brown hair, partially covering a scrunched, tense face with deep ridges on her brow. The snapshot revealed Kris biting her index fingernail, totally absorbed by the process, slobbering her sleeve cuff while at it.

"God-awful," she reacted, then pressed the option to delete.

"No!" Carl said, pulling the phone from her hands. "I like it!"

"There's nothing to like. There," she said, relaxing a little, and arranging her hair briefly with her long, thin fingers. "I'll pose for you." She smiled.

Carl took a few pictures. She looked gorgeous, against the backdrop of fiery skies, pink sand, and turquoise water. He took image after image, as she got into it and made faces, danced, and swirled in front of him, laughing.

The sun's first piercing ray shot out of the sea, just as Kris shrieked, a blood-curdling scream that got Carl to spring to his feet and run to her.

Speechless, Kris pointed a trembling hand at the lifeguard tower. Underneath the tower, between the wooden posts supporting the elevated structure, was the naked body of a young woman. She appeared to be kneeling, as if praying to the rising sun. Her hands were clasped together in front of her in the universal, unmistakable gesture of silent pleading.

Holding their breaths, they approached carefully, curious and yet afraid of what they stood to discover. The growing light of the new morning revealed more details with each step they took. Her back, covered in bruises and small cuts, stained in smudged, dried blood. Her blue eyes wide open, glossed over. A few specks of sand clung to her long, dark lashes. Her beautiful face, immobile, covered in sparkling flecks of sand. Her lips slightly parted, as if to let a last breath escape. Long, blonde hair, wet from sea spray, almost managed to disguise the deep cut in her neck.

No blood dripped from the wound; her heart had stopped beating for some time. Yet she held upright, unyielding in her praying posture, her knees stuck firmly in the sand covered in their footprints, and her eyes fixated on the beautiful sunrise they came to enjoy.

~~~End Preview~~~

Like *Dawn Girl?*

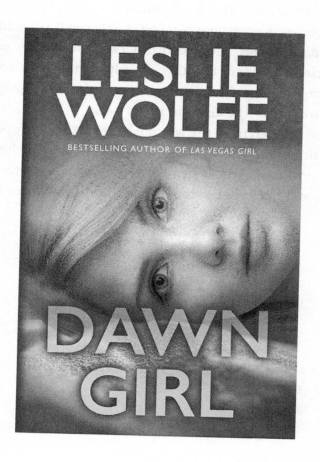

Buy it now!

ABOUT THE AUTHOR

Leslie Wolfe is a bestselling author whose novels break the mold of traditional thrillers. She creates unforgettable, brilliant, strong women heroes who deliver fast-paced, satisfying suspense, backed up by extensive background research in technology and psychology.

Leslie released the first novel, *Executive,* in October 2011. Since then, she has written many more, continuing to break down barriers of traditional thrillers. Her style of fast-paced suspense, backed up by extensive background research in technology and psychology, has made Leslie one of the most read authors in the genre and she has created an array of unforgettable, brilliant and strong women heroes along the way.

Reminiscent of the television drama *Criminal Minds*, her series of books featuring the fierce and relentless FBI Agent **Tess Winnett** would be of great interest to readers of James Patterson, Melinda Leigh, and David Baldacci crime thrillers. Fans of Kendra Elliot and Robert Dugoni suspenseful mysteries would love the **Las Vegas Crime** series, featuring the tension-filled relationship between Baxter and Holt. Finally, her **Alex Hoffmann** series of political and espionage action adventure will enthrall readers of Tom Clancy, Brad Thor, and Lee Child.

Leslie has received much acclaim for her work, including inquiries from Hollywood, and her books offer something that is different and tangible, with readers becoming invested in not only the main characters and plot but also with the ruthless minds of the killers she creates.

A complete list of Leslie's titles is available at LeslieWolfe.com/books.

Leslie enjoys engaging with readers every day and would love to hear from you. Become an insider: gain early access to previews of Leslie's new novels.

- Email: LW@WolfeNovels.com
- Facebook: https://www.facebook.com/wolfenovels
- Follow Leslie on Amazon: http://bit.ly/WolfeAuthor
- Follow Leslie on BookBub: http://bit.ly/wolfebb
- Website: www.LeslieWolfe.com
- Visit Leslie's Amazon store: http://bit.ly/WolfeAll

Made in the USA
Las Vegas, NV
12 February 2024

85680993R00132